*They were at the same impasse
that had split them apart.*

"You put your father's well-being before mine. He meant more to you than I did. That was impossible for me to accept," Peter said.

Clearly, the point of pride still rankled ten years later, Tess realized. She wanted to deny that she'd loved her father more than him, but she knew there would be no convincing Peter. They faced each other over a fathomless breach.

"Hashing over old memories doesn't resolve a thing," she protested unhappily.

"We need to, Tess," Peter replied. "We need to talk about the feelings we've bottled up all these years."

He paused, gazed into her eyes, then added quietly, "I never got over you."

Dear Reader,

Welcome to the Silhouette **Special Edition** experience! With your search for consistently satisfying reading in mind, every month the authors and editors of Silhouette **Special Edition** aim to offer you a stimulating blend of deep emotions and high romance.

The name Silhouette **Special Edition** and the distinctive arch on the cover represent a commitment—a commitment to bring you six sensitive, substantial novels each month. In the pages of a Silhouette **Special Edition**, compelling true-to-life characters face riveting emotional issues—and come out winners. Both celebrated authors and newcomers to the series strive for depth and dimension, vividness and warmth, in writing these stories of living and loving in today's world.

The result, we hope, is romance you can believe in. Deeply emotional, richly romantic, infinitely rewarding—that's the Silhouette **Special Edition** experience. Come share it with us—six times a month!

From all the authors and editors of Silhouette **Special Edition**,

Best wishes,

Leslie Kazanjian
Senior Editor

# CAROLE HALSTON
# Unfinished Business

*Silhouette Special Edition*

Published by Silhouette Books New York

**America's Publisher of Contemporary Romance**

SILHOUETTE BOOKS
300 East 42nd St., New York, N.Y. 10017

Copyright © 1989 by Carole Halston

ISBN: 0-373-09567-8

First Silhouette Books printing December 1989

Printed in the U.S.A.

**Books by Carole Halston**

Silhouette Romance

*Stand-In Bride* #62
*Love Legacy* #83
*Undercover Girl* #152
*Sunset in Paradise* #208

Silhouette Special Edition

*Keys to Daniel's House* #8
*Collision Course* #41
*The Marriage Bonus* #86
*Summer Course in Love* #115
*A Hard Bargain* #139
*Something Lost, Something Gained* #163
*A Common Heritage* #211
*The Black Knight* #223
*Almost Heaven* #253
*Surprise Offense* #291
*Matched Pair* #328
*Honeymoon for One* #356
*The Baby Trap* #388
*High Bid* #423
*Intensive Care* #461
*Compromising Positions* #500
*Ben's Touch* #543
*Unfinished Business* #567

# CAROLE HALSTON,

a Louisiana native, resides on the north shore of Lake Pontchartrain, near New Orleans. She enjoys traveling with her husband to research less-familiar locations for settings but is always happy to return home to her own unique region, a rich source in itself for romantic stories about warm, wonderful people.

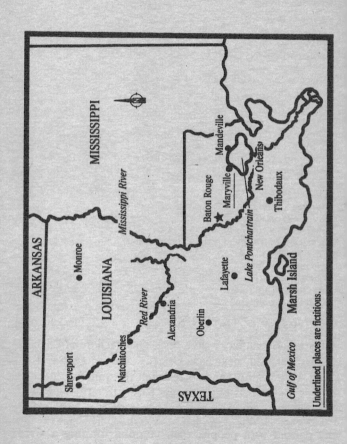

ARKANSAS

MISSISSIPPI

LOUISIANA

TEXAS

Shreveport

Monroe

Natchitoches

Red River

Alexandria

Oberlin

Lafayette

Mississippi River

Baton Rouge

Maryville

Mandeville

New Orleans

Lake Pontchartrain

Thibodaux

Marsh Island

Gulf of Mexico

Underlined places are fictitious.

## Chapter One

Dixieland jazz blared from *Good Times*, the big power vessel directly ahead of *Seabreeze* in the long procession of boats. Rousing strains of "When the Saints Go Marching In" blended with the gay voices and laughter of Peter's companions aboard *Seabreeze*, whose tall rigging was strung with gaudy banners of purple and green and gold, the colors of Mardi Gras. Peter was largely oblivious to the music and the conversation. He was untouched by the general mood of revelry. As the sailboat rounded a bend in the broad river, their destination, the little town of Maryville, came into view. The sight claimed his total attention.

Gazing hard through the eye slits of his black mask, he noted the size of the crowd eagerly awaiting the arrival of the boat parade. The length of the town riverfront was solidly packed with people, their clothing forming a vivid, dense mosaic from this distance. Les Morgan, the owner of *Seabreeze*, had remarked that the annual local event was popular, drawing people from Baton Rouge and New Orleans, as well as nearby small towns on the North Shore. But Peter hadn't been prepared for a crowd as large as this. Why, there must be ten thousand people at least jammed into the small town.

If Tess were among them, he might never catch a glimpse of her.

Peter's shoulders sagged beneath his swashbuckling pirate's costume as he struggled to suppress a wave of disappointment that was absurdly strong, considering that just moments ago he had been tense with dread at the possibility that he might very well spot Tess in the crowd. His own state of emotional upheaval baffled and exasperated the hell out of him. He should have gotten her completely out of his system by now. It had been ten years.

He had long since put his brief marriage to her into perspective. He had faced up to the truth dispassionately and wasn't bitter toward Tess. She had honestly believed herself in love with Peter when she married him, but at nineteen she had simply been too young and immature to make an adult commitment. She had spoken her wedding vows sincerely, including the promise to "forsake all others" for Peter. Tess hadn't known herself that parental devotion was far stronger than the affection she'd felt for her young bridegroom.

Before a year was up, unforeseen circumstances had put her to the test. She had been forced to choose between doing what was best for a bereaved father and what was best for Peter. It hadn't been an easy decision for her. She had been torn by her conflict, but the daughter in her had won out over the wife.

Peter wasn't without blame, of course. Looking back, he always cringed at the memory of himself as a husband. He had been possessive and demanding, expecting Tess to cater to him the way his mother always had to his father. Admittedly, his expectations in a wife had been old-fashioned and selfish, but that hadn't been at the root of the problem. Peter could have adapted if Tess had rebelled and insisted upon a more modern domestic role for herself. What he couldn't accept was not coming first with her.

It had been a brief episode in Peter's life. He had met Tess in his junior year at college. They had married the following summer, over the objections of both sets of parents, and separated eleven months later, when Peter was finishing his degree in petroleum engineering and starting his career. The split had been simple and clean. There hadn't been any community property to squabble over. Tess hadn't asked for alimony.

Peter hadn't seen her or spoken to her since they had separated. He had gone to Denver to take his new job, and she had returned home to Maryville and her father. Pride and hurt had made him hold out from contacting her when she hadn't telephoned or written him. Eventually the divorce documents had arrived in the mail.

After the first couple of years, no news of Tess had come to Peter, and he had never sought out information. There was no doubt in his mind that she had remarried. As pretty and personable and desirable as Tess had been, it was unthinkable that she would have stayed single. Peter's guess was that she had matched up the second time around with a local man who met with her father's approval. It wouldn't surprise him to learn that Jake Davenport lived with his daughter and her husband and children in the same house that had been Tess's childhood home.

Perhaps the husband even worked for Jake, helping to run the marina and fuel dock that Tess, an only child, would inherit someday. She, no doubt, still knew the family business inside out and pitched in on holidays and busy weekends, selling ice and beer to fishermen and pleasure boaters. Her children would be totally at home in the marina, skipping along the wooden piers, as she had done, and hailing all the boat owners by name.

Peter hoped, for Tess's sake, that the life he imagined for her was true. He hoped that her husband was a good man and deserved her, that she had beautiful, healthy offspring, that she was happy and content. If he caught a glimpse of her today and saw worry and sadness and disappointment etched into her face, he wouldn't gloat. He would be deeply dismayed.

He wished the very best for Tess and harbored no fantasies whatever about turning back the clock with her. But he obviously still had a hang-up where she was concerned. Otherwise, he wouldn't be in this state of turmoil over the prospect of seeing her today. Nor would he have suffered such powerful mixed feelings about transferring to his company's New Orleans office, where he would be in close proximity to Maryville.

Peter intended to deal with his problem, which he suspected might be a large part of the reason that he hadn't fallen in love again or made a permanent commitment to another woman. He planned to look Tess up while he was in New Orleans and close the book on the past. Not today, though. Today he wasn't ready to come face-to-face with her.

If Tess saw him among the costumed crew on the sailboat, she wouldn't recognize him, Peter reminded himself as the boat parade neared shore and he joined perfunctorily in the hubbub of preparations. Finding a place on the starboard deck, he looped a generous supply of brightly colored strings of beads over his left arm to toss into the crowd, which had already erupted into a frenzy, waving arms and shouting the traditional litany of Mardi Gras spectators, "Throw me something, mister! Throw me something, mister!"

The parade passed as close as safety would allow to the riverfront bulkhead. Peter's eyes searched the sea of faces as he methodically arced beads and doubloons over the intervening strip of dark water, not bothering to note who snatched them out of the air. Several times his heart leaped when his gaze would come to a laughing, dark-eyed, dark-haired young woman, but none of them was Tess.

None of them was even close to Tess's present age, Peter realized. He was looking for a twenty-year-old, whose picture he still carried in his wallet, not a mature woman of thirty. It was possible that Tess could have changed enough in appearance that he wouldn't recognize her in the crowd. The thought at first disturbed Peter and then soothed him. Perhaps seeing Tess again would instantly cure him of his hang-up, he reflected. Chances were that she might not even appeal to him anymore.

Replenishing his supply of beads, Peter began to relax and enjoy himself. The loud music was suddenly infectious, and he was aware that the mild weather made being outdoors in mid-February a pleasure. Last year, according to Les, it had been windy and cold, but today was perfect for the boat parade, with the temperature in the high sixties and the sun breaking out from behind the clouds.

With his anxiety eased, Peter took in the scene before him and felt at home. After living in other states, he could appreciate the spontaneous and fun-loving nature of his fellow native Louisianians, who would seize any excuse to throw a big celebration with music and food and drink. Down in the Acadian country, where Peter was from, Mardi Gras wasn't as big a seasonal event as it was here in the New Orleans area, but nearly every small town had an annual festival that brought out the whole population from miles around. The more, the merrier was the general attitude.

It was good to be back in Louisiana. Peter had paid lip service to that sentiment during the two months since he had moved to New Orleans, but now he was boosted by his first real sense of gladness. If he could let go and have a good time in Maryville, of all places, that must mean that his old scars were better healed than he had thought. Just a few blocks away was the church where Tess had walked down the aisle to meet him, looking like a dark-haired angel in her white wedding dress.

Peter deliberately held the picture in his mind for a few seconds to test himself and was jubilant when he felt nothing more painful than nostalgia. Picking up a whole handful of doubloons, he hurled them with a broad sweep of his arm, sending a shower of shiny aluminum coins into the outstretched hands of the clamoring crowd.

"You're getting into the spirit of things, Peter!" a female crew member on Peter's right-hand side called to him. A buxom blonde, she wore a scullery maid costume with a low-cut neckline that showed a generous amount of cleavage. They evidently had been invited for each other, since they were the only single people aboard. Earlier Peter had been too tense and absorbed to be interested. Now he grinned at her and tried to recall her name as he answered, accentuating the faint trace of a Cajun accent that lingered in his speech.

"I just discovered that I'm back in Louisiana, *chère*, where folks know how to loosen up and have a good time."

The blonde smiled back at Peter delightedly. "Welcome to the party!"

They both tossed beads absently to the crowd while they got acquainted, raising their voices to carry over the noise. Peter learned that she lived on the North Shore in a nearby

country-club subdivision. Originally from Illinois, she had
relocated to Louisiana seven years ago with her husband,
now her ex-husband.

"I wouldn't think of moving back up North," she declared. "I love it down here. There is so much local color
that it's an interesting place to live. Plus the food is wonderful. It isn't even necessary to drive over to New Orleans.
We have marvelous restaurants on the North Shore. Some
of them are little hole-in-the-wall places. Like Marvin's,
over there." She was pointing to one of the buildings on the
opposite side of the street that ran parallel to the riverfront. "It's one of my very favorites. You'll have to drive
over soon, and I'll take you . . ."

Her voice went on, but Peter didn't hear anything else she
said. The loud music and din of the crowd receded, as
though someone had turned down the volume. In the fore-
ground of his vision, arms waved and bodies shifted, but he
didn't see the movement. His eyes were focused upon the
porch of the restaurant where a slender brunette stood at the
railing. She was looking out toward the river, directly at
him, it seemed.

*The woman was Tess.*

Peter stared, paralyzed but not numbed by his instant
recognition. Every powerful emotion that Tess had ever set
off in him seemed to hit him full strength: desire, tender-
ness, possessiveness, jealousy, anger, rejection, frustration. He tore his gaze free of her long enough to scan the
faces of the men on the porch. Was one of them her husband? The thought was intolerable to him.

Seeing her, even at a distance, ruled out any chance that
she hadn't remarried. At thirty she was still pretty and vi-
vacious. Peter's memory acted like a zoom lens on a cam-
era, giving him a close-up view that added sharp regret to his
clash of emotions. He could visualize so clearly the lively

play of expression on her features as she made some smiling comment to the woman next to her. Her dark brown eyes would be alight with whatever amusing thought she had shared.

God, how he had missed her. They had had so much fun together when they were dating and during those first few months that they were married, before her mother had fallen ill and reality had set in.

She had kept her hair long. One of the few issues upon which Peter and her father had agreed was that she shouldn't cut it, as she had threatened to do. Today she wore the dark, wavy tresses pinned up in a topknot, one of the hairstyles she had favored when she was Peter's girlfriend and then his wife. Curly tendrils escaped, the way he remembered. He had wound the tendrils around his finger. When he was undressing her, he had delighted in pulling out the pins and taking down her hair.

Did her husband do the same thing now?

Peter clenched his hands into fists, fighting a wave of jealous rage combined with an overwhelming sense of betrayal. He ground his teeth together so hard that his jaw ached as he tried to keep from crying out recriminations that welled up inside him. *How could you let another man touch you, Tess?* he demanded of her silently. *How could you give yourself to someone else, after the promises that we made to each other?*

"Peter, are you okay?"

The blonde's worried inquiry penetrated Peter's consciousness, making him dimly aware that he was standing rigid and immobile, totally unresponsive to the crowd and oblivious to the sailboat's slow progress. His head was turned at a sharp angle now so that he could keep Tess in sight.

"No, I'm not okay," he stated, each word requiring an enormous effort.

"I wondered earlier if you weren't bothered by the motion," she said sympathetically.

Peter didn't answer, letting her error go uncorrected. His ailment had nothing to do with seasickness. It was a serious case of self-delusion that had been affecting him all these years.

Deep down, he had never believed that everything was over and finished between him and Tess. In his heart of hearts, he was still her husband and she was still his wife.

That was the real reason that Peter had kept his wedding ring, although he'd given various other, cynical explanations. It was the reason that he transferred Tess's photo to each new wallet, the reason he hadn't fallen in love again, remarried and had the family that he wanted.

Peter had to divorce himself from her at long last and get on with his life. He had to sever the emotional tie, silence the voice inside him that was insisting, this very moment, *She's mine*. He had to conquer, once and for all, the need that was a physical ache inside him to take her into his arms and hold her tightly.

For now, he could only brace himself against the anguished emotion that engulfed him as the parade advanced downriver and he lost all sight of her.

"The boat owners certainly went all out this year with costumes and decorations," Evelyn Laird observed brightly. "Some of the boats actually look like floats, don't they? If you were a judge, which one would get first prize, Tess?"

"I'm too biased to be a judge, since several of the boat owners rent slips from me." With a grateful smile at her well-intentioned friend, Tess evaded giving an answer. Without commenting directly on the fact that Tess wasn't being very good company, Evelyn was trying to draw her into the conversation and distract her from her thoughts.

Not just Evelyn, but all of Tess's other friends on the porch of Marvin's were sympathetically aware that occasions like today were difficult for her. She was inevitably reminded of her father, who had been prominent at any big local event, but he had especially been in his element at this one, with a number of his marina tenants participating.

It was impossible for Tess not to call up images that brought a glaze of tears to her eyes. Through the blur, she could just see him down there on the riverfront in the thick of the crowd, shaking hands and greeting countless friends and acquaintances, swapping yarns with cronies, politicking.

Later, when the boat parade was over and most of the boats had circled back to tie up at the town dock and continue the festivities, she would be flooded with more memories if she stayed around. Her father could never get away until dark. He had been singled out by one captain after another, hailed by crew members and urged to come aboard for a drink. Tess would meet with the same genuine welcome herself, but she had too much weighing on her mind to shed her troubles and get into the spirit of Mardi Gras.

Her father's death a year ago had left a huge gap in her life, and she still missed him terribly. In addition to the loneliness, though, she found herself faced with pressures that she just couldn't seem to deal with, decisions that she just couldn't seem to make. Whenever she would try to force her mind to confront the future, it would balk and take her on a senseless journey backward in time.

Tess had to give Will a definite yes or no answer about whether she would marry him. He had proposed to her six months ago and had been very patient. Her problem was that every time she began a mental list of all the points in favor of marrying Will, she was besieged with old, bittersweet memories of Peter that had no bearing on her decision, but left her more uncertain than before.

And now recently, like a bolt out of the blue, had come a grave new development that she hadn't confided to even her trusted friends, like Evelyn and Joe Laird. Only Will, who was also her attorney, knew that Tess might have to share her inheritance with a half brother, whose existence had been totally unknown to her.

Up until a north Louisiana attorney contacted Will two weeks ago, Tess had believed herself to be an only child. As far as she knew, her father's only marriage had been to her mother. But this alleged half brother claimed that he was born in wedlock and, in addition to his birth certificate, could produce a copy of his parents' marriage certificate to prove it. Will was in north Louisiana now, checking the validity of the documents. Tess was on pins and needles, dreading to hear the outcome of his investigation.

As incredible as it seemed, under Louisiana law, which made children the ''forced heirs'' of their parents, this stranger was entitled to a sizeable portion of Jake Davenport's estate, if, indeed, he was her father's son.

Aside from the dire financial implications, Tess was deeply disturbed to think of what public reaction would be to the news that Jake Davenport had had an offspring from a previous marriage and had never acknowledged him. She couldn't bear having her father censured posthumously. There was absolutely no doubt in Tess's mind that the true facts of the case, whatever they were, would exonerate her father, who had been a good, honorable man. But the true facts might never be known, and people had a way of believing the worst of their fellow humans.

And, too, it was going to hurt if Tess learned that her father had kept such a secret from her. They had been so close.

He could have trusted her with any disclosure of his past, even something shameful, without fear of losing her love and loyalty.

Tess prayed that the half brother was an imposter. In the meanwhile, until she learned the verdict, she was trying to prepare herself for the economic realities if he wasn't. The marina and fuel-dock business, along with the house that had been her home as long as she could remember, made up the bulk of her inheritance. She had a limited amount of money and would have to raise the cash to satisfy his claim, if it held up.

That would mean either mortgaging the marina to the hilt and saddling herself with debt for years to come or else selling a large interest in it and taking on a partner. Both alternatives were appalling enough without the worrisome intuition that she was going to find herself in a very untenable position, on further investigation.

Property values were generally low, because of the depressed state and local economy, and she suspected that her cash-flow situation wouldn't impress a bank or an investor. With the competition being what it was, she had to keep her slip rents modest. There had been an overbuilding of marinas on the North Shore just prior to the slump in the oil and gas industry. Much newer marinas than hers had empty slips.

Tess had a comfortable income at present, but she might not be able to make ends meet with a huge mortgage payment. Taking on a partner and splitting the proceeds would probably be preferable from a financial standpoint, but she could barely tolerate the thought of having to answer to someone else and put up with interference. The marina was *hers*. It was more than just a piece of property and a business. It was a legacy of hard work and pride and independence that her father had always meant for her to have.

Will had told her not to worry. He would make her a personal loan for whatever amount she needed, if it came to that. "Your daddy was a friend of mine as well as a client. I promised him on his deathbed that I'd look after you," Will had declared sincerely. Then he had smiled and added with blatant hopefulness, "Of course, if you do decide to make me the happiest man in the world and become my wife, I'd cancel out any debt as a wedding present."

In other words, he wasn't above trying to bribe her. Tess appreciated his honesty in forewarning her of his motives. She was honest enough with herself to admit that her inheritance problems just might end her vacillating and tip the scale in favor of marrying Will. He seemed crazy about her, and she liked and respected him and enjoyed his company, even if she didn't love him passionately, the way she had loved Peter. It was doubtful that she was going to experience that kind of love again anyway. She wasn't even sure she would want to. It had brought her more pain than happiness.

Will would make her a good companion. The fact that Tess wasn't turned on by the thought of being sexually intimate with him bothered her a little, but she wasn't repelled by him and knew from experience that sexual attraction wasn't the basis for a successful marriage. If it was, Tess would still be Peter's wife.

All the anger and hurt and disappointment that had broken her and Peter apart hadn't lessened any of their physical attraction for each other. Theirs had obviously been a special chemistry between a couple of young, immature people because Tess hadn't reacted to another man the same way since then. After all these years, her pulse quickened and her body came alive when she recalled making love with Peter.

"Tess, look at the tall pirate on the big sailboat that's just passing. The one who's just standing there, like a zombie and staring up here in our direction. Is he someone you know?"

Evelyn was making another effort to divert Tess, who didn't have to search out the pirate in question. With no conscious thought of observing him, she had been noting his odd behavior and finding him vaguely familiar. Now she realized that the pirate's height and lean body build were similar to Peter's.

"No, I'm sure he isn't anyone I know," Tess denied, cross with herself. Not only was she constantly dredging up memories of Peter, but she was starting to single out strange men who physically resembled him. "Judging from the way he's acting, I doubt that he will remember whether he had a good time today or not," she added, but the statement failed to dispel the certainty that was strengthening and sending strange ripples down Tess's spine: The pirate had singled *her* out, too. *She* was the one whose face had caught his attention, for whatever reason.

Any number of times she had seen individuals who were riding in Mardi Gras parades in an alcohol or drug-induced stupor. They tended to fix their gazes on a person in the crowd. It caused an eery sensation to be the object of prolonged scrutiny by a stranger staring through the slitted eyeholes in a mask. Tess had experienced the feeling before, but never as strongly as now, when she couldn't even tell for sure that the man's eyes were trained upon her face.

There was a disturbing intensity about his gaze. It was ridiculous, but she sensed currents of powerful emotion that tugged at her. Deliberately she looked away, attempting to break the contact, but her eyes were drawn back to verify what she could feel in her pores: he was continuing to stare back at her as the sailboat took him downriver farther and farther away.

Tess drew in a little sigh of relief when he finally disappeared from sight. Would the sailboat be among those boats that stopped and tied up to the dock on the return trip back up the river? she wondered uneasily and then roused herself and made a determined effort to be more sociable.

After the parade was over, the crowd immediately began to thin. Cars were parked for several miles along the highway in both directions. It would take at least an hour for the partial evacuation, Tess knew. There would be a solid stream of automobiles across the drawbridge, which would open intermittently all afternoon to accommodate the busy boat traffic on the river. With the congestion eased, the partying would go on all along the waterfront.

Tess was more than ready to join the exodus, but she was sure to meet with opposition if she openly announced her intention of leaving and going home. It would be better to separate herself from her group of friends and then slip away.

"I'm really not hungry," she said when the consensus was to go inside Marvin's and have something to eat and another round of drinks. "Mr. Buddy Koepp has looked up here several times. His feelings will be hurt if I don't go and say hello to him." Tess didn't have to explain that the elderly man she'd mentioned had been her father's contemporary and friend.

"Well, come back and sit with us," Evelyn urged. "By then, you may have worked up an appetite."

A half hour later Tess was having doubts about the wisdom of her escape plan. Every few steps she ran into someone else she knew and had to stop and chat. Several people made gentle mention of having missed her father's presence at the boat parade, and she had to contend with a lump of emotion in her throat.

A number of others inquired about Will's whereabouts that day, plainly assuming that if Will weren't with Tess, he hadn't attended the event. "He's in north Louisiana on business," Tess explained, swept by fresh anxiety over the nature of that business and the identity of Will's client, herself.

Just about the time that she thought she might finally make her getaway, her name was blared out loud enough so that everyone on the waterfront must have been able to hear it. Ed Graham, one of her marina tenants who had been in the parade and now had his boat tied alongside the town dock, had spotted her and was addressing her, using the amplified hailing system that was installed on vessels for safety purposes. He obviously had had quite a bit to drink and issued an insistent public invitation for Tess to come over and join his party aboard his powerboat.

Not wanting to make even more of a scene or hurt his feelings, Tess went reluctantly. On the way she noticed that the large sailboat tied up in front of Ed was the same one with the tall pirate among its crew. They had shed their masks and were having drinks out on deck, but Tess couldn't pick him out among them. Probably he was down below, passed out in a stateroom.

Standing elbow to elbow with Ed's other guests in the powerboat cockpit, Tess sipped the can of cold beer that was pressed into her hands and forced a smile. The raucous laughter and high-pitched voices combined with loud music made her head throb. When half a dozen newcomers swarmed on board a few minutes after her arrival, she took advantage of the confusion and eased ashore.

As she hurried past the sailboat, hoping that she could manage to get to her car without being stopped again, she glanced over and still didn't see the tall pirate in evidence anywhere. He apparently had missed the dockside celebration. Judging from the activity on deck and the sound of the motor running, the sailboat was about to depart.

"Is everybody accounted for? We're about to cast off," the man standing at the wheel in the cockpit called out in a midwestern accent.

"What about Roussell?" answered a male voice. "Is he down below?"

"He left," a woman piped up to explain. "He asked me to tell you, Les, that he would find a way by land to get back to your house to pick up his car. Poor guy was so seasick he was green," she added sympathetically.

Tess had come to a complete standstill, unable to believe her ears. Her heart was pounding. The absent crew member under discussion was the tall pirate. She just knew it.

His name was Roussell.

Could he possibly be *Peter* Roussell? A thrill of disbelief chased up and down Tess's spine.

No, of course, he wasn't. The physical resemblance and the name had to be a coincidence. The man's seasickness was proof positive of that. Peter was an experienced boater. He had grown up in south Louisiana and gone shrimping and fishing with his father and brothers from the time he was a small boy. A calm sailboat ride wouldn't bother him, not even if he'd had too much to drink. And, the man's behavior had been entirely atypical of Peter. She couldn't imagine anything throwing him into that kind of catatonic state. Tess shivered, remembering.

Peter had been deeply emotional, but he had never held his emotions in check. He slammed doors when he was angry. He pounded tables with his fist when frustration welled to unmanageable levels. Jealous and hotheaded, he had turned aggressive in a heartbeat if some other guy had even looked at her the wrong way. Tess had had some anxious moments when she'd feared that Peter would pick a fight on her behalf and get the worst of it.

At the other end of the emotional spectrum, he hadn't been able to contain himself when he was happy and elated. Tess's pulses quickened with the memory of being swept up in Peter's arms and waltzed around the floor. Those exultant moods had inevitably erupted into passion. . . .

Tess drew in a breath and let it out in a sigh. No, that man today on the sailboat hadn't been Peter.

Yet it was conceivable that Peter could have been riding in the boat parade. On the short drive home, Tess dwelled on that realization. Major oil companies, including the one that had hired Peter right out of college, still had offices in New Orleans. Tess didn't doubt that he had stayed in petroleum engineering and survived all the severe cutbacks in the suffering oil-and-gas industry. Peter had been smart and had loved his field. By now he would have gotten an advanced degree, the way he had planned, and he would have been promoted. Tess felt a little glow of pride at the certainty.

By now, Peter would also have remarried, of course. He undoubtedly was a father. From a large family himself, he had wanted at least three or four children. Tess had been intrigued but daunted at the prospect of a household with more than three people.

Tess just couldn't imagine that the Peter who had been married to her, ever so briefly, would have participated in an all-day event on a weekend if it hadn't been a family outing. The insight into his character squeezed her heart with old painful regrets, but awoke warm approval, too.

Along with his faults, Peter had had many good traits. He had surely made some lucky woman a wonderful husband. Tess hoped that he was happy, wherever he was and whatever the circumstances of his life. Someday she would like to get news of him. Someday she would like to see him again and talk over old times.

Someday, but not now.

## Chapter Two

The riverfront presented a totally different view at mid-morning on Wednesday. There wasn't a person in sight and not a single boat tied up at the dock. On Sunday Peter hadn't paid any attention to the huge old live oaks with Spanish moss dripping from their outspread branches. In contrast, several other deciduous trees, also handsome specimens, looked conspicuously bare of foliage.

Between the street and the neat wooden dock, a generous expanse of grass was visible, dotted by the occasional bench and old-fashioned drinking fountain. Forming a backdrop, the buildings facing the street were painted white with only an occasional sober-colored exterior.

If Peter had been driving through, he probably would have been charmed by the whole scene. With time to spare, he might have taken a left turn across the bridge and stopped at Marvin's anyway, on sheer impulse. But there was no element of pleasure or choice for him today, just a sense of grim purpose.

He had taken the day off from work to come to Maryville and pay Tess a visit. Seeing her on Sunday had been a necessary kind of shock therapy, Peter told himself. Now three days later, he thought that he was recovered enough to take the follow-up treatment, encountering her face-to-face.

Stopping at Marvin's wasn't all procrastination, although, admittedly, it was partly that. Peter dreaded his mission and needed to shore up his courage, but from a practical standpoint he also needed information. Tess's married name, for example. Without knowing it, he couldn't even use a telephone directory to look up her number and find out her current address.

Peter didn't want to embark on a blind search to track Tess down, since the obvious starting point would be the marina or her father's house. He might find her at either place, but the chances were even better that he would run into Jake Davenport. Peter was braced for a meeting with the old man and would shake his hand and be civil, if it occurred, but he would avoid putting himself through that particular ordeal, if at all possible. He was going to have enough to handle carrying on a conversation with Tess and getting an update on her husband and kids.

The only vehicle parked outside of Marvin's was a sporty pickup truck with oversize wheels. Even without the gun rack visible through the cab windows, it made a macho statement about the owner. Peter left ample room between it and his BMW, got out and took a moment to glance around.

He had driven along the street with Tess on his first visit to Maryville to meet her parents. She had given him the grand tour, taking him through the heart of her hometown, which was really nothing more than a small village, and pointing out the tiny post office, a bank branch that wasn't any bigger, a grocery store, a filling station, a drive-up hamburger joint. Down here on the riverfront there had been a couple of seedy-looking bars, Peter recalled. Tess had mentioned them derogatorily as rough male hangouts.

He was fairly certain, thinking back, that Marvin's must have been one of them, but it had apparently been upgraded in respectability. At close range he could see that the porch was quite obviously an addition, built on to a plain-fronted, windowless facade. MARVIN'S BAR & RESTAURANT was painted in huge block letters across the whole upper portion of the building above the porch. The name could easily be read by motorists on the drawbridge and boaters on the river, but it had completely escaped Peter's notice on Sunday. His eyes had been locked on Tess's face.

Today his powers of observation were fully in operation, though. Walking to the porch with a long-legged stride, he noted that the door of Marvin's all but confirmed that the establishment had known more disreputable days. A single small pane of glass was located at eye level. Whatever restricted view it afforded of the interior was obstructed by the word DIXIE spelled out in red neon. Peter hadn't lived out of state so long that he needed to have explained to him that the owner wasn't being patriotic to the old south, but reminding his patrons that he served Dixie beer, bottled in New Orleans.

The brand name touched off memories of college parties. Tess hadn't really liked beer, but she'd tried to cultivate a taste for it, since it was the popular, affordable beverage. Peter had a sudden clear mental picture of her wrinkling up her nose and shivering as she forced down a sip.

Resolutely clearing away the image, he mounted the steps and stopped to look out at the river, a frown of concentration cutting lines between his dark eyebrows. This had been Tess's vantage point on Sunday. Had he attracted anything more than her idle notice?

It wasn't likely, he decided, and Tess would have had no inkling of his real identity anyway. She didn't know that he was living in New Orleans, and he was the last person she would ever expect to see participating in an event in Maryville. Peter would be safe in not making any mention of having ridden in the boat parade.

Inside he saw that Marvin's was definitely not a family eating establishment. A long bar extended across most of the back of the room. Above it a menu board announced the limited fare: boiled seafood in season, poboy sandwiches and fried-seafood plate dinners.

A plaintive country-western tune was coming from the jukebox, drowning out the sounds of a pool game that was in progress in a back room. Peter had a glimpse of a brawny upper torso poised to make a shot with a pool cue. The driver of the pickup truck had presumably taken on the owner or whoever had opened up, since nobody was tending bar.

Marvin's was exactly the kind of place that Peter had been hoping that it was, and the whole situation was made to order for his purposes. Sucking in his breath and then exhaling audibly, he headed over for the open door. Reaching it, he stopped and watched silently while the same muscular fellow, the younger of the two men in the room, put the eight ball in an end pocket to win the game.

"Nice shot," Peter remarked, leaning casually against the door frame. He suffered the quick scrutiny of both men without any qualms. Dressed in jeans and a rugged plaid shirt, he would meet with as much acceptance as any stranger could expect.

The older man, who had the looks of a proprietor, cursed his grinning companion, addressing him as Buster, and went over to return his pool cue to the wall rack.

"Come on, Marvin, don't be such a sore ass," implored Buster, retrieving the balls from the pockets. "That was just a little run of luck there."

"I got work to do," Marvin growled. "I can't spend all day shooting pool with you, Buster."

Buster looked over at Peter questioningly.

Peter shrugged, as though to say he had nothing better to do than to shoot a few games of pool. While he was selecting a pool cue, he wished fleetingly that his only motive in taking Buster on was to kill some leisure time in friendly competition. He could have enjoyed the opportunity to test his rusty skills. Peter had done his share of hanging around local pool halls with adolescent buddies and had been a pretty good pool player at one time.

Marvin was staying to watch, Peter saw, as he stepped up to one end of the table, where Buster stood waiting to lag for break, standard procedure for determining which player got to go first.

For the moment Peter pushed aside his reason for being there in Marvin's on a Wednesday, early in the day. He concentrated all his attention on the pool table, first planning the sequence of shots, executing them one by one in the watchful silence and ending up with sinking the black eight ball, thus winning the game.

Plainly challenged, Buster offered to buy Peter a beer, and Peter accepted, seconding Buster's request for a long-necked bottle of Dixie. Marvin got a beer for himself, as well. Peter took advantage of the interlude to volunteer an explanation of his presence.

"I'm looking around for a marina over here on this side of the lake where I could keep a boat and not have to worry about it being safe," he announced after he'd taken a big swallow of ice-cold beer. "If possible, I'd like to find a small operation where the owner keeps an eye on things."

"There's Tess Davenport's marina," Buster said thoughtfully.

Marvin nodded. "Tess lives practically next door to her marina, and she's there every day, just like her old man was, when he was alive."

Peter nearly choked on his second swallow of beer. "I don't know about doing business with a woman," he managed to get out, even though his mind was reeling. Jake Davenport was dead. Tess owned the marina now. Buster had referred to her by her maiden name. Could that mean that she was unmarried? Peter fought a wild surge of hope. "Is there a husband in the picture?" he asked.

"There ain't one in the picture now, but I hear tell there's gonna be." Buster looked to Marvin for verification of the rumor.

"Put it like this. Wouldn't come as no big surprise to anybody," Marvin stated wisely.

Tess wasn't married to some other man. But she was seriously involved with someone. Peter took in the two separate revelations, feeling as if he'd just been given a delay in execution. Looking from Buster to Marvin inquiringly, he had to bite back a righteous demand for a full explanation, *Tell me the facts, dammit. Who the hell is the guy you're expecting Tess to marry?*

"Personally, I'm of the same opinion as some other folks that Will Buford's robbing the cradle," Buster remarked to Marvin.

"Tess ain't no spring chicken anymore," Marvin pointed out imperturbably.

"She was a year behind me in school, and I was thirty-one my last birthday. Buford's pushing fifty," Buster retorted. "Why, he's got grown kids."

Marvin's sage expression didn't change. "Tess could do a lot worse. Will's well thought of, and he's not exactly a poor man, either."

"What does he do for a living?" Peter put in tersely. Both men had been pursuing the conversation and ignoring him. They looked at him now with vague surprise at his interest.

"Buford's a lawyer, but he's big in parish politics and has his fingers in lots of pies," Buster explained with mixed admiration and contempt. He went on in the same tone, "Drives a big Cadillac and owns a fancy boat with twin screw engines. He keeps it in Tess's marina. Guess he'll be getting free rent soon." He grinned at his own humor and eyed Peter curiously. "What kind of boat do you have?"

"Right now, I don't own a boat," Peter admitted. "But I'm seriously considering buying a sailboat." The truthful disclosure of his intention met with no empathy from the present company, not surprisingly. But Peter had already learned enough and now there was a sense of urgency in locating Tess. He would find out the rest of the story from her.

"Never could understand the attraction of a sailboat," Buster declared, shaking his head. "Me, I'd rather have my fishing skiff any day." He downed the last of his beer and picked up his pool cue, ready to resume play.

Peter couldn't just walk out, but his concentration was totally gone. He lost his turn on the break, not managing to sink a ball, and mentally urged Buster on to victory. Buster missed after making several shots, and the two of them alternated back and forth until it seemed that the game would drag on forever. Apparently bored with the mediocre level of play, Marvin abandoned his spectator's role and went about his business in the other room.

Finally, Buster won, sinking the eight ball under the interested eye of another local patron who had strolled in. Peter made his escape, paying for beers for both men on his way out.

On the porch, he glanced out at the river view that he had passed earlier to scrutinize through Tess's eyes. It was no longer a matter of concern that she might make a connection between him and a strange-acting man in the boat parade on Sunday. With the news that there hadn't been a husband here on the porch with her or somewhere in the crowd, Peter had completely changed his mind about keeping his presence in Maryville three days ago a secret.

His whole outlook on paying Tess a visit was entirely different now. He intended to hide nothing, present or past. His pride had controlled him eleven years ago, but his pride could be damned.

Relying on memory, Peter easily found the street that ran roughly parallel to the river and would take him past her house to the marina, a short distance farther on. As he drove, he pondered what her unguarded reaction would be to having him appear without any warning.

Aside from the normal surprise, what would she feel on seeing him? Would she be flooded with old emotions, as he had been on Sunday, or had all those emotions long since dulled and died away? Despite the long separation, Peter thought that he would sense almost immediately whether Tess had gotten over him.

If she had, how would he deal with it?

That was a question he wasn't prepared to answer. Peter was acting on sheer instinct at this point and not trying to look into the future.

He slowed down when he came to the house, but didn't pull into the driveway when he didn't see a car or evidence that anyone was home. The house was still painted white with blue trim. Maybe it was his imagination, but it had a bleak, lonely air. It would be large for one person, Peter reflected, wondering for the first time, as he drove on, how long it had been since Jake Davenport had died.

The marina was smaller than he remembered and even more rustic. The rough creosoted pilings stood askew at slight angles, and the wooden docks didn't look in the best repair. The tin roofing over the covered slips had obviously been through more than one hurricane and was ruffled and uneven. Peter's general impression was that the whole place was rather run-down.

It apparently wasn't at full occupancy. Following the rutted driveway that wound back to the office and fuel dock, he saw half a dozen empty slips and recalled Les Morgan's having mentioned that there was an abundance of boat slips available on the North Shore. Was Tess feeling the squeeze of competition?

Peter's heart lurched at the likelihood that he might soon have all his questions answered. As he rounded a curve, the office came into view, and someone was there. A car was parked next to the one-story structure perched on the water's edge. Made of weathered cypress and covered with a tin roof, the building was smaller and more dilapidated than he remembered, too.

As he drove the remaining distance, Peter concentrated on recalling the interior layout. The door opened into a main room that Jake Davenport had kept stocked as a convenience store with beer and soft drinks and snack foods. It could also be entered from the fuel dock outside. Over to the left were restrooms and a storeroom. On the right was a smaller room with rudimentary office furniture.

Wherever Tess was inside, she should be alerted to his arrival, Peter reflected. The sound of his tires crunching the embedded clam shells was so loud and abrasive that it made him wince. He slammed his car door quietly, but the noise reverberated in his ears, almost deafening him as he walked the few steps to the building, opened the door without knocking and stepped inside.

One quick glance around told him that no one was in the main room. Before he had time to cope with the knowledge and call out to inquire if anyone was on the premises, Tess's voice came through the open doorway on his right.

"Will, is that you? I'm in here, in the office."

Her familiar husky cadences washed over Peter, bathing him in pleasure and pain. He stood rooted to the spot, incapable of speaking while he struggled to contain the same powerful mixed response that had overwhelmed him three days ago, when he had seen her at a distance.

"Will?" Tess called out again, this time with a note of uncertainty.

The harsh scrape of wood on wood brought Peter out of his paralysis. Tess was pushing back her chair, intending to come out to see who her visitor was. He headed toward the open doorway as he answered, "No, it isn't Will, Tess."

Silence came from inside the room.

Peter felt a fierce satisfaction, along with a fresh surge of bittersweet pleasure, as he came to a stop just inside the smaller room, where Tess waited for him. She had made it around to the side of a battered old wooden desk before she'd been halted by her recognition of his voice. Her dark brown eyes were wide with shock, and her expression mirrored her inner turmoil.

For several seconds they looked at each other. It was time enough for Peter to confirm what his first glance had told him. At thirty, Tess had lost none of her physical appeal for him. More womanly now than girlish, she was still slim and just as sexy in old jeans and a sweatshirt that only hinted at the curves underneath. She had the same vivid coloring that made her pretty without makeup, the same expressive features, the same tender, kissable mouth. Peter focused on the latter as Tess found her voice and whispered his name.

"Peter..."

"Hello, Tess," he said gently, fighting the impulse to go over and take her into his arms. She would feel so right. The knowledge was an ache inside him.

"That *was* you in the boat parade Sunday," she murmured.

It took a second for her observation to sink in. Peter stared at her, taken completely off guard. "But you couldn't possibly have recognized me," he pointed out incredulously. "I was in costume and wearing a mask."

She nodded in agreement that she hadn't been able to see through his disguise. Peter was absurdly disappointed and not altogether convinced. There was something vaguely defensive about her manner as she collected herself to explain.

"After the parade I overheard your friends on the sailboat talking about you. Of course, I assumed that it was another man with the same name, especially when someone said that you had gotten off the boat to get a ride because you were seasick. I knew that you had never had a problem with seasickness."

It had disturbed her to be reminded of him and to consider the possibility of his proximity. Peter could read the admission in her eyes and voice, along with her unspoken question: What had been wrong with him?

"I still don't have a problem with it," he told her simply. "That was just the best excuse that I could come up with at the time. I saw you watching the parade from the porch of Marvin's and my emotions got the best of me. When I accepted the invitation to ride in the boat parade, I thought I was prepared for seeing you again, but obviously I wasn't."

Tess drew in a deep breath and backed around to stand behind the desk. "How does it happen that you got the invitation?" she asked.

"The owner of the sailboat is a company man. I was transferred to New Orleans a couple of months ago."

Her somber expression told him that he was merely confirming what she'd already guessed. "You're still in petroleum engineering?"

Peter replied that he was and, anticipating her next question, added that he was also still employed by the same oil company that had hired him right out of college.

She nodded, once again not surprised. "You've been happy and successful in your career then. I'm glad to hear that. Naturally I thought of you when I would hear of oil companies cutting back on employees the last few years." She sat down in the chair behind her and confessed with a wan smile, "My knees are a little weak. In the back of my mind, I've always assumed that the two of us would meet again someday and catch up on each other, but I never imagined that you would just drop in like this. Lately I've had more than my share of surprises."

Peter made an apologetic gesture when what he really yearned to do was go around behind the desk and touch her reassuringly. "I should have called and given you some advance warning, but I took it for granted that you had married again, and I couldn't get your telephone number from information without knowing your husband's name," he pointed out.

"I haven't remarried. My number is listed under Tess Davenport. I took back my maiden name."

"I was sure that your father would insist on that before the divorce was final." Peter couldn't keep a tinge of bitter resentment from creeping into his voice, even with the knowledge that Jake Davenport was dead.

"Actually I waited a couple of years," Tess informed him. "By then I figured that there was another Mrs. Peter Roussell."

"But there wasn't. I haven't married again, either," he told her.

"You stayed single?" She looked him over skeptically, absorbing with difficulty his first startling news about himself. Peter's body responded to her examining gaze. "Any minute I was expecting you to take out your wallet and show me pictures of your wife and children. One reason that I didn't think the Roussell in the boat parade could be you was that I was so certain you would be a family man now. You wanted at least four kids."

Peter shrugged, acknowledging the reminder, but sidestepping an explanation of why he had remained a bachelor. He couldn't just blurt out the true reason, and he didn't want to be glib and insincere. "It seems that we both pictured each other as parents," he remarked. "I drove over today, prepared to find you involved in Girl Scouts and PTA and the local booster club for junior sports."

Tess shook her head. "Isn't it ironic? We were in such a hurry to get married when we were too young, and here we've ended up staying single past the age when we should be settled down." Before Peter could reply, she went on sadly, without any transition, "My father died a year ago."

Peter inclined his head in deference to her loss, but conventional words of condolence wouldn't form on his lips. Did you ever regret your decision, Tess? he wanted to ask her. Did you ever think that your father was wrong and selfish, coming between us?

"I'm sure you miss him a great deal," he finally managed to get out.

"I do," she said, matching his formal tone. "How are your parents?"

"They're fine."

"They must be happy that you're back in Louisiana and can get home often."

"Yes, they are." Peter listened along with her to the sound of a car door slamming. Fortunately, it didn't come from immediately outside. He hoped that the driver was a boat owner and wouldn't interrupt them.

"That's probably Will Buford," Tess said, both her face and her voice gravely troubled. "He's an old friend and also my attorney. He'll be over to discuss a legal matter that he's handling for me."

"I gather that it's something serious," Peter commented, torn between concern and the jealous awareness that he was about to meet the man she was expected to marry.

"Very serious."

He frowned, visualizing the run-down state of the marina. "You're not being sued by one of your renters?"

"No, I'm not being sued." She hesitated. "I'm having some inheritance problems."

"Inheritance problems?" Peter queried skeptically. "Your father owned the marina, free and clear, didn't he? As his only child, you should automatically inherit everything."

Tess sighed. "It's not something that I want to be public knowledge, but I've found out recently that I'm not my father's only child. A half brother who lives up in Shreveport has come out of nowhere and is demanding his share of my father's estate."

"A half brother," Peter echoed, staring at her. "Your father had an illegitimate son?"

"No, apparently he was married briefly to another woman up in north Louisiana when he was in his early twenties."

"And your father never mentioned any of this to you?" Peter was too incredulous to be disapproving.

Tess shook her head.

"He didn't keep it secret from your mother, too?"

"I don't know whether he did or not," she admitted unhappily. "I prefer to think that he didn't. Whatever the true story is, I have to believe that it wouldn't reflect badly on him, but you can understand why I'd rather protect his memory and just keep the whole matter secret."

"But how are you going to keep something like this a secret? Your brother will want to come to Maryville to meet you, won't he?"

"He hasn't expressed any desire to meet me, and he isn't my *brother*. He didn't even come to my father's funeral," Tess added resentfully when Peter raised his eyebrows at her disclaimer of kinship.

"It's possible that he wasn't informed of your father's death," he pointed out.

"Well, he certainly found out about it somehow," she retorted cynically. "He must have been keeping tabs through the years, like a vulture. Now I have to figure out a way to raise the money to pay him off."

"You do intend to meet him?"

"No, I don't intend that at all," she denied. "What would be the point? I'll let Will handle it. Please, Peter, if you should happen to run into people who know me, don't mention any of this."

Peter made an impatient gesture. "Tess, of course, you can trust me to keep your personal business confidential. As for running into people who know you, it's very probable that I will be doing that. I'm planning to buy a sailboat and will, more than likely, keep it over here on the North Shore."

She was silent, absorbing that information. "A sailboat," she said finally with a kind of resigned interest.

"Yes, I've gotten hooked on sailing since I moved to New Orleans, but it's almost impossible to rent a boat slip in the city marinas. They have long waiting lists."

"You won't have any trouble renting a slip over here. A number of marinas have been built in the last seven or eight years. There are several over in Mandeville, near the Causeway, and a couple of nice little yacht clubs, too, that aren't so exclusive like those in New Orleans."

"I'm not much of a yacht-club type," Peter demurred. "Racing in regattas doesn't really appeal to me, at least not right now. Sailing is enough challenge in itself. I noticed when I was driving through the marina that you have some empty slips," he commented without a pause.

The idea that Peter might rent a slip from her obviously hadn't even crossed Tess's mind. "You want to keep a boat in *my* marina?" she blurted out.

"Why not?" Peter asked.

Before she could answer, the outer door to the main room was thrust open. Peter turned to see a beefy man in his late forties enter. The broad smile on the man's face faded at the sight of Peter, and he crossed the room with an aggressive stride.

Nodding briefly to acknowledge Peter's presence, he stopped in the doorway to look at Tess with an indulgent, proprietorial eye. "Hi," he said, managing to make the one-syllable greeting an intimate communication. "Busy?"

Peter had to unclench his hands, which had knotted into fists. The man's manner infuriated him. "Peter Roussell," he said in an assertive tone before Tess could introduce him. "You must be Will Buford, Tess's attorney. She was just telling me that you're handling her legal affairs."

"Roussell." Buford switched his gaze to Peter and made the minimal response. He frowned slightly, as though searching his memory, and looked inquiringly back at Tess.

She nodded, answering his unspoken question. "The same Peter Roussell that I was married to when I was a teenager," she told him before explaining for Peter's benefit, "Will was my father's lawyer, too, and took care of all the paperwork for our separation and divorce."

That information would have been reason enough for Peter to dislike the man, who quite obviously reciprocated Peter's antagonism.

"It's amazing, isn't it, hon, who can turn up when there's been a death in the family and a sizable inheritance is involved," Buford drawled to Tess.

Peter's temper hadn't flared up so hotly in years. It wasn't just the insinuating remark that made him want to take a swing at the lawyer, but the use of the endearment in a casually possessive tone of voice.

Tess sprang up out of her chair and came around the desk, talking nervously. "Peter is a petroleum engineer. He's been transferred to his company's New Orleans office. Before you came in, Will, Peter was just mentioning that he's in the market for a sailboat." She looked from one man to the other, imploring them both to take her lead and treat each other with civility.

"He shouldn't have any trouble finding one to buy, especially in the smaller size range. Sailboats are a dime a dozen, with all the layoffs in the oil patch." Will directed his faintly condescending reply to her and then glanced pointedly at his watch. "I'm due back at my office in an hour and a half, hon. We have important business to discuss."

Tess apologized mutely to Peter, her dark eyes shadowed with worry again. "It was good to see you—" She broke off as Peter reached to his hip pocket of his jeans and took out his wallet.

"What do I owe you for a month's slip rent?" he asked. "Or do you charge by the quarter?"

"No, I charge by the month," she answered uncertainly. "How much?"

She told him the amount and then protested as he began to pull out bills, "You don't need to reserve a slip ahead of time. I have enough vacant that there should be one available when you need it."

"But I'd rather not take any chances," Peter said resolutely, and walked over closer than necessary to give her the money. She went tense and kept her eyes on his hand as she accepted the payment. When he didn't move back, she let out her breath and looked up at him. Peter held her gaze, his whole body responding to her nearness and her awareness of him. Buford shifted and cleared his throat impatiently, reminding them both that he was there in the background.

Tess closed her eyes and swallowed. Then she went around behind the desk and sat down with a little plop, as though her knees had given out on her. "I can always give you a refund, if you find a marina that suits your purposes better," she said, opening a drawer noisily and putting the money in it.

"I won't," Peter told her softly. "Buford." He nodded at the other man, who glowered at him and stood aside to allow him room to pass.

## Chapter Three

Will, if you don't mind, could we talk later...this afternoon or maybe tonight?" Tess asked weakly, sagging in her chair. Her whole body was limp, and she wanted desperately to be alone to recover from Peter's surprise visit.

"Sure, hon," Will agreed in his low rumbling tone, but he stood firmly planted, without making a move to leave. "I picked up some lunch for us. Let's go over to the boat where it's more comfortable and have a bite to eat." He made a beckoning gesture.

"I'm sorry, but I couldn't possibly eat anything right now. It was a shock seeing Peter after all these years, and my nerves are too jangled. But you go ahead."

He scowled, eyeing her with concern. "There's no big hurry. I can wait until you settle down. Come on over with me, and I'll fix you something to drink."

"Will, *please*, I'm not in the mood for company right now!"

"Okay, hon, I'm going." He turned to leave and then looked back at her again, heaving a sigh of worry and frustration. "You're not going to give this guy another shot at breaking your heart, are you, Tess? He didn't care a thing about you, hon, or he would have tried to keep you. You haven't heard one word from him in all this time."

"The fact that I'm upset over seeing Peter doesn't mean that I would allow myself to get involved with him a second time. I have no intention of making the same mistake again."

"Then you ought to give him his money back the next time he comes around and tell him to go rent a boat slip in somebody else's marina."

Tess opened her mouth to argue and then closed it. He was right, of course, even if she did need all the income that she could get from the marina now. Still, she couldn't quite bring herself to promise him that she would follow his sage advice. "Just give me a few minutes to pull myself together, Will, and I'll be over," she promised instead.

"Good girl." He smiled and winked at her encouragingly and finally left her alone.

Tess slumped deeper into her chair, conscience-stricken at how relieved she was to be rid of Will so that she could think about Peter in privacy. Will had been her bulwark the last year, always there to comfort and advise whenever she needed him. He was kind and considerate and utterly dependable. He seemed to care about her genuinely and wanted to marry her. Despite her appreciation for his solid qualities, though, the shallow woman in her preferred Peter over Will.

Peter had hurt and disappointed her, but she still responded to him as strongly as before. Her heart beat faster and she felt a surge of pleasure as she called up a mental picture of him. He was even handsomer now in his early thirties than he had been when she'd met and fallen for him. Everything about his appearance and his physical presence pleased her, his voice, his clean-cut looks, his height and build and the way he carried himself, his whole brand of masculinity.

The attraction wasn't one-sided, either. Tess still appealed to Peter. He had wanted very much to touch her. She had sensed his restraint and had had to fight herself to keep from giving him the merest signal that would have snapped his control. If he had tried to take her into his arms, Tess doubted that she would have been able to resist him, as shameful as the admission was. Just the thought of being held by him, of being kissed by him, caused an ache of pure yearning now.

Peter would still be able to arouse her and satisfy her sexually. . . .

Tess stood up abruptly before her imagination could test out her instinct. He was undoubtedly an even better lover now, with all the practice that he'd had, making love with other women since her, she told herself contemptuously, calling on pride to come to her rescue.

The question was whether it would hold up as a strong enough protection if she were faced with the temptation of intimacy with Peter. Based on her reaction to his visit today, Tess didn't trust herself, and she had problems enough in her life at the moment without getting involved in an affair with her ex-husband.

Even if she treated him impersonally and Peter took the hint and made no overtures, Tess would find it very disruptive to have him coming and going in the marina. Her best course of action was to do what Will had recommended. She would refund Peter's rent money at the first opportunity and state plainly that she preferred not to have any more contact with him while he was living in the New Orleans area.

Meanwhile Tess had other pressing matters to think about and to deal with. She left the office and walked over toward Will's boat, a big twin-engine sports-fishing yacht with a flybridge on top. Because of the boat's size, it took expert maneuvering for him to get it into the slip. But Will liked large boats and large luxurious cars. Parked in front of his covered slip was his white Cadillac. The sight of it made Tess wonder what kind of car Peter drove now that he was successful.

A wistful smile curved her lips at the memory of his transportation in college, a battered VW Beetle with fenders of different colors. The body had been assembled out of parts from junkyards, but he'd kept the engine tuned, and the little car had started at the turn of a key and had run faultlessly. She had loved driving it, but Jake Davenport had worried about accidents and insisted upon giving them a heavier, safer secondhand car after they were married.

Peter had stubbornly refused to sell his car or use the one provided by his father-in-law, she recalled, sighing. But then they had needed two cars after her mother died and Tess was going home every weekend to take care of her grief-stricken father.

If her mother had remained healthy and lived and their marriage hadn't been subjected to such stress almost from the first, would Peter and Tess have had a good chance of staying together? She had asked herself that question numerous times in latter years and always concluded that it wasn't likely. Theirs hadn't been a resilient, lasting love, but the wildly passionate, consuming kind that would have burned itself out eventually anyway.

It certainly wasn't the kind of man-woman relationship that Tess wanted or needed at this stage of her life, even if it could be fanned into flames again.

But, on the other hand, would she be happy and satisfied with what Will offered her, a bland, stable relationship that was completely free of all the sharp tension and all the excitement, too?

Tess was no closer to a yes or no answer after the few minutes in Peter's company. Skirting the bulk of Will's car, she could see the name painted on the glossy transom of his boat, *Mary IV*. Will had named all of his boats after his wife, Mary, who had died of cancer a year and a half ago.

Will's reputation, whether deserved or not, had always been that he had an eye for the ladies, but he had earned universal admiration for the way he'd taken care of Mary during her lingering illness. Tess knew that he had grieved over his wife after she was gone and kept her very fondly in his thoughts, even if he didn't cling to the past. It was a bond between him and Tess that they'd both lost dear ones and felt free to talk about them.

Tess hadn't been close to Mary Buford, but she'd considered her a pleasant, likeable woman and felt as if she knew her much better now, through Will's eyes. He and Tess's father had gotten on famously. It warmed her heart to listen to Will's anecdotes describing Jake Davenport as a crusty individual.

She had known Will for literally half of her life, since he'd kept a succession of boats, each bigger than the last, in the Davenport marina for fifteen years. One of the pleasures of his company was that he had always spent a lot of time in the marina and thus had shared in much of her background. Any marina happening or colorful personality that she recalled would strike a chord of memory with him, and vice versa.

It was too bad that she and Will couldn't just continue their present relationship, Tess reflected regretfully, walking with sure feet along the uneven pier. She liked seeing him often and being his regular date, but she didn't know if she wanted to spend the rest of her life with him.

Will came out into the rear cockpit in response to her tap on the side deck. "Come on aboard, hon," he invited, and waited for her. When she came close, he opened his arms, and she went into them with no repugnance, but with no rush of eagerness, either. Hugging him around his middle, she was conscious that he had a slight paunch, and she tried hard, without succeeding, to blot out the awareness of how different it would feel to be in Peter's arms and pressed against his taller, leaner body. Guilt made her give Will a tighter squeeze.

"I missed you while you were in Shreveport," she told him fervently.

"I missed you, too, baby. With a welcome like this, I might go away more often," he declared in a pleased voice. "How about a hello kiss?" He slackened his embrace just enough for Tess to submit to his request and bent his head the necessary few inches so that she didn't have to rise up on her toes.

Tess closed her eyes as she met his lips, remembering how Peter had handled their difference in height when they would kiss. He had lifted her and held her so that their faces were on the same level. Tess had wrapped her arms around his neck and kissed him until they both were breathless. His lips had been firm, not fleshy. His tongue had been ardent, the contact sweet and hot....

"Come on, hon, you can do better than that," Will chided disappointedly as Tess pulled back.

"Someone may drive up," she said, trying to free herself of his hold. "Besides, I'm starving."

Both excuses rang hollow. Tess stopped struggling when he wouldn't let her go. She met his frustrated gaze apologetically and watched his expression harden.

"I'd like to get my hands on Roussell. He really did a number on you, didn't he, hon?"

"I'm sorry," Tess murmured, appalled that she had been so transparent and communicated somehow that she was kissing Will and thinking about Peter.

Will went on, his voice gentling. "Don't be sorry. I'm not blaming you, but I can help you get over this, hon, if you'll just trust me and give me a chance. It puzzled me why a good-looking woman like you hadn't found herself another man," he explained hesitantly. "Then after we started going together, I suspected what the trouble was."

"Trouble?" Tess echoed, puzzled by his embarrassed air.

"Don't make out like you don't understand, hon," he pleaded. "We need to talk about it. You don't mind touching and kissing, as long as there's no danger of it leading anywhere, but you freeze up in a second when we start getting aroused."

Will thought she had a problem with sex. "I don't 'freeze up,'" she contradicted, biting back the rest of the denial. She hadn't ever begun to get aroused with him. "I just know enough to play fair and not let things get out of hand with a man."

He sighed and reluctantly released her. "Have it your way, hon. Just answer me one question. Isn't it the sexual part of married life that's keeping you back from becoming my wife?"

"That and the fact that I don't really love you, not the way that I loved Peter," Tess told him honestly, enormously relieved to get her feelings out into the open, as much as she hated hurting Will.

He made an impatient sound. "That was puppy love, hon. We're both past the age for it, and it didn't make you happy, anyway, did it?"

"No," Tess admitted. "But I can't leave you with the false impression that Peter gave me a hang-up about sex, because he didn't. He let me down in other ways, but not in that one."

"This is enough discussion on an empty stomach," Will declared, putting his arm around her shoulders. "Let's have some lunch."

He obviously was unconvinced, but Tess gladly dropped the subject for the time being. Inside the comfortable main cabin she saw that he had set the teak table with nautical-design place mats, cutlery and insulated cups. There was the aroma of food and freshly brewed coffee.

Tess sniffed appreciatively. "Something smells too good to be hamburgers and French fries."

"I worked up a real hunger for some highly-seasoned food while I was up in north Louisiana the last few days," Will replied. "Those folks go in for bland cooking."

He had bought a quart of seafood gumbo and a separate container of steamed rice from a popular seafood restaurant, which didn't stint on the fresh oysters, shrimp and crabmeat that went into the savory concoction. Tess always ordered gumbo, which was one of her favorite dishes, when she and Will ate at the restaurant. Even though he didn't say as much, she knew that he'd planned the noon meal as a surprise treat for her.

Then he'd arrived at the marina and walked in on the scene with her and Peter. Tess was twice as sorry for the way that she had treated Will after Peter's departure.

"Why didn't you tell me that you had the best gumbo in town for lunch?" she said, pretending to scold him. "I'd have been over sooner."

At her insistence that she could handle the simple preparations more speedily, he went over to sit down out of her way and watched with an indulgent eye while she warmed up bowls of gumbo and rice, using the microwave in the well-equipped galley. It was cozy and relaxed. They chatted about inconsequential topics. After the delicious meal, Tess served them both coffee and broached the subject of Will's trip to Shreveport on her behalf.

She already knew his findings from telephone conversations with him, but he restated them calmly. Her half brother's inheritance claim was valid. The documents supporting it were authentic, not forgeries, as Tess had hoped. The next step was determining the monetary worth of his share of her father's estate, which would involve getting appraisals of property value.

"You don't worry your pretty little head about a thing," Will urged her, patting her on the hand. "I'll take care of what has to be done. You can depend on me to look out for your interest."

"I know that I can, and I'm very grateful," Tess said. She hesitated, nibbling at her lower lip as she recalled a portion of her conversation with Peter. "Do you think that I ought to meet my half brother, Will?"

He frowned at the idea, immediately shaking his head. "Personally I would advise against it. You might be opening up a whole can of worms. If he got even a hint of how concerned you are about not letting any news of him leak out, he could have us over a barrel."

"You mean he could blackmail me into paying him more."

"Exactly."

"And he obviously doesn't have any desire to meet me, or he would have gone about this differently. He could have contacted me himself instead of going through a lawyer."

"This guy's only interest in his family tree is cashing in on it," Will stated cynically. "In a way, that's fortunate. We won't have to worry about him turning up and visiting your father's grave. You'll never hear from him again after he's been paid."

She nodded, reassured. "You said that you didn't uncover any details about my father's first marriage."

Will patted her hand again. "Hon, I didn't even try. If you wanted to uncover the whole story, you could hire a private detective, but what would be the point? You and I both know that your daddy was a good, honest man who wouldn't shirk his duty. He must have left north Louisiana with a clear conscience. Maybe there was another man in the picture who was going to adopt the boy. Maybe the woman's family was well-to-do. There are numerous circumstances that could account for your daddy's having peace of mind about that early chapter in his life. I, for one, am confident that he didn't have anything to be ashamed of and am perfectly satisfied just to leave the matter there."

"That's what I plan to do," Tess said, warmed by his stout defense of her father's character. She was sitting next to him on the L-shaped settee that provided seating along the back side and one end of the table. Feeling a surge of gratitude and affection, she leaned over and kissed him on the cheek. "Thank you for everything."

His arm closed around her, drawing her close and making her regret the impulse. The last thing she wanted at this particular moment was to have to reject a physical advance. She was afraid that her relief showed on her face when he gave her a hard hug and then allowed her to scoot away, putting a few inches between them again.

"I'd understand if you started dating other women, Will," she told him.

He didn't pretend not to understand. His expression dismissed the idea. "You've been under a terrible strain, hon," he said gruffly, massaging her neck with thick, strong fingers. "First, your daddy passing away and then all this recent worry."

Tess was saved from answering. The polished brass ship's clock, mounted with a barometer on a bulkhead in the main cabin, took that moment to chime the hour. Will glanced at his watch to verify its accuracy and reluctantly withdrew his hand.

"I'd love to spend the whole afternoon with you, but I really shouldn't take off," he said on a resigned note.

Tess offered to do the minimal amount of cleaning up, and he left. While she washed the few dishes, dried them and put them away, she thought about the excuses that he had offered for her lack of interest in sex with him. They didn't hold up. Tess had been over the worst of her grief before learning about her father's first marriage and the existence of a half brother.

The truth was that Will didn't turn her on physically, and she hadn't been tempted to go to bed with him. If she did, she didn't think that she would be revolted, but doubted that she would be satisfied, either. That would be hard on Will's ego because Tess wasn't going to lie to him and pretend.

Perhaps her intuition was wrong, though, and she was holding out mentally, just as Will thought. If she made up her mind that she was going to have sex with him and went through with it, she might discover that he was a wonderful lover. The intimacy could possibly erase all her doubts about marrying him.

For the second time that day, but for a different reason entirely, Tess didn't give her imagination free range.

She finished quickly, locked Will's boat with the spare key he'd given her and went back to the office and called Evelyn

Laird to arrange an impromptu shopping expedition for that afternoon instead of on Saturday, when they'd planned to go. Both of them needed to buy a wedding present and a gift for a baby shower.

"What happened? Can't Billy work Saturday?" Evelyn asked. Billy Batson was a high-school youth Tess employed part-time.

"No, it's just dead here in the marina and I haven't had a single customer at the fuel dock today," Tess explained. "I did paperwork and bookkeeping all morning. I'm restless and need to get out around people."

"Well, I'm glad to hear that," Evelyn said, pleased. "Lately you've turned into a regular hermit. I'm in the middle of cutting out a pattern, but, sure, I'll go shopping."

"Thanks, Evelyn. You've saved my sanity," Tess declared fervently.

It was imperative that Tess get out of the office, out of the marina. She didn't want to think about Peter's visit. She didn't want to think about her lunch with Will. She just wanted to do something ordinary and feel like her old outgoing self again.

Besides, she needed to be around on weekends. That was when Peter would most likely return. Since he'd given her cash, not a check, she couldn't mail his rent back to him with a letter.

"From the looks of the weather forecast, you probably won't need Billy this weekend," Evelyn commented on the drive over to Slidell to a shopping center. "A front is coming down from Canada, and it's supposed to be nasty, with freezing temperatures. Nobody in his right mind will be out on the water."

"Those weather forecasters are right about half the time," Tess replied gloomily. "I don't usually bother to watch the weather portion of the news."

She watched it faithfully during the next two days, though, and read the daily weather forecast in the *Times Picayune*, the New Orleans newspaper. The cold front came in on Friday afternoon, right on schedule. Before she went out that night, she called Billy and freed him for the weekend. It would be too cold in the office, which wasn't insulated or well-heated, for him to do stocking or cleaning to occupy his time.

Saturday morning Tess awoke about seven and got up to see that it was gray and blustery outside, with a temperature reading in the low thirties on the outdoor thermometer on her screened back porch. She went back to bed and slept until nine. Dressed in her warmest robe, which was also her oldest and shabbiest, and a pair of heavy socks, she made coffee and then dashed out to get the newspaper at the end of the driveway.

By the time she had read the paper and drunk several cups of coffee, it was nine-thirty. She considered getting dressed and then decided that she would have some breakfast first. A real breakfast, not just cereal or toast. For company, she turned on the TV in the kitchen, flipped very quickly through the channels playing cartoons and found a cooking program on the public television station.

It was on days like this that Tess knew for certain that she couldn't spend the rest of her life living alone. She just wasn't the kind of person to thrive on solitude. As she checked the pantry and found a box of pancake mix, she mulled over the idea of calling Will and asking him if he'd like to brave the cold and have breakfast with her.

A knocking sound caught her attention. She went over to the TV and turned down the volume to listen. The knocking came again from the front of the house. After a moment's hesitation, she went to see who was at the door. She retied the sash of her robe on the way and shook back her long hair. Fortunately she had given it a few strokes of the brush before going outside earlier.

Through the shirred lace covering the glass upper portion of the door, Tess could see that her caller was a man, wearing a blue hooded parka. She pushed aside the edge of the curtain for a better look and peered into Peter's dark eyes. He smiled at her and clapped his gloved hands against the chill.

"What on earth—" Tess murmured, unlocking the door with nervous fingers. She opened it just wide enough to stick her head out and greet him. "Peter." The statement of his name conveyed that he'd taken her off guard once again.

"Did I get you out of bed?" he asked, sounding more interested than apologetic.

"No, I've been up awhile. I just had the TV turned up loud. I was watching a cooking program," she hurriedly explained when his eyebrows quirked.

"You don't have to be ashamed to admit to me that you were watching cartoons," he chided.

"I haven't watched cartoons in years. I've grown up since we were married, Peter," Tess said with dignity.

"Not even the old Looney Tunes cartoons?"

"Every now and then, if I happen to tune in accidentally," she admitted.

"Do you still turn on cartoons on Saturdays?" The question came out sounding wistful.

"Very seldom." He clapped his hands together again. "You wouldn't happen to have some coffee made, would you? I could sure use a cup."

"I'm not dressed for company," Tess protested, but opened the door wider and stood back for him to enter. He stripped off his gloves, stuck them in the pocket of his jacket and took it off, too, and hung it on the coat tree in the hall. "You came to Louisiana prepared for the cold weather," she remarked lamely. When he smiled at her, he looked incredibly virile and handsome in his bulky sweater and jeans.

"I wondered about bringing a down jacket, but on a day like this, it feels pretty good," he replied, his dark eyes inspecting her.

Tess was self-consciously aware that she couldn't have looked any less sexy if she'd tried. The ruffled neck of her flannel nightgown was visible in the vee of her fleecy old robe. It was a faded pink, while her socks were brown-and-tan argyle. Underneath all the layers, her body tingled.

"You must have needed warm clothes in Denver. Have you been there the whole time?" she asked. "The oil company employees I've met seem to get transferred often."

"I spent seven years in Denver, all told. I was transferred to the Houston office twice and back to Denver each time."

Tess counted on her fingers. "So you're moved five times."

"Six, if you count the original move from Lafayette," he corrected. "You've kept your hair long."

"One of these days I'm going to have it cut." She tossed her head to dispel her reaction to the satisfaction in his voice. A movement of his hand set off a panic, and she started down the hall, talking as she went, "Come on back to the kitchen. I'll give you a cup of coffee and then I'll excuse myself to go and put on some clothes. I want to give you back your rent money while you're here. I don't think it's a good idea for me to rent you a slip."

"I can help myself to coffee," Peter said from behind her.

Tess led him into the kitchen anyway, got down a cup and saucer and filled the cup with dark brew. She handed the coffee to him. "The sugar bowl is on the table. I'll get you some milk from the refrigerator."

"Don't bother. I drink my coffee black now," he told her, holding the saucer in lean, supple hands.

"You do?" He had once added two heaping spoons of sugar and a generous amount of milk.

"The coffee out in Denver was so much weaker than what I was used to drinking that I couldn't stomach it sweetened or diluted. Our dark roast coffee has a different taste entirely."

"I hope that's not too strong." Tess's thoughts gave her voice a sad, wistful undertone. It would have been an adventure going with him to a different geographical area, if only things had worked out differently.

He took a sip. "It's good."

"I'll just be a few minutes. Turn the TV to another channel, if you want, and the *Times Picayune* and the local paper are both there on the table."

"If the local paper has a classified section, I'll look at the boat ads."

Tess could feel his gaze following her as she made her exit. Closing the door of her room behind her, she thought about locking it but didn't. The decision made her heart beat faster. Her ears strained for the sound of footsteps while she stripped down to bare skin and dressed, but Peter didn't intrude on her privacy. When she returned to the kitchen, it was with an almost let-down feeling.

He was standing at the back door, looking out. He turned around when she entered. The tenseness in his posture made her doubt that he had sat down in her absence. She suspected that he had been pacing restlessly. Had he been bothered by the knowledge that she was dressing in a nearby room with the two of them alone in the house? She knew, meeting his dark gaze, that the answer was yes.

"Did you find any promising boat ads?" she asked.

"One," he replied. His gaze lingered on her red sweater as he gave her an appreciative once-over. "I took the liberty of using your telephone and talked to the owner. He told me where the boat is located. You look as pretty in red as I remembered," he said, changing the subject without a pause.

Tess was all ready with a defensive explanation for having opted for the color that he'd always liked best on her. She had made it to herself in the bedroom. "This is the warmest sweater that I own," she declared, walking over to the coffeemaker. "It's part wool. So far this winter, the weather hasn't been cold enough for me to wear it. Would you care for another cup of coffee?" She turned with the pot in her hand, prepared for him to be closer behind her than he was.

"Why don't we go out somewhere and have breakfast?" he suggested tersely.

Tess looked around for her box of pancake mix, trying to cover the fact that she was at a loss. She had been expecting to have to fend him off, and he wanted to go out to a restaurant. "I was about to make breakfast when I heard you at the door," she said, locating the pancake mix over by the TV. "I was thinking about having pancakes and bacon." Somehow the information took on the guise of a half-hearted invitation for him to join her.

"Now you won't have to go to the trouble of cooking."

He obviously wasn't in the least tempted by the prospect of a home-cooked meal prepared by her. "I have eggs in the refrigerator and grits and oatmeal in the pantry, if you'd rather have something besides pancakes. I haven't turned into a gourmet cook, but I can put an appetizing meal on the table now," Tess informed him.

"I'm sure you learned to cook all of Jake's favorite foods the way he liked them," Peter speculated. His note of accusation finished out his thought: she hadn't stuck with him long enough to learn to cook the foods that he liked.

"I did my best, which is all anyone can be expected to do," Tess replied, tilting her chin to a defiant angle. "My father appreciated my efforts, but, of course, if he'd had any say in the matter, my mother would have been cooking his meals for him. Life just doesn't always go according to our plans."

"That's an understatement," Peter agreed tersely.

Holding her breath Tess waited for him to speak the question she could read in his eyes. *Were you ever sorry, Tess?* She had her own question ready for him. *Were you, Peter?*

He drew in a deep breath. "So how about letting me buy you some breakfast? Afterward, if you don't have plans for the afternoon, I'd appreciate it if you'd come with me to the various marinas in the area. Some of them, I'm told, aren't easy to find."

"No, that's true," Tess agreed, drooping at the realization that he wasn't going to put up any argument about getting another boat slip. Would he put up any resistance to not seeing her again? She doubted it. "You could waste a lot of time driving around. No, I don't have any plans for this afternoon. I'll get my jacket."

"You'll need to dress warmly. Do you have a wool cap and some lined gloves?"

"You have a heater in your car, don't you?"

"Sure, but I'd like to get out and have a closer look at the boats that have For Sale signs on them. I'll jot down the telephone numbers if I see some interesting prospects and call for more information later."

"If you were lucky enough to find the right boat in a marina that suited you, you could kill two birds with one stone," she pointed out.

"Wednesday I didn't notice any newer sailboats for sale in your marina in the thirty-to-thirty-five-foot range, which is what I'm looking for," he remarked, not replying to her observation. "Have you done any sailing?"

"Not much. I've gone out a few times over the years. Actually, I haven't done as much boating as you'd think, considering that I practically grew up in a marina," she added after a brief, awkward pause when he didn't speak up to say what both were thinking: He could invite her out sailing after he became a sailboat owner.

If he had said that, she could have cleared the air with an open discussion, found out exactly what his intentions were in regard to her and stated her position. Tess was not only disgruntled at the missed opportunity, she also felt rejected and jealous. Without a doubt he would be taking women out sailing with him.

"Shall we go?" Peter asked.

"I guess so," she said shortly, and marched out of the kitchen, leaving him to follow behind her.

## Chapter Four

His car was a sporty BMW, obviously brand-new. It had leather upholstery and a handsome interior that was roomy enough to be comfortable, but seemed confined as soon as Peter slid behind the wheel.

"This is a very nice car," Tess complimented, finding it disturbingly familiar to be his passenger again.

"It handles well," he said, starting the engine. "So far I'm really pleased with the way it performs." He glanced at her conservative sedan parked ahead of them in the driveway.

She fully expected him to make some comment to the effect that the car showed her father's taste in automobiles, but he shifted the BMW into reverse and backed out, not speaking his thoughts.

"How long did you keep your VW after you drove it out to Denver and started your new job?" she asked, partly because she wanted to know and partly because she wasn't willing to pass over sensitive subjects.

He shifted into forward and accelerated before he answered. "I bought a new car as soon as I had enough money saved up for a down payment."

"That must have been kind of sad for you in a way, leaving the VW on the lot," Tess said, sounding sad herself as she visualized the little car. "It must have looked so rejected."

"I didn't trade it in," Peter said tersely.

"Did you sell it to some high school or college student?"

"No, I didn't get rid of it."

Tess gazed at his profile in surprise. "You were that sentimentally attached to it?"

"I couldn't have gotten but maybe a couple of hundred bucks for it. Where would you like eat? You'll have to give me directions."

"When we get to the main highway through town, turn right. There's a nice little restaurant in Mandeville that serves a late breakfast on weekends. What happened to the VW eventually? You don't still have it?" She refused to be sidetracked. Her instincts told her that she was on the trail of something he didn't want to reveal. Had he kept the VW for a second car in the hopes that she would join him in Denver? If so, she wanted to hear him say it.

"I had it painted and fixed up. When my brother Dave started college, I gave it to him. He passed it on to our nephew, and the last I knew, it was still in the family. Speaking of cars, I gather that the white Cadillac I saw in the marina Wednesday belongs to your lawyer, Buford."

"Yes, that was Will's car." Tess was angry with herself for her own feeling of letdown. She was a fool to have latched on to the idea that his reason for keeping the little car had something to do with her. He hadn't called her or written from Denver or registered one objection to the divorce.

"What's your relationship with him?"

"Aside from being my attorney, he's a good friend, and I go out with him on a regular basis. He's asked me to marry him, and I'm giving his proposal serious thought."

Peter seemed to be mulling over her crisply matter-of-fact answer. His jaw set. "Then you sleep with him on a regular basis, too."

"Whether I sleep with him at all is none of your business," Tess retorted stiffly, feeling the color rise in her cheeks. She met his searching glance with a defiant glare.

"Did you see him last night?"

"As a matter of fact, I didn't," Tess informed him, reading his train of thought. She'd evidently slept alone in her bed the previous night. If she had seen Will, she must have sent him home to sleep in his. "Will had a meeting to attend, and I had other plans. We are having dinner together tonight, in case you're interested." Actually she and Will were invited to a casual supper at the home of Sherrie and Wayne Myers, friends of Tess's, but she wanted to give the impression that they would be dining alone. "Tell me about your job," she suggested.

He complied after a brief, silent battle of wills that Tess found both nerve-racking and stimulating. His unwillingness to drop his interrogation on the subject of her sexual relationship with Will was somehow satisfying to her ego. There was a suggestion of righteous reproach in his manner, as though Tess owed him a full revelation.

She put in questions to encourage him to elaborate about his present position, not just to make conversation but because she was genuinely interested and also because she took pleasure in hearing him talk. His voice had a pleasant masculine timbre and wasn't pitched as low as Will's. Peter's speech was more succinct than Will's, not rumbling. She could still catch the faint suggestion of a Cajun accent.

He was from New Iberia, which had a large Cajun population, as did all the small towns in the Lafayette area. The Acadians, originally from France, had settled in the marshland of south Louisiana after leaving Canada. The Roussells, like most Cajun families, weren't pure Acadian or Peter and all three of his brothers wouldn't have been above average height. His grandmother on his father's side was descended from north European stock and was a big, tall woman.

When Tess met Peter at the University of South Louisiana in Lafayette, he had been living at home and commuting. His parents had contributed what they could toward his tuition, and he had applied for student loans and grants to pay the rest and to cover the expense of books and supplies. Holding down a part-time job to earn gas and spending money, he had managed to maintain a B-plus average and still be popular and enjoy his share of campus social life.

Tess had admired him and been proud to be his girlfriend and then his bride, while at the same time she'd envied him his drive and sense of direction. She felt those same emotions now.

"You've done extremely well, Peter," she commended him sincerely when they had arrived at the restaurant and were about to get out of the car. "Not that I'm surprised. You certainly deserve your success. Even though your parents were supportive, you supplied your own incentive. Whether or not the oil-and-gas market improves, I'm sure that you'll continue to be promoted up the ladder."

"I got into the right field for me, even though the industry is having lean times," he replied. Inside, when they were seated and had looked at menus and ordered, he inquired,

"What about you, Tess? Did you go back to school and finish your degree?"

"No, I never did. There was no good excuse. I could easily have commuted to Southeastern in Hammond, but I just wasn't ambitious enough. If you remember, I wasn't exactly a dedicated student at USL. I had picked it because of its reputation as a party school and majored in having fun." Tess shifted the position of the salt and pepper shakers, wondering if he weren't thinking, too, that they never would have met if she'd frivolously decided upon some other school.

"You were bright enough that you were able to pass your courses with a minimum of studying," Peter reminded her. "You had a C average your freshman year."

It was her sophomore year when her grades had plummeted. They both waited tensely while their waitress poured them cups of coffee and then moved away. Tess took a sip of hers before she answered.

"My main motivation was to convince my parents that they weren't wasting their money sending me to college, even though I knew deep down that they were. When I enrolled at USL, I had no real interest in learning or getting a degree." She had confided as much to him, along with all her other most private personal thoughts.

"The same is true of a lot of entering freshmen who go on and get degrees. If you had been able to concentrate on school your second year, you might have settled down and gotten more serious."

"I doubt it. I only pretended that I wanted to continue with my education so that my father would pay for an apartment for us to live in and continue to give me an allowance." An arrangement Peter had gone along with reluctantly because it would last less than a year until he could support them. He had swallowed his pride. "It didn't occur to me that I could have dropped out and gotten a job. I was a pampered only child—or so I thought—and figured my parents should be glad to spend their money on whatever would make me happy." Tess made a little grimace at her self-centeredness.

"Whatever your father spent on you, it was a smart investment on his part," Peter said harshly.

"That's a terrible way to put it!" Tess protested. "My father didn't buy my love!"

"I apologize," he said immediately in a taut, disgusted voice. "That was pride talking. I meant to reimburse him with interest for everything he spent on our living expenses after we were married. Plus I had every intention of paying him full price for that damned gas guzzler that he bought for you, and then I was going to trade it in as soon as we could afford to buy a second car." He picked up his cup of coffee and took a large swallow. "After you divorced me, I sent a check to him through your lawyer, but it was never cashed."

"I tore it up." Into tiny little bits, while she sobbed her heart out. "You didn't owe my father any money. It didn't cost him any more than he would have had to pay for my room and board and personal expenses. The rent on our apartment was practically nothing, and we didn't eat steak. You paid for at least half of our food and entertainment with what you earned from your job."

"I would have felt less like a freeloader if he'd cashed the check," Peter said. "The way things turned out, I was just a roommate who didn't split the rent."

"How do you think I felt, Peter? You didn't make a single effort to communicate with me, not one note or phone call. Then you send my father a check, as if settling up some account with him. It was humiliating."

"What was I going to say that you didn't already know, Tess? That I was a thousand miles from home and starting a future I'd worked hard to prepare for. That you were my wife and I needed you there with me."

"I watched for the mailman day after day and ran to answer the phone when it rang, hoping that it was you." Tess's voice was full of scorn for herself as well as reproach for him.

"You could have called me or written."

"I didn't have your address or your telephone number!"

"Your divorce lawyer didn't have any problem locating me." Peter sighed. "I should have sent you some notification of how to contact me. Instead I made sure that the information was easily available through my parents and the company personnel office."

"Your number was listed. I was able to get it from information without any trouble," Tess confessed wanly. "I guess we both just knew that there wasn't anything to say that we already hadn't said to each other dozens of times. We'd begged and argued enough, and nothing had changed."

Peter nodded. "I had this illusion that you were going to see that you were wrong and come around to my way of thinking. I made plans that included you." His smile was humorless, his voice edged with self-contempt as he admitted what she'd tried to pry out of him earlier. "That's why I kept the VW. And I held off from buying anything except a car so that we could choose things together. Then the divorce papers came in the mail, and I finally faced up to reality."

Tess swallowed a big lump in her throat. "I wish I'd known. I imagined you having a good time and dating. Filing for divorce was the last desperate card I had to play. You were supposed to wake up, like a character in a soap opera, and come to the realization that you couldn't live without me." She shook her head at her own adolescent thinking.

"But, of course, you didn't. We were a couple of immature kids, Peter, and had no business getting married. I take the main responsibility. I wanted to sleep with you and play house. If we'd waited, as both our parents wanted us to do, we would have broken up instead of getting divorced. It would have been less painful."

He acquiesced with his silence, and Tess was irrationally hurt that he didn't take issue with her. What had she wanted, for him to disagree with her and argue that they could have made a go of their marriage?

Their waitress came with a loaded tray, giving Tess a few moments to conquer her emotions while they were being served.

"Have you had a job, Tess, aside from working for your father in the marina?" he asked, opening up a less stressful subject. When she answered that she had held down several jobs and told him what they were, he showed such interest that she found herself describing her stints of employment in detail during the meal.

Tess hardly tasted her food. She had all she could handle keeping up her defenses while she allowed herself the temporary pleasure of being in Peter's presence. It was so *good* to be with him again.

She put down her fork with a little clatter and asked in a strained voice, "How long do you expect to be in New Orleans? A year or two?"

He laid his fork down, too, and carefully pushed aside his plate. "Probably no longer than a couple of years, but there's no predicting exactly."

"Where will you be going next?"

"Back to Houston is my guess, but I can't be certain about that, either."

Tess picked up her coffee cup, but it was empty. She took a sip of water instead. "Do you have any say?"

"Can I refuse a transfer? Yes, but it wouldn't be a wise career move. If I pass up a promotion, I might be over-looked in the future."

"I see how it works. Before now you haven't been offered a position in New Orleans then."

"No, I lived with the possibility that I could be, but, fortunately, I wasn't. During the first few years especially, I might have turned down a promotion that meant moving back to Louisiana." A mistake he would have later regretted, he implied. "It must have occurred to you that I might be relocating to New Orleans eventually, if I stayed in petroleum engineering."

"It did," Tess admitted. "I even considered that you might live on the North Shore." Along with his wife and children.

"Would you like more coffee?" their waitress inquired, arriving to clear the table.

"No, thanks. I've had enough." Tess regretted the interruption.

"None for me, either," Peter said.

The waitress left, promising to return with the check. Tess wanted to resume the conversation where they'd left off, but didn't quite know how.

"It must be difficult, moving every few years," she remarked. "You have to leave your friends and everything that's familiar, meet all new people and get used to a place where you don't expect to live permanently."

"I guess you do find the notion strange," Peter said.

There was nothing critical in his voice, but his thoughtful note made Tess defensive. She suspected he was wondering whether she would have been able to adjust to changing locations with him. "Aside from those two years off at college, I've not only lived in the same little town, but the same house I grew up in," she elaborated on his comment. "The whole extent of my travel is a few trips to Florida and the Smoky Mountains in Tennessee. The Mississippi Gulf Coast hardly counts, it's so close to home. Oh, and Hot Springs, Arkansas. I nearly forgot."

"Who did you go on vacations with?"

"Friends. What about you?"

His gaze fell away before hers, confirming what she'd expected. He had taken a woman companion, of course. Tess felt a sharp stab of jealousy and glanced away, pretending to make a survey of the other people in the restaurant. A woman at a table on the opposite side immediately got up and headed over, smiling. Tess curved her lips and tried to look welcoming rather than dismayed.

"Tess, I thought that was you!"

"Hi, Sherrie. I didn't see you and Wayne and the kids come in," Tess told her friend from high school days, who was also her hostess for that evening.

"We just came from a parade in Covington." Sherrie indicated the strands of Mardi Gras beads around her neck. "There was a good crowd in spite of the weather." She gave Peter a glance full of curiosity and then looked a little harder at him, evidently trying to place him.

"Sherrie, you remember Peter," Tess said as casually as she could manage. "Peter, Sherrie was a guest at our wedding a hundred years ago. Peter is working in New Orleans and dropped over to say hello," she explained to a wide-eyed Sherrie, who took full advantage of her more extended view of Peter as he stood up politely to shake hands with her.

"I knew you looked vaguely familiar. Please, sit back down," she urged him. "I'll let you get back to your conversation. Excuse me for butting in."

"That's quite all right," he said pleasantly, smiling his attractive smile at her. "Tess and I will be spending the afternoon together."

Tess stood up, too. "It won't take that long to drive around to all the marinas," she objected, and then directed her words to her friend, who looked exactly the way she did when she was discussing the latest development on one of her soap operas. "Peter is in the market for a sailboat. He was curious to see what's available over here on our side of the lake, but he isn't familiar with the North Shore." And doesn't intend to become familiar with it, Tess tried to imply.

"It's too bad you don't have a better day for it," Sherrie lamented. "But you two have fun. Nice to see you again after all these years, Peter." Her friendly gaze took on a discreet cast as she looked from Peter to Tess. "Goodbye now."

"Will is picking me up tonight at seven-fifteen. We'll be at your house at seven-thirty. Is that okay?" Tess asked although she hadn't needed to reconfirm the time. It just seemed necessary to bring up Will's name and destroy any wrong impression that Sherrie had intruded upon a romantic meeting between Tess and Peter.

"Fine. That's when Ann and Roy and Evelyn and Joe are coming. See you tonight, Tess." Sherrie gave Peter a faintly apologetic parting glance, as though to say she would have liked to include him among the guests.

Their waitress, meanwhile, had unobtrusively brought the check.

"Now I won't have to take out an ad in the paper," she said when they were outside, bundled up again in their heavy jackets. "The whole world will know that I was out with my ex-husband. Sherrie has a heart of gold, and I love her, but she couldn't keep a secret if her life depended on it."

"Then you definitely haven't mentioned anything to her about what you told me Wednesday."

Tess had been all primed for him to question the need for secrecy where he was concerned. Then she would tell him that she had no intention of becoming involved with him during his temporary residence in New Orleans. Irked as well as disappointed that he was opening up another avenue entirely, she followed his glance at a couple getting out of a car and understood his deliberate vagueness. He didn't know if that couple might not be friends or acquaintances of hers, too.

"Aside from yourself, I haven't mentioned that to anyone except Will. Nor do I intend to," she stated, appreciative of his caution.

Assuming that she would be his passenger again, she started automatically to walk around the front of his car. When he stopped her, catching her arm and suggesting, "Why don't you drive," Tess looked up at him in surprise.

"You trust me to drive your new car?"

"Sure. That way I can notice better exactly where we're going and get my bearings."

"Okay," she agreed, not at all averse to driving. He gave her the key to the ignition, on a key ring with his other keys, including, Tess assumed, the one to his home. She didn't know what part of the city he was living in or whether he was renting or buying. They hadn't gotten around to discussing that, dwelling upon the past more than the present.

"I could manage to steer all right, but I might need to put on the brakes," she told him as she tried unsuccessfully to figure out how to slide the seat forward. She demonstrated that she was just barely able to reach the pedal.

"Let's see. Isn't there a lever under here...?" While he talked, he was leaning over, his upper body twisted so that he faced Tess and feeling around with his right hand underneath the front of her seat. "Yes, here it is."

"I felt it and tried moving it, but I was afraid to force it," she explained, intensely conscious that his jacket was touching the front of hers.

"I have the seat pushed back all the way. The mechanism may be jammed."

"I was probably just too gentle." She would try again—as soon as he moved and got out of her way.

He read her message, but he didn't straighten up. Now that he was there, positioned conveniently with his face less than a foot from hers, he was going to kiss her. With her heart beating wildly, Tess met his dark searching gaze. Whatever he saw in her eyes didn't discourage him.

"Peter..." she murmured as he made a movement closer, focusing on her mouth. A rush of pure longing swept through her. She closed her eyes and turned her head aside.

"Are you sleeping with Buford, Tess?"

His voice came from so close that she could feel the warmth of his breath. She shook her head, keeping her eyes tightly shut. "No, I'm not. I mean, I haven't so far."

He drew in an audible breath and sat up. Not looking over at him, Tess manipulated the lever forcibly and slid her seat forward. She couldn't explain her own sense of rejection, as though she had been the one rebuffed, not him.

"How long have you and Buford been a regular two-some?" Peter inquired as they both clipped on their seat belts.

She glared at him resentfully, glad that his prying gave her an excuse for her emotion. "Why don't I just give you a full case history, and then maybe we can close the subject of my relationship with Will. He was widowed six months before my father passed away a year ago. We had just started going out. We've been a comfort to each other in addition to the fact that we enjoy each other's company. There's a great deal more between us than physical attraction, which wasn't the case with you and me."

"Tess, you don't mean to tell me that you're seriously considering marrying a man who can't interest you in going to bed with him in a whole year," Peter scoffed, ignoring the comparison between her current relationship with Will and her past relationship with him.

"Sex is not the basis for a marriage, Peter, and it takes more than being a good lover to make a good husband." Lessons that she had learned the hard, painful way, Tess added silently.

"I couldn't agree with you more," Peter agreed soberly, regret in his voice. "But you and I had more than sex going for us, Tess. One big plus was that we had both been raised Catholic and didn't have any conflict about religion. We were married in the church," he reminded. They had been joined together before God as man and wife, and the bonds of holy matrimony couldn't be severed by a divorce court. Wasn't that a problem for her?

Tess started up the car, totally frustrated that she couldn't sting him into a confrontation. "Will is a Catholic, too," she said, avoiding his gaze as she shifted into reverse gear. "We usually go to Mass together on Sunday. Because I was so young when I married you and because our marriage lasted less than a year, I shouldn't have any trouble getting a dispensation," she said, referring to the special church permission to remarry. "I've discussed it privately with Father John, my pastor."

When Peter didn't respond, she had no choice but to back out of the parking space.

"How old is Buford?" he asked when she had shifted into forward and accelerated with a spurt. His car was more responsive than hers to pressure on the gas pedal.

"Forty-seven. He's in excellent health. Aside from an occasional cigar, he doesn't smoke, and he's a moderate drinker. He may be a few pounds overweight, but he's quite active and vigorous."

"How solid is he financially?"

"I haven't asked him his net worth," Tess replied with a touch of sarcasm. "But in addition to his law practice, he has income from commercial rental property, and he's chairman of the board of a local bank, which tells me that he must own a big chunk of stock in it."

"Did he and his wife have any kids?"

"Two. Both boys," she said shortly, giving him a look of exaggerated patience. "Will Junior is twenty-five and married. Greg is twenty-three and in law school at LSU in Baton Rouge. I get along very well with them. They've made a point of telling me how much they would like to see their father settled down with someone who will make him happy."

"How do they feel about a little brother or sister?"

"I wouldn't know. I haven't discussed it with them. Before you ask, yes, Will and I have talked about children. He is agreeable to starting a second family, if I want to be a mother. Whether I do or not is something that I'll decide if or when I marry him." Would Peter care to probe further into matters that were none of his business? Tess asked with a pointed glance.

It gave her no satisfaction whatever when he didn't seem to take offense and guided the conversation into impersonal channels, remarking upon the route that she was taking to the marina that was nearest the restaurant. He didn't bring up Will's name during the rest of the afternoon, nor did he try to kiss Tess again, even though there was more than one charged moment, in the car and outside of it, when they looked at each other and she knew that he was restraining himself.

Each time she had to contend with the same surge of longing and turn her head or walk away to keep from giving in to the weak desire to feel his mouth on hers, his arms around her. Each time she experienced the same contradictory disappointment that he showed control when he must have been able to sense her inner struggle.

He hadn't come across the lake on a pretext. That in itself seemed somehow a slight, though Tess didn't mind at all getting out of the car at each marina and walking the docks with him. She took full advantage of the opportunity to observe him surreptitiously while he inspected sailboats that were for sale in the size category in which he was interested and admired others that caught his eye.

Having grown up around boats and boat owners, Tess was used to hearing boats referred to as though they were females. She was also used to the male tone in bestowing compliments on a craft, but she'd never felt a tinge of jealousy before as she did when Peter whistled several times and exclaimed, "Isn't she pretty?" or "Wouldn't I love to have her?"

As he jotted down telephone numbers and descriptive information, he used terminology that revealed how knowledgeable he was. She questioned him just to hear him talk about what obviously fascinated him, not because she really cared to differentiate between a sloop and cutter rig.

How much was he thinking of paying for a sailboat? she wondered and finally, in one marina, gave in to her curiosity. He told her without any hesitation and went on to mention his current salary.

"You can certainly afford an expensive car and a boat then, especially being a bachelor," Tess remarked.

"At the rate I'm going, saving to send kids off to college isn't a major priority." There was genuine regret in Peter's voice, as well as irony.

Before she could decide what to say, he had turned his attention back to the boat beside which they were standing. Why hadn't he married by now? she wanted to ask, knowing that she would be leaving herself open to hearing about the women in his life since her.

She would also be opening herself up to the same question. Why hadn't *she* married by now?

When they stopped for something hot to drink in mid-afternoon, Peter brought up her half brother's inheritance claim and inquired about her father's estate. Exactly what had her father left her that she would have to divide?

Tess didn't mind answering and outlined her own financial situation for him, admitting that until the appraisals were done on the marina and her parents' house, she had only a vague idea of the monetary worth of her inheritance.

"If he gets half of your father's portion, that would mean he comes in for a fourth. You should be able to borrow that amount with no trouble, since there's no outstanding mortgage," Peter suggested, his whole manner interested, but objective.

"It gets more complicated than that," Tess explained. "Unfortunately, my father had acquired the property on which the marina is built before he married my mother."

"Oh, so your brother gets half of the current market value of the property, minus the improvements."

Tess started to correct him that she didn't have a *brother*, but then didn't. "Right, and I have a sinking feeling that the marina isn't going to appraise for a lot more than the property worth. You've seen already how many newer marinas there are on the North Shore that are in much better repair."

Peter nodded. "You're looking at having to spend some money in the near future on rebuilding docks and replacing pilings, aren't you?" It was more a reflective comment than a question.

"Yes, and the covered slips all need to be reroofed." Tess sighed. "It's going to be an enormous expense, I know. That's one reason I've procrastinated on getting an estimate on the whole job. I hated to go in debt, and now I'm going to have to mortgage everything to the hilt just to hang on to the marina the way it is."

"If you met your brother and laid all the facts on the table, he might turn out to be a reasonable person," Peter pointed out. "Perhaps he would agree to being a silent partner or to letting you pay him in installments over a long period of time."

"*Half* brother, and I don't want him as a partner," Tess objected strongly. She had been expecting Peter at least to verify that selling out wasn't an option for her. "I don't want an arrangement that means keeping up any kind of contact with him. It's too risky."

"You're afraid that he might show up and not keep his identity a secret." Another thoughtful observation, carefully free of any opinion. "Isn't that a possibility anyway? You said that he lives up around Shreveport. It isn't all that far to travel from the northern part of the state. I wonder why he hasn't come down to see for himself what he's inherited, even if he had no desire to meet you. Unless he's bitter toward his father."

"I assume he has some sort of job or maybe he owns a business. He could be tied up. Whatever the reason, I'm just glad that he's letting his attorney look out for his interests." Tess didn't care to engage in any speculation that made her half brother the wronged party and her father a culprit.

"What's his name?" Peter asked.

"He was named after my father." She disclosed the information grudgingly.

"And his last name is Davenport? He wasn't adopted?"

"Apparently not."

"Have you had any explanation of why he didn't put in a claim sooner?"

"No. I can only guess that he didn't learn that my father had passed away until recently. What does it matter? The fact is that he has put in a claim for an inheritance that he's legally entitled to, even if he doesn't deserve it, in my own biased opinion. I have no choice but to do what the law requires and pay him his share, but then I want to blot all this out," Tess stated unequivocally.

"In that case, you are better off leaving the questions unanswered and not coming face-to-face with him," Peter said, obviously not agreeing with her, but steering clear of any argument. He hesitated. "You have considered that he may resemble your father?"

She nodded reluctantly, unable to hide from his discerning eyes how the thought had disturbed her. "I can read your mind, Peter. Without knowing any of the facts about my father's first marriage, you're ready to believe the worst of him, just because you bear him a grudge," she accused. "Deep down you're glad, aren't you, that something has come out to call into question the kind of man he was."

Tess wanted him to go on the defensive, but instead he looked guilty and even ashamed. "I do have hard feelings toward your father, even though he's dead. I admit it. For a number of years, I despised him," Peter confessed gravely.

"But you shouldn't have blamed him, Peter!" she protested, dismayed as well as reproachful. "What happened wasn't his fault!"

"Lots of men lose their wives, Tess, and carry on. I can't be objective, it's true, but I don't think I'm being too harsh in thinking that your father was selfish and weak to lean on you the way he did. If he had coped with his grief, you would have been able to live your own life. We wouldn't have split up."

"Not then. Can you honestly tell me that you think we would still be married now, except for my father?"

"We would have had a shot, anyway," he replied with as much regret as bitterness.

"Isn't that copping out, Peter? Sure, it was a tough situation for a couple of newlyweds our age to handle, but we could have ridden it out. There were temporary solutions that we could have considered. You could have taken the job in Denver and gone by yourself until I had helped my father through his bad time. We could have lived apart for a while and stayed married. Other couples have coped with separation, during war time, for example.

"But it was all or nothing with both of us," Tess went on. "One person had to give in. You weren't very understanding, perhaps because you were from a large family and not an only child. Maybe it's different being a son, too, rather than a daughter. In your defense, I guess I expected too much, asking you to postpone making the best career decision for yourself. You had worked hard for your education. We were too young, Peter, too immature, and what we felt for each other obviously wasn't enough."

"Was divorcing me your father's idea?" Peter asked, seemingly unmoved. "Tell me the truth."

"No, it wasn't his idea at all," she denied. "I've already told you. I filed for divorce as a desperate way of forcing your hand. We failed, Peter, you and I. My father wasn't responsible for our divorce, and whatever the true story is behind his first marriage, I just know in my heart that it wouldn't reflect badly on him. Will feels exactly the same way," she added stoutly.

Peter's jaw hardened as though he were keeping his mouth clamped shut to prevent himself from making a sharp retort. When he did answer, he had his voice carefully under control and spoke thoughtfully, ignoring her deliberate reference to Will.

"Even if your father weren't blameless, that doesn't mean that having the story come out would destroy the good opinion of his friends and neighbors. Most of them probably made mistakes when they were young, too." Just as he and Tess had. "So whatever you do, whether you stick by your decision not to meet your brother or change your mind, I hope you'll act on your own instincts." Not by what he or anyone else—including Will—advised her to do or not to do.

"You think I should meet him."

He shrugged, evading committing himself. "As you pointed out a moment ago, I'm from a large family. I can't put myself in your shoes. Personally I enjoy big holiday get-togethers with my brothers and their wives and kids. I get a kick out of being an uncle."

Tess stared at him, following the train of thought that he'd opened up. Her half brother might have children. If he did, they would be her nieces and nephews. "I may be an aunt," she murmured, trying to adjust to the notion, which she found disturbing.

"You could call your bro—half brother," Peter amended. "On the basis of a telephone conversation, you'd probably know whether you wanted to follow up and meet him and his family, if he has one. To be fair, don't you think he deserves the benefit of the doubt, as much as your father does?'' Peter asked reasonably. "He could be a hell of a nice guy. Whether he is or not, he didn't have any more say than you did about who his parents were. This isn't a scheme that he hatched up, if his birthright is valid. You seem to be taking that point of view, though I can understand that this all came as a shock to you and puts you under financial strain.''

"I'm satisfied that he is who he claims to be," Tess said in a troubled voice. "And I guess I am reacting very emotionally, but I don't want to meet him or talk to him. I resent the very fact that he exists. I've been an only child for thirty years. You have no idea of what a burden and a responsibility that is.''

"You've paid the price for your inheritance, and he gets his scot-free."

"Why do you have to word things so cold-bloodedly!'' she protested. "I was a good daughter because I loved my father. There was never any motive of earning my inheritance, but I do deserve it.''

"Maybe your half brother might have liked a chance to earn his by being a good son," Peter suggested.

"*You* would prefer to believe that because you would like nothing more than for my father to be damaged in my eyes. You still hate him, don't you, Peter?'' Tess accused, dismay as well as challenge in her voice. "You still blame him for our breakup. In spite of what I've said today, you won't agree that you and I were responsible for our own actions.''

"I do agree," he contradicted, his calm voice at odds with the intense emotion in his dark eyes. "That's why I hated your father in the first place. Actions speak louder than words. In a nutshell, you put his well-being before mine. He meant more to you than I did. That was impossible for me to accept.''

And it was still a problem for him ten years later.

Tess wanted to deny that she had loved her father more than Peter, only differently. There would be no convincing him, though. They were at the same impasse that had split them apart, facing each other over a breach that could never be healed.

"This has been so *painful* today," she protested unhappily. "Hashing everything over doesn't resolve a thing, and somehow I always thought it would."

"We needed to say all of this to each other, Tess," Peter replied. "I've kept feelings bottled up all these years and never got over you."

Would he be able to get over her now? Tess couldn't bring herself to ask him, and he didn't volunteer to tell her.

## Chapter Five

He didn't suggest cutting short the tour of marinas, and neither did Tess. They both steered clear of any conversation about their past relationship, and neither of them made even the most casual reference to a future relationship of any kind.

"It was a pleasure driving your car," she said sincerely as she pulled into the driveway and turned off the engine. "Now I won't be happy with my stodgy one." Manipulating the lever beneath the front of her seat, she pushed the seat back the way it had been and reached for her purse.

Peter unclipped his seat belt. "Why don't you come over to New Orleans tomorrow? Then you can try it out in city traffic," he offered.

Tess was opening up her purse and taking out her wallet. She paused in surprise and looked at him searchingly. "You don't need a guide to take you around to the city marinas."

He rented a condo at West End, where the marinas were located, she'd learned during the course of the afternoon.

"I don't have in mind putting you through another day of walking up and down docks and looking at boats," he explained. "We can go to a parade, see a movie. Instead of going to church here, you could drive on over early and go to Mass with me."

Tess delayed answering while she took out several folded bills, the very same ones he had given her. "I'm sorry, but I have plans tomorrow." She put her wallet back in her purse and closed it. "I want to give you back your money. You need to rent a slip from someone else, Peter. There are too many unhappy memories connected with my marina. Every time you drove in, you'd be reminded of my father. It would put a damper on your pleasure in having your own sailboat, and I wouldn't want that. I would feel bad on your account, in addition to getting all stirred up emotionally myself." She held out the money to him. "Please, you know I'm right."

He drew in a breath, reluctance written all over his face, but he took the money, crushing it in his gloved hand. Tess felt a sudden overwhelming bleakness and turned to open the door, but he reached over and stopped her with an urgent, "Wait."

She sat back tensely.

"Were you just putting me off by saying you have plans tomorrow?" he asked.

"No, but even if I were free to come over and spend the day with you, do we really want to put ourselves through a repeat of today?" Her question was a kind of despairing plea.

"Spend one day with me, Tess, for old times' sake, if nothing else," he urged. "We'll put out of our minds how everything went sour between us and just have a good time.

Have you forgotten how much fun we used to have together?''

Of course she hadn't forgotten. Tess bit her lip, torn.

"How about Tuesday?" Peter went on. "Mardi Gras Day? We'll go downtown on Canal for Zulu and Rex, take in the scene in the Quarter. My company has a hospitality suite at one of the French Quarter hotels. There'll be a party going on there. We can drop in on it. If we hold out, we'll even see Comus when he rolls that night. Come on, Tess. You can't refuse."

"It's supposed to warm up by Tuesday," she said weakly, as though the weather were a factor in her capitulating, against her better judgment. They hadn't ever done Mardi Gras in New Orleans together. There shouldn't be any painful déjà vu, she reasoned.

Peter gave her his address and telephone number, and they settled on a time early in the day on Tuesday when she would meet him at his condo, where she would leave her car safely parked. They would ride downtown in his. With the date definite, they both got out, and after another of those breath-quickening interludes when he obviously resisted the urge to kiss her, Tess went inside, her knees weak and her pulses fluttering.

Not trusting himself to stand there and watch her leave him, Peter got back in the car. After managing somehow not to reach for her and take her in his arms up until now, he didn't want to weaken and catch up with her in a couple of long strides. Once his control snapped, there wouldn't be any holding back. It would be like a dam bursting loose, and there was too much at stake to risk making a wrong move.

God, what an ordeal the day had been, he reflected, tossing the wad of bills onto the passenger seat and starting the engine. But it had been a gruelling pleasure all the same, being with Tess, despite the conversations that had been like probing into old, festered, unhealed sores.

She was right. Nothing was resolved after all these years of living apart from each other. Nothing was changed. At rock bottom, no matter how much she regretted the outcome, Tess couldn't honestly say to Peter that she should have made a different choice, and he couldn't honestly tell her that he could have acted differently, as much he regretted the outcome, too.

The question was how they were going to deal with the impasse now, ten years later. Could they put all the hurt and disappointment behind them and go from there? It wouldn't be easy, and they would have to iron out major problems that a reconciliation posed.

Backing fast out of the driveway onto the street, Peter spun the wheel to the right so that he was headed in the wrong direction, toward the Davenport marina rather than the highway. As he drove the short distance to the marina, following a grim impulse, he thought about Tess's words when she gave him back his rent money.

She had hit right on the mark. The prospect of keeping a boat in Jake Davenport's marina was repugnant to Peter. Today while he and Tess were going from marina to marina, he'd wished that there was some way he could avoid being her tenant, but there wasn't. Just now when he'd taken the money, he was only giving the impression of conceding to avoid an argument and address the more immediate matter of seeing her again.

The marina looked bleak and depressing in the gray wintry light. The boats tied up in the slips had an abandoned air. Peter drove back to the fuel dock and office, passing Buford's boat, and turned around. On a sunshiny, warm day with people around and traffic on the river, the whole scene would be different, cheerful. The marina's slightly run-down condition would only add to the weathered, salty charm. Its location on the lake side of the drawbridge was a plus. There would be just a short motoring trip up the river to the channel and then open sailing . . . with Tess.

Peter fantasized a moment and then relinquished the vision and focused again on his surroundings. After several months of coming and going in the marina, he would gain a feeling of familiarity. The unpleasant associations would fade. He could handle the idea of keeping a boat there.

If he knew that it was only for a year or two.

But what if it were for an indefinite length of time? How would he handle that? How could he handle the idea of working permanently in New Orleans, of bringing his career to a dead halt, of tying himself down to this area?

Peter didn't really have an answer, and yet he knew, going in, that a future with Tess almost certainly hinged on his making all those adjustments and sacrifices.

It would be very difficult for her now to pull up roots and cut close ties. She wasn't ever going to want to part with the marina and probably wouldn't be happy living anywhere else.

Tonight she would be spending the evening with friends in Buford's company. The thought stirred fierce jealousy in Peter and roused him out of his reverie.

Driving past Tess's house after he left the marina, he suffered one last temptation. She would be getting dressed for her date with Buford. Peter could stop on some pretext. Or he could stop, without one. She might come to the door wearing a robe that she'd hastily put on. Underneath it . . .

He stepped hard on the gas.

Opening the door to Will when he came for her promptly at seven-fifteen, Tess greeted him with extra warmth to make up for the awareness that the sight of him didn't affect her at all the way seeing Peter standing in the same spot had affected her that morning.

She settled herself next to Will in his car, much larger and plusher than Peter's and tried not to think of how differently she had felt being Peter's passenger. This was much more pleasant, much more relaxed, she told herself. There was none of the tension, none of the uncertainty that had kept her on edge in Peter's presence, attuned to every inflection in his voice, every expression on his face.

Will inquired about what Tess had done that day, and she told him. He frowned disapprovingly throughout her accounting until she ended with the news that she had returned Peter's rent money to him.

"Good for you, hon," he said in a satisfied tone. "You did the right thing. Did he put up an argument?"

"None," Tess replied, unable to feign being pleased over the ease of the transaction.

"That surprises me," Will said. "I had him figured for a stubborn, headstrong cuss. If he gave you any problems, I was prepared to step in and deal with him."

"He used to be very stubborn and headstrong," she said a little wistfully. "Hot-tempered, too. He would fly off the handle very easily. I could egg him into a fight with a sarcastic comment. But he's developed self-control." Though Peter had spoken openly and honestly today, he hadn't spoken rashly, refusing to let antagonism rise to the surface.

"He didn't rough you up when you were married to him?" Will questioned, scowling.

"Heavens, no. Peter never laid a hand on me to hurt me, and I did provoke him," Tess admitted. She had even attacked him physically a few times, but she didn't mention that, remembering how those bouts had gone, with Peter defending himself and restraining her and then making love to her when anger exploded into passion.

"Well, I hope that's the last you see of him, but I wouldn't count on it."

"I'm not worried about his forcing his attentions on me," she said truthfully, feeling some guilt as she passed over the opportunity to tell Will about her date with Peter on Tuesday. "On a different subject, do you have my half brother's address or telephone number, just in case I should decide to try to communicate with him? It isn't likely that I will," she added when he gave her a sharply questioning glance.

"I strongly recommend against it, Tess," he said. "This is the kind of situation that's best left in the hands of lawyers. The sooner it's taken care of, the better. The sooner forgotten, the better. To answer your question, I don't have his address or telephone number." And he wouldn't be party to obtaining them for her, his whole manner implied.

Tess let the matter drop, but she was even more in a state of doubt, oddly enough. It was probably just contrariness on her part, she reasoned. Will hadn't stated his position quite so emphatically on previous occasions, and Tess was open to advice, but not to being told what to do, by Will or Peter.

Will's refusal even to discuss opening up communication with her half brother made him seem close-minded and undermined Tess's confidence in him ever so slightly. She didn't question that he had her best interests at heart, but was no longer certain that he was giving her the best advice.

Tess had to follow her own instincts, as Peter had urged her to do.

It was difficult to be grateful to Peter for making her decision less cut-and-dried, while admitting his own bias. It was also disturbing to realise that he was the one that she could go to, not Will, if she wanted to do her soul-searching aloud.

The evening brought other upsetting insights. When Tess and Will arrived at the Myerses' home, the other two couples who had been invited, the Lairds and the Robinsons, were there. Sherrie had already confided to the women, also old friends of Tess's who had attended her wedding, about running into Tess and Peter.

Out of the range of Will's hearing, Tess was put through the third degree and had to admit that, yes, Peter was even better looking now than he had been when he was younger. Yes, he had done very well and was successful in his career. Yes, he was single. No, he hadn't ever remarried, either.

"He expects to be in New Orleans only a year or two. Then he'll be transferred elsewhere," she put in at the first opportunity. "You know how it is with the big oil companies. They move their employees from one place to another, wherever they need them."

All three women nodded, immediately ruling out the possibility of a romantic matchup between Tess and her handsome ex-husband.

"That's no kind of life I'd want to lead, even if it did mean moving from one gorgeous house to another in high-priced subdivisions," Evelyn Laird remarked.

The North Shore had several subdivisions that were built around golf courses and had country clubs. They were populated largely by corporate types who owned and occupied the large homes temporarily and then sold them to others like themselves when the time came to relocate.

"No, I'd rather have my nice little ranch-style house and a husband who works away at his steady job," Sherrie agreed. "Going off to a different part of the country on vacation is one thing, but I'd be miserable away from my friends and family."

"So would I," Ann Robinson chimed in. "Roy would have to make a fortune to pay for my plane tickets home to visit."

Tess didn't add her sentiments, and her friends interpreted her silence as total agreement with their views. She was just as glad that they didn't press her. It would be difficult to keep a note of poignant regret from creeping in when she admitted that she thought she might have adapted to changing locations with Peter when she was younger, but not now, of course.

Or could she?

Tess was shocked that she would even ask herself that question. She had trouble putting it out of her mind as the women joined the men and she sat next to Will.

What would it be like to go to a dinner party at the home of new acquaintances where all the other guests were complete strangers, instead of good old friends? Tess tried to imagine it. What would it be like to get in her car and run errands, knowing that she wouldn't wave at anyone along the way or blow her horn in friendly greeting? To go shopping and know that she wouldn't see a single familiar face or encounter at least a dozen people to stop and chat with?

Tess's little pang of homesickness seemed to be her answer. She was a small-town person and was where she belonged. She had lived her whole life in Maryville, aside from the two years of college at Lafayette.

But during that first year especially, she had thrived on meeting new people and living in a totally different environment, Tess remembered. She hadn't suffered from homesickness or been lonely at all. Then she and Peter had started dating, and it wouldn't have mattered to her where she was....

Tess cut off the train of thought and concentrated on the conversation.

When it came time to serve dinner, Tess and Evelyn and Ann helped Sherrie with the last-minute preparations. Sherrie brought up Peter again, talking in a nostalgic vain.

"I had forgotten, Tess, what a cute couple you and Peter made. When I got home today, I went through my old albums and found your wedding picture. You were such a pretty bride, and Peter was so handsome." Sherrie sighed. "You two looked so radiantly happy."

"It was a beautiful wedding," Evelyn put in.

"It cost enough that it should have been," Tess said, trying for a light, cynical tone and failing.

"I remember thinking that you and Peter were certain to have kids with dark brown eyes and dark hair, whether they got your features or his. It was a shame that things happened the way they did, your mother dying and all," Sherrie said regretfully. "With you being an only child, you came in for the full brunt when your daddy went all to pieces. If you'd had a brother or a sister to share the load, things might have worked out altogether differently."

Evelyn and Ann both concurred.

Tess had had an older brother who might have helped to console their father. Appalled by her little stab of resentment that accompanied the reflection, Tess spoke hurriedly. "It's all water under the bridge now. I couldn't have gone off to some other state in another part of the country and left Daddy. This tossed salad looks scrumptious, Sherrie." Tess had been adding the homemade dressing and tossing the salad. "Do you want me to go ahead and dish it into the salad bowls?"

"Why don't you? We can call the men to the table. This cream sauce for the broccoli is done. The rolls are hot. The pork roast is sliced on the platter. We're ready to sit down and eat."

Sherrie Myers was a good cook, and it was a delicious meal, but Tess ate without any real enjoyment and participated in the dinner conversation with an effort. She felt too guilty and ashamed over the discovery that her old streak of self-centeredness evidently wasn't dead. Her father hadn't asked her to sacrifice her happiness for him. She had done it of her own volition, acted according to the dictates of her own conscience. Tess had no cause to feel cheated just because the knowledge of a brother had been kept from her.

For her own peace of mind, Tess had to at least talk to her half brother on the phone and put to rest the possibility that things could have been different. Out of fairness to her father, she couldn't let the little seed of doubt grow.

As much as she would have liked to blame Peter for having planted it, she knew that she couldn't. She could blame him, though, for wanting to nurture it out of a vindictive impulse.

Tess got up with the other women and pitched in to clear the table and serve dessert and coffee. She braced herself for Peter's name to be brought up again, out of shot of the men's hearing. Her friends' sympathetic glances at her and their tone when they spoke to her was evidence that she hadn't fooled them with her attempt at acting normal. They had sensed her troubled abstraction.

It touched her that they didn't say anything and that they only made a show of objecting, calling her a party pooper, when she made excuses about not feeling well and asked Will to take her home as soon as dinner was over.

"I hope you're not coming down with the flu, being out in this nasty weather," Sherrie said, giving her a warm hug at the door. "If I don't see you at church in the morning, I'll call and check on you when I get home."

"I made a huge pot of beef-vegetable soup today," Evelyn spoke up from the living room. "Let me know, Tess, if you want me to bring you some."

On her way out to Will's car, Tess had to blink hard against a glaze of tears. She was lucky to have friends who genuinely cared for her and could be depended upon to rally to her support.

Will was solicitous, helping her into the passenger seat. His touch was steady and comforting. Tess smiled at him when he got in behind the wheel and she scooted over closer when he put his arm along the back of the seat.

"You do look a little peaked tonight, hon," he observed in a concerned voice.

Tess turned aside her head and offered him her cheek when he leaned over to kiss her on the mouth. "If I am coming down with flu, I wouldn't want to give you my germs," she said apologetically.

The guilty knowledge that she wasn't being honest with him only added to Tess's churned-up emotions. The truth was that she didn't want Will to kiss her the way she'd yearned for Peter to do today.

"I'd like to ring Roussell's neck for dragging you out in the cold and dampness," Will growled.

At her house, he walked her to the door, embraced her and held her after he'd given her another kiss on the cheek. "You know I'm crazy about you, Tess, don't you?" he asked gruffly.

"I think a lot of you, too, Will," she told him with sincere affection.

Closing the door behind her, Tess leaned against it and shut her eyes, listening to Will's footsteps as he crossed the porch and went down the steps. It occurred to her that she had followed the same pattern of behavior that afternoon when she'd entered her house after parting with Peter.

Except that her heart had been beating fast, and her body had been alive with dissatisfaction. Hearing Peter's car start up, she had sagged with disappointment that he was leaving, heading back to New Orleans. The sound of Will's Cadillac's engine only intensified her relief that she'd been able to avoid a passionate good-night scene with him, without hurting his feelings.

Peter had scoffed at the notion that she was seriously considering marrying a man who hadn't gotten her into bed with him in a year's time. Tess was awfully afraid that he was right and that she wasn't going to be able to talk herself into marrying Will.

Tonight she was too confused and emotionally exhausted to think clearly. It was better to postpone making a decision anyway, until after Tuesday. Tess needed the protection of her uncertainty when she went over to New Orleans to spend Mardi Gras Day with Peter.

## Chapter Six

It promised to be a beautiful day. The sky was azure blue, without a cloud in sight. The sun shone brightly, backing up the weather forecasters' promises of temperatures rising into the sixties by noon.

Tess could feel her spirits rise as she made the twenty-four-mile drive across the Lake Pontchartrain Causeway. By the time she neared the tollgates on the Metairie side, she had cleared her mind of her worries and let go of the pressures that had been weighing her down. She would pick them up again on her way home, but today she was going to get in the mood of Mardi Gras.

It had been so long since Tess had felt carefree that she'd almost forgotten the giddy, buoyant sensation.

At West Esplanade, she took a left and drove to West End, finding Peter's multistoried condo complex with no problem. In the parking lot, she glanced up and saw him standing out on his balcony on an upper level. He evidently was watching for her and waved.

"Hi. You're right on time."

He sounded as though he didn't have a care in the world, either. Tess's heart gave a little leap of pure gladness. "I'm ready and raring to go," she called up to him. "I've been warming up my voice all the way over so that I won't get hoarse, yelling 'Throw me something, mister!'"

"I won't hold us up, then. I'll be right down."

Tess waited for him by his car on the passenger's side. He emerged and walked over with a long, loose stride to unlock the driver's door. They both got in, and he started the car immediately, as though it was the most normal thing in the world for them to be setting out on an excursion together.

"You dressed exactly right," he said approvingly, giving her an inspecting glance when they were driving along.

Tess had noted that they were dressed similarly, both wearing jeans and a windbreaker over a light pullover sweater and a shirt. They might have consulted on their attire.

"We'll be shedding these jackets pretty quickly," she said.

"Probably the sweaters, too, but then we'll be putting them back on when the sun starts going down."

The complacency in his voice warmed Tess. It was only nine-thirty. He was looking ahead to a long day that would go on after dark. So was she. "I brought some bags for all the loot," she told him, pulling a wad of plastic grocery sacks out of her jacket pocket and then stuffing it back in after he'd looked over, grinning.

"That was good thinking. Aren't you being a little optimistic, though?"

"Not with three parades to go to. I'd give my eye teeth to catch a Zulu coconut, but that's not very likely," she lamented.

The prized favor from the flamboyant Zulu parade was a decorated coconut sculpted into a head with African facial features. Zulu was an old, predominantly black organization, or *krewe*. Its members who rode in the parade, which according to custom rolled first on Mardi Gras Day, blackened their faces, and the keynote was vaudevillian.

"You have to know somebody riding on a float to get one of those, don't you?" Peter asked.

Tess nodded. "They don't really throw them. They hand them to their friends." She went on to explain how a few years ago the threat of lawsuits had put an end to tossing the coconuts into the crowd. Parade goers had raised such a fuss when the unique favors were eliminated altogether that Zulu was now permitted to hand them down. "New Orleans people won't stand for having their Mardi Gras traditions tampered with," Tess remarked.

"Mardi Gras isn't a tourist event, is it? The tourists are welcome to come and join the party, but it would go on without them."

"I think that's why it draws so many outside people. It isn't staged for them."

The drive downtown seemed to take almost no time. They parked at the Superdome, took a shuttle bus and went to Canal Street, where a large crowd was gathered. They found a spot on the broad median, commonly called the "neutral ground" in New Orleans, the origin of the term dating back to when the historic old street had marked the dividing line between the French Quarter on one side, where the Creoles lived, and the American settlement on the other side.

"Our timing was *perfect*!" Tess said exultantly, clapping her hands in rhythm to the loud, brassy music of a high-school band that was marching by. Behind it was a colorful float raining beads and doubloons and a whole variety of other throws to right and left.

There was no explaining the Mardi Gras madness of parade goers to anyone who hadn't ever experienced it firsthand. It was a good-natured fever that stripped away inhibitions and galvanized a crowd of people into screaming, jostling but friendly competition for trinkets of relatively small value.

Tess lifted her arms into the air as the float approached, jumped up and down and added her voice to the frenzied chorus of "Throw me something, mister!" that welled up louder and louder into a crescendo as the float arrived and caused bedlam. She scrambled for objects that fell to the ground and took a second or two to display her prizes to Peter, who, with his height advantage, was doing much better catching the airborne treasures.

"I got a Frisbee!" she yelled. "And a cup!"

"Great going!" he said, an exultant grin on his face. Reaching up, he snatched a long strand of beads and hung it around her neck, instead of adding it to the several other shorter strands on his arm. Then he bent and took a quick kiss in payment.

Tess reacted spontaneously. With both her hands full, she put her arms around his neck and kept him from straightening up. He looked into her eyes and murmured her name before he kissed her again, lingeringly and then hard and with passion. She kissed him back, tightening her arms as he picked her up and held her against his body, the way she remembered.

"Damn!" he muttered when they were suddenly pelted with throws. Drawing in a breath, Tess reluctantly opened her eyes and turned her head to follow his gaze. Several rid-ers on the departing float were pointing at them and grinning broadly. She smiled sheepishly and waved.

"It was a good way to attract their attention, but we didn't catch anything," she complained unsteadily to Peter.

They were also the focal point of attention on the ground in their immediate vicinity. There were joking requests to be allowed to stand close to them when the next float came along. Tess blushed as Peter took his time about setting her down on her feet. She got out a plastic bag and dropped her cup and Frisbee into it.

"You held on to those, I see," Peter observed. His tone was lightly teasing and intimate. "I dropped my beads."

"You didn't!" Tess pretended consternation.

"Here. I caught a couple of doubloons." He fished in the pocket of his jacket. Tess held out the bag for him to add them to her meager collection. He dropped the aluminum coins in and then put his arm around her shoulders, and they turned their attention to the street, where another band was marching by.

"I wish we had thought of bringing along a sack, honey," a woman next to them said wistfully. "We should have at least worn clothes with lots of pockets."

"We're not veterans at this, dear," replied her male companion. "This is our first Mardi Gras."

Tess glanced over with a smile at the couple, both in their fifties, she would guess, and obviously husband and wife. From their appearance, she would have spotted them as tourists, even if she hadn't overheard the snatch of conversation.

"I have an extra bag. You're welcome to it," she told the woman, pulling out a bag and offering it to her.

"Are you sure?" The woman was taken aback by Tess's generosity, but delighted. "This is so nice of you," she said, taking the bag. "We have grandchildren, and we want to bring them some Mardi Gras souvenirs. We're from Virginia,'' she volunteered.

"Do you folks live here in New Orleans?'' the man spoke up, addressing the friendly inquiry to Peter, who replied that they didn't live in the city proper, but in the New Orleans area. Tess knew that he had probably left the couple from Virginia with the impression that he and Tess lived together, but she really didn't care. She didn't add to his explanation or engage the couple in conversation, even though they seemed to be nice people. Another float was in sight.

Tess craned to see it, standing in the circle of Peter's arm. She wasn't in the least troubled by the kiss. There was no significance to it. Kissing Peter in a state of euphoria not surprisingly was still pure sensual delight. After all, he was as physically attractive to her now as he had been when she met him, twelve years ago. Tess didn't doubt that there might be another unpremeditated kiss or two during the day, but she wasn't worried or anxious.

Mardi Gras was all about letting loose and living in the moment.

By the time Zulu was over, Tess and Peter were both feeling pangs of hunger and decided to walk to the French Quarter and get something to eat. They could come back and catch part of the Rex parade, which would be along shortly. Tess looked around and spotted the couple from Virginia. They hadn't done nearly so well in their combined efforts at catching throws.

"We don't want to carry all this stuff, do we?'' she asked Peter, holding up their bulging bag.

He had followed her glance and read what was in her mind. "No, why don't you give most of it to them. The fun's in catching it anyway.''

Tess kept a few doubloons and a dozen or so strands of beads, hanging half of them around her neck and the others around Peter's. He bent down obligingly, the devil-may-care expression in his dark eyes daring her to kiss him. People were milling around now, awaiting Rex, and it was anything but private, but she accepted the challenge and kissed him on the mouth. He didn't pick her up this time, but he did frame her face with both hands and brought her lips back to his for a lingering kiss that deepened briefly with one sweet coupling of their tongues.

They both pulled back reluctantly. Peter drew in a deep breath as he straightened, and Tess had to take just a moment to overcome her body's protest over ending the second kiss.

The people from Virginia were thrilled to accept the rest of the contents of her bag. Tess had taken off her jacket by now and, like Peter, had tied the sleeves around her waist. She stuffed the empty bag back into a pocket, and they set off down a side street in the direction of the French Quarter, holding hands.

There had been some parade watchers on Canal wearing costumes, but the heart of the French Quarter was like a huge masquerade party that had been in swing for several hours, with all the self-invited guests promenading in the streets, toasting one another with drinks in plastic cups. Peter dropped Tess's hand and put his arm around her protectively as they entered the crush.

"It looks like the California Raisins are in vogue this year," she remarked as a second group of revelers passed by, in purple garb, dancing down the middle of the street and doing a musical rendition of a California Raisins television commercial.

They threaded their way through a sea of clowns and bears and belly dancers, stopped to listen to a jazz group giving an impromptu performance on a street corner, then walked on, calling each other's attention to particularly bizarre or spectacular or ribald costumes. After several tries, they found a restaurant that wasn't filled to capacity and sat down at the one remaining table.

It didn't matter that service was slow and the atmosphere raucous. They both agreed that it was good to get off their feet and that their Bloody Marys were worth waiting for, when the waitress finally brought them. The oyster poboys they had ordered were long in coming out of the kitchen, but the sandwich loaves of crusty French bread were delicious, the fried, breaded oysters fresh and succulent. Meanwhile, they'd had a second round of Bloody Marys.

They didn't make it back to Canal Street for Rex, choosing instead to walk around some more in the French Quarter, where the tempo was picking up. On every block it seemed that there was live music playing for dancing in the street. Tess didn't need any urging when Peter twirled her around and started dancing with her. Neither of them had ever been the type to hold back at a party, and this was just one big party open to anyone who wanted to come.

It was four-thirty, and they were ready for a rest when they eventually found themselves at the French quarter hotel where Peter's company had a suite that employees and invited guests could use as a convenient base, coming and going as they pleased. He introduced her simply as Tess Davenport, and Tess got no hint that he might have talked about her to any of his co-workers who were present, except one, a man named Les Morgan.

A big sandy-haired man with keen blue eyes and an easy, genial manner, he regarded her with frank curiosity as he shook her hand, saying, "I'm pleased to meet you, Tess. I motor past your marina quite frequently in my sailboat."

"Les lives on the North Shore. He has a great place on the river with his own dock," Peter told Tess and left her to chat with Les while he stepped over to a bar to get them drinks.

"Does your sailboat have a bright red hull?" Tess asked him, putting two and two together and guessing why he seemed vaguely familiar. She had heard his voice last Sunday.

"Yes, she does. Her name is *Seabreeze*."

Tess remembered the name lettered on the transom. "I noticed her in the boat parade on Sunday. She's a lovely boat."

He smiled ruefully. "I'd rather hear that than a personal compliment any day. *Seabreeze* is the apple of my eye."

No follow-up on the subject of the boat parade. No mention that Peter had been among his crew.

"Did you give Peter the sailing fever?" Tess inquired lightly, her intuition telling her that Peter must have confided in Les Morgan. She thought the sailboat owner knew that she was Peter's ex-wife. "He's very enthusiastic about getting his own sailboat."

"He had been sailing a few times when he was with the Houston office, I believe, but, yes, I have to admit that I have encouraged him to become a sailboat owner. He was a little reluctant about investing in a boat because he will only be in New Orleans a year or two."

"Yes, that's what he told me."

"Peter is a very bright lad and works hard. He's going to go far with the company, despite the squeeze in the industry."

Tess couldn't tell whether she was supposed to take his words as a recommendation or a warning.

"I have no doubt that he will," she said. "He likes his work very much. He's one of those people who picked the right field for himself."

Peter joined them, interrupting the exchange that Tess found rather odd. Les Morgan, who was about Will's age, she would guess, had spoken with an almost paternal air.

She assumed that he was farther up the company ladder than Peter. It was obvious to her that he liked Peter and that the feeling was mutual. While there was no coolness whatever toward her, she wondered if he altogether approved of her.

Since there was no shop talk, she didn't learn until later, when she and Peter had left the hotel and she had a chance to question him about Les, that Les was Peter's superior several levels up.

"I would never have guessed that he was someone you had to answer to," Tess remarked. They were walking along without having discussed a destination, but heading generally in the direction of Bourbon Street. "You two seem to be friends."

"Les and I hit it off right from the first," Peter replied. "He kind of took me under his wing."

"He certainly has a high opinion of you, you'll be glad to hear."

"I have a great deal of respect for him."

But he wasn't particularly interested in talking about his boss and friend now with her. Tess nibbled her bottom lip, knowing that she was about to get them in dangerous territory, but she wasn't ready to drop the subject of Les Morgan. She kept her voice casual as she asked, "Does he know that you and I were married? Somehow I got the impression that you might have filled him in."

"I told him the whole story," Peter admitted. "He knew that I wasn't seasick last Sunday when I jumped ashore. We had been out sailing on his boat a number of times. He was very concerned, and I owed him an explanation."

Did the "whole story" include Peter's feelings about her now and his thoughts about a present relationship between them? Tess wondered, thinking back to her brief conversation with Les. In retrospect, her perception was even stronger that he hadn't spoken idly in outlining Peter's career prospects. With hindsight, she was also even more certain that she hadn't met with Les's approval.

"I had the paranoid notion when I was talking to Les that he wasn't really taken with me," she commented, covering up an absurd sense of rejection with a rueful note.

Peter hesitated before answering, and he didn't make the denial that she was expecting. "Les was married and divorced when he was in his early twenties, too. He got back together with his ex-wife a few years later, and they ended up divorcing again. Based on his own experience, he's not an advocate of taking a second chance with the same person. He's convinced that the same problems will crop up."

"And he doesn't want you to make the same mistake that he did."

"Right. There was nothing personal against you." Peter was holding her hand and gave it a little reassuring squeeze. "What's next on our agenda? Should we think about finding ourselves a good spot on the Comus parade route? Or should we get something to eat first? I'm wondering if we're going to run into trouble finding a restaurant open later on tonight."

Tess discussed immediate plans with him and put the encounter with the owner of *Seabreeze* out of her mind for the time being.

With nightfall the temperature was cooler, and they put their sweaters and jackets back on as they awaited the arrival of Comus on a corner at the intersection of Poydras and St. Charles. In either direction on St. Charles, a crowd was lined up on both sides of the street as far as they could see. A little leg-weary, Tess stood in front of Peter, leaning against him. Both his arms were wrapped around her.

"Cold?" he inquired with a tender note.

"No," she replied, but he hugged her tighter anyway, as though she needed his body warmth.

The sky had been clear all day and was now studded with stars. Tess happened to look up and notice and called the fact to Peter's attention. They gazed up at a brilliant canopy that would go unappreciated as the procession of bands and floats and equestrian groups passed. Tess heard the faint music of the first band and regretted that the waiting was almost over. As the strains got louder, though, she came to life again and was soon rejuvenated by the noise and color and collective energy as she succumbed to the magical element of a night-time Mardi Gras parade.

Like all the rest of the crowd along the jammed parade route, she and Peter were volunteer subjects, paying homage to His Majesty, King of the Mystick Krewe of Comus, the oldest secret Carnival organization, formed in 1857. He was making his traditional night march to the Municipal Auditorium for a ceremonial meeting with Rex, the King of Carnival, who awaited his arrival.

At midnight, Carnival was over, after the weeks of balls and parades. Tomorrow the Lenten Season began, with fasting and sobriety.

"Do you want to go back to the Quarter, along with the diehards?" Peter asked Tess when the parade had gone on by them.

"No, I've had enough," she admitted.

They started walking in the direction of the Superdome, then when they'd gone a few blocks, they caught a taxi that took them the rest of the way.

"I'm so glad that you asked me to come over," Tess told Peter after they were settled in his car and on the interstate. "I had a marvelous time." She didn't try to keep from sounding exactly the way she felt, fortunate for having had the day and sorry that it was over.

"I wouldn't have missed it for anything," Peter said, on the same wavelength with her.

Traffic was heavy, and he wasn't able to drive the speed limit. They rode awhile in silence. Tess looked out at the city lights and yawned, fatigue settling in.

"Tired?" he asked, sympathy in his voice and in his glance.

"All of a sudden, I am. I have a sneaking suspicion that I'm going to have some sore, stiff muscles tomorrow," she predicted ruefully. "Not just from this walking, but from the jumping up and down and not acting my age."

"Your high school missed a good bet when you didn't go out for cheerleader," he remarked with a kind of amused indulgence.

It was too comfortable and relaxed, winding down with him after the day's emotional highs. Tess had to disrupt the harmony, as much as she hated to. Sitting up straighter in her seat, she sighed and then lamented, "Now if I only had an automatic pilot on my car and could program it to take me home."

Peter looked over at her comprehendingly, rebuking her with his dark gaze for being roundabout, rather than open about the issue that worried her—how this evening would end. Tess welcomed her defensiveness, needing whatever protection she could muster.

"I won't let you make that drive across the causeway alone this late at night," he stated quietly but definitely.

"It's perfectly safe," she argued. "The police will be patrolling, and there are call boxes, in the unlikely event that I break down. My car is very dependable, and I have good tires. It was a foregone conclusion when we stayed for Comus that I would be driving home at this hour." If he had made any other assumption, that was his mistake, she added with her tone.

He gave her another eloquent look, full of reprimand for talking all around the subject and then not speaking the last aloud. His firm, quiet reply invited no further haggling. "If you want to go home tonight, I'll drive you."

"Then my car would be over here," Tess protested. "I'd have to put someone to the trouble of bringing me back tomorrow so that I could get it. Plus, you'd have to make the trip home by yourself, even later at night, and I'd be worried about you."

"My car is brand-new, but if I did have a blowout or engine trouble, I could handle the situation far better than you could."

"You can't tell me that you're not tired, too," Tess persisted. "You could fall asleep at the wheel and have an accident. Besides, don't you have to get up early and go to work in the morning?"

"I'm really not all that tired or sleepy," he denied, his tone wearily patient. "And I don't have to work tomorrow, so I can sleep as late as I want. It's no problem for me to take you home, Tess."

Evidently he considered the matter settled. He didn't take the Bonnabel exit when they came to it. Tess sighed, her dissatisfaction welling up. "It really is silly for you to do all this extra traveling. The sensible thing would be for me to sleep on your sofa tonight, get up and drive my own car home in the morning."

"Neither one of us has to sleep on the couch. I have a daybed in the room that I use for an office. I'll sleep in there, and you can have my bedroom."

"No, I won't take your bedroom," Tess objected, her whole body responding to the idea of sleeping in his bed.

"It has an adjoining bath. The other one doesn't."

"That's okay. The daybed will be short for you, and you'll be uncomfortable. It'll be plenty long enough for me."

"Okay, have it your way," he relented.

They rode for several minutes in silence.

"You certainly have changed a lot and become a far more reasonable person," Tess observed when she thought she had her frustration under control, but the remark still came out sounding more like a complaint than a commendation. "I don't suppose that you can say the same about me."

"All you'd have had to do, Tess, was tell me outright that you didn't want to sleep with me tonight. Then we could have discussed our alternatives like two mature adults and arrived at these same arrangements."

"It's not a question of 'want,' Peter," she confessed earnestly. "It's a matter of what's best for both of us. I know that having an affair with you wouldn't be good for me, and I don't think that it would be good for you, either."

"I agree."

"I thought you would," she said when she had swallowed the huge lump in her throat. The real explanation for her behavior was crystal clear to her, as it must be to him. She had simply lacked the courage to raise an honest discussion and have him concur that they had no future together.

The least disturbing of her emotions as she accompanied him into the building was curiosity about the place where he lived and his life-style.

"You must not buy any more groceries than you can carry up at one time," she suggested as they took the elevator to his level, the fourth floor.

"No, I don't," Peter agreed. "But then, for one person, it doesn't take a lot. I notice that the couples who live here tend to do their grocery shopping together."

"Probably the extent of your cooking is TV dinners, anyway. Or do you mostly eat out?"

"I eat lunch out during the week. At night, I usually fix myself something. You'd be surprised," he said. "I've gotten fairly handy in the kitchen."

"Have you?"

It was the perfect opening for him to say that he would cook her breakfast the next morning and show her. When he didn't, Tess felt rebuffed, even though she would have responded by stating her intention to be up and gone very early. She didn't dare trust herself to laze around his condo with him the next day. Evidently he wasn't entertaining any such ideas.

When he didn't make any efforts at picking up the conversation, Tess stubbornly said nothing more. Inside his condo, she broke the silence, falling back on her curiosity again.

"This is very nice," she complimented sincerely as she looked around the combination living room and dining room, furnished and decorated attractively, but in a plain, masculine style. It was obviously a man's home. "Is the furniture yours? And the pictures?"

"Yes. I like having my own household things."

"You have very good taste," Tess remarked approvingly and then wished she hadn't when the jealous thought occurred to her that he might have had some female help in making his selections.

Peter obviously wasn't interested in standing around and chatting. "The kitchen's over here," he said, leading the way. "Help yourself to anything you can find to eat or drink. There's liquor in the cabinet next to the refrigerator, and I have milk and beer and soft drinks." He stopped in the doorway to turn on a light switch, then stood aside. Tess barely had time to glance into the kitchen before he was telling her to follow him and he would show her where the bathroom was and the room where she would be sleeping.

"Unless you've changed your mind and would like to take my bedroom," he said over his shoulder.

"No, I haven't," she informed him, a little provoked with the way he was acting. "Just give me some bedding, and I'll do fine. If you don't mind, I will borrow one of your old T-shirts to use as a nightgown."

"The daybed is already made up with clean sheets and a blanket," he answered, seeming to step up his pace. He didn't make any reply to her request other than, "I'll be right back."

Tess had scarcely had time to look around before he returned, holding a folded T-shirt. "You have a computer," she remarked. "Everyone has been telling me that I ought to get a computer for the marina."

He dropped the T-shirt on the bed and went back to the door. "You would probably find one handy, after you learned to use it." He grasped the doorknob. "Well, I'm going to turn in. I'll see you in the morning."

"You may not, unless you're up early," Tess said. "But I promise I'll be very quiet leaving. Now I'm glad that I didn't listen to you earlier and let you drive me home. You were a lot more tired and sleepy than you admitted." Judging from his great hurry to go to bed.

"I'm not nearly tired and sleepy enough," Peter warned her softly.

"Good night, Peter," Tess told him hastily, her heart beating wildly with panic and pleasure.

"Good night, Tess."

He closed the door behind him.

## Chapter Seven

Tess drew in a deep breath to combat the feeling of letdown. Not even her hot wave of shame could flush it away, as she thought of how contradictory and how transparent Peter must find her. She said one thing to him and then gave out entirely different signals.

Was it pride that made him heed her words when he must be able to sense that she had no real powers of resistance? Right now, if he came through the door, took her into his arms and started making love to her, she might murmur protests, but she would respond helplessly. Just the possibility awoke longing.

Picking up his T-shirt, Tess shook it out, then gathered up the soft folds and held the garment against her cheek. It smelled fresh and clean from the laundry, with no faint musky male scent, the way it would have smelled if he had stripped it off after wearing it.

With a sigh, she laid the shirt down again while she took off her jacket and her sweater, draping both of them on Peter's swivel chair at his desk. After a moment's deliberation, she decided that she would undress in the bathroom and put on the shirt there. The chance that Peter might emerge from his bedroom just as she was returning to hers without a robe made her heartbeat quicken and brought her body alive.

In the bathroom Tess ran water for a bath while she brushed her teeth, using a new toothbrush and a tube of toothpaste that she found in a drawer, along with other feminine toilet articles, including hand lotion and shampoo.

They all appeared to be newly bought or at least they didn't seem to have been used previously. Did Peter make a habit of being prepared for female guests? she wondered jealously. Or had he thought ahead to her possibly staying overnight?

After her bath, Tess towelled off, slipped on the shirt and took her hair down and brushed it. When the tub had emptied with a loud gurgle, she rinsed it out before gathering up her clothes and leaving the bathroom.

Back in her room, she turned the covers down on the daybed, shut out the light and was about to lie down when she thought of how good a soft drink would taste. Opening her door very quietly, she left it ajar. Her bare feet made no noise on the carpeted floor, but she tiptoed to the kitchen anyway. The refrigerator door made a sucking sound, both opening and closing, and the pop top on her soft drink can released with a small explosion.

But if Peter heard her moving around, he didn't come out to investigate, and Tess gave him plenty of time.

She didn't think that she had ever been more awake in her life, but she lay down on her back and closed her eyes. If only she had some assurance that Peter was asleep, that might help her to relax, but, short of tiptoeing to his bedroom and peeking in, she had no way of telling. He probably had a king-size bed, or at least a queen-size. The double bed in their rented apartment had been short for him, but it hadn't been too narrow for the two of them. They'd slept, cuddled closely together, with room to spare.

Even when they'd fought and gone to bed with their backs to each other and not touching, they would wake up the next morning with Peter's arm thrown over her and hugging her to him or with her curled against his back and hugging him. The memory flooded her with sweetness and reawoke an ache of longing.

Tess turned on her side, raised her head and pummeled her pillow. This was hopeless. She wasn't ever going to fall asleep, especially not lying there and torturing herself with thoughts of past intimacy with Peter.

Tess sighed and moved her cheek deeper into the pillow, then came alert. Had she heard something? Getting out of bed, she went quickly over to the door and opened it enough to stick her head out and listen.

A faint sound, not from the direction of Peter's bedroom but from the kitchen. Had Peter gotten up to get himself something to cure his own case of insomnia?

If he had, he could come along the hallway any second. Tess should go back to bed and bury herself under the covers. Instead she just stood there, shivering and gripping the doorknob until, against her will, with her heartbeat jolting her breastbone, her feet took her out into the hallway and, step by step, to the kitchen doorway.

One glance confirmed that she had guessed right. With his back to her, Peter was drinking a glass of milk. The gallon jug was on the counter. He was barefoot and wore nothing except dark cotton knit briefs that rode low on his hips. Tess could have turned around and fled back to her room, her presence undetected. Instead she swallowed, working up her nerve and inquired wistfully, "Could I have a glass of that, too?"

His split-second reaction to her voice was visible. He went still and rigid with the awareness that she was there, behind him.

"Sure." He put his own glass down and got another one from the cabinet. He poured milk into it before he turned around and looked at her.

"I hope I didn't disturb you a while ago, using the bathroom. I tried to be quiet as a mouse," Tess assured him, conscious that her hair tumbled down around her shoulders and that she was naked underneath his shirt, which rode high on her thighs.

"You didn't wake me. I wasn't asleep."

"I also helped myself to one of your soft drinks earlier, after my bath."

"I heard you when you got the drink."

"That pop top sounded like an explosion. It's funny, isn't it, how loud everything sounds when you're trying to be quiet?"

He didn't answer. Tess could feel her nipples, hard against the cloth of his shirt. She folded her arms across her chest and shivered, as though being chilly explained her body's state of stimulation.

"Do you know if milk really does have any sleep-inducing effect?" she asked as she walked over to the counter near him.

He sucked in his breath. "Recently I read that it does."

Tess took a sip of her milk, put it back down and hugged herself, saying, "That's cold!"

"If it isn't warm enough for you in here, I'll turn up the thermostat," Peter offered in a low, strained voice.

"I'm warm enough under the covers. I guess I should go back to bed and make another try at getting to sleep. Do you want me to put away the milk?"

"No, what I want is to take you to bed with me, and you damned well know that, Tess." He picked up a tress of her hair and held it in his palm as he went on, his voice softer, but still frustrated and accusing. "What do you think I'm made of, baby?" Tess melted at his use of the old tender endearment. "It was bad enough imagining you with your hair down and wearing my shirt. Why did you come in here, looking like that, when you knew what it would do to me?"

Tess met his dark searching gaze and spoke the truth, "When I heard you out here, I couldn't stay in my room. I couldn't help myself. Just now I couldn't force myself to go back, before you saw me." She made a move toward him, murmuring, "Oh, *Peter...*" His arms opened and closed tight around her as she went into them.

"Tess, baby, I want you so much." His urgent low tone was full of longing. "It was sheer hell, lying in my bed and knowing that I could be holding you tonight."

"It was just as bad for me. I want you to hold me tonight, Peter. I want you to make love to me. Tomorrow I'll be sorry, but I don't care."

He picked her up and held her against him, demanding huskily, "Kiss me, baby." Tess hugged him tightly around his neck and answered the passionate hunger of his lips and tongue with her own hunger. The T-shirt was hiked up so that only the cloth of his briefs separated their hips. She could feel his arousal pressing against her bareness and wanted him inside of her.

"Take me to bed, Peter," she begged. "It's been such a long time."

"An eternity," he said fervently, sliding her down his body slowly and setting her on her feet. "It'll be as good with us as before, Tess. You turn me on the way no other woman can."

He was caressing her beneath the T-shirt while he talked, his low, soft tone making sexual promises even without the words. Tess moaned as he slid his palm across her stomach and then moved both hands higher to fondle her breasts.

"Your hands feel so good, Peter. You always knew exactly how to touch me."

"*You* feel good to me, baby. Do you taste as sweet as I remember?" He bent down and bit one hard nipple and then the other one gently through the clinging folds of material.

Tess gasped with her pleasure and clasped his head, pressing his mouth hard against her breast. She waited helplessly as he slid one hand lower, passing the palm over her stomach and then farther down.

"That makes me too weak to stand up," she complained.

He straightened, withdrawing his hands and taking both of hers down low to his body. "Touch me, baby," he requested with soft urgency.

They both watched her stroke him intimately without any shyness. "Oh, baby," he said weakly, caressing her shoulders.

"Let's go to your bedroom, unless you want to make love in the kitchen," she urged, and blushed when her words came out sounding like an ultimatum.

He smiled, tender reminiscence mingling with the desire in his dark eyes. His voice revealed the same emotion, as he reminded, "It wouldn't be the first time we made love in a kitchen. That apartment of ours was small, but we made good use of all the rooms, if you remember."

Tess smiled back at him. "How could I forget?"

"That was cruel of you to take a bath tonight," he accused. "I lay there and thought of how soft and pink you would be when you got out."

"You were always very helpful about drying me off after I had been soaking in the tub." Tess eased her fingertips beneath the waistband of his briefs and tugged them down an inch, silently posing her question again, the kitchen or the bedroom?

Peter took her hands in his and squeezed them. Then he picked her up in his arms, giving her his answer.

"I can walk," Tess protested, hugging him around the neck as he carried her out.

He didn't put her down, observing, "You haven't put on any weight."

"Yes, I have. Three or four pounds."

"Then that must bring you up to about 114. You weighed 110."

"You always had a very good memory for facts and figures." Tess was absurdly pleased at the accuracy of his recall.

"A good memory can be a curse," he said. "I can't walk past a jewelry store without remembering your ring size. I could tell you to the penny how much that cheap little set of wedding rings cost."

"I loved those rings. I thought they were beautiful," Tess protested, and thought about how through the years, in weak moments, she had taken the rings out of her jewelry box and slipped them on her finger. "As it turned out, it was a good thing that you couldn't afford a more expensive set of rings. You'd only have been wasting your money. I'm really sorry, Peter, about...everything." Filled with regrets for the past and the future, she reached up and caressed his face with her fingertips. "And yet here I am in your bedroom, getting us both involved in another no-win situation.''

Peter hugged her tight to him. ''Tonight isn't any more your doing than it's mine. It had to happen, Tess, sooner or later. You and I both knew that Wednesday when I came to the marina.''

Tess couldn't deny it. Mute, she looked up into his face as he released her. ''I had been thinking about you so much the past few weeks, remembering.''

''While you were trying to make up your mind about marrying Buford,'' he said, pulling the T-shirt over her hips.

She nodded and helped him as he took off her shirt. He was very careful not to pull her hair. When the shirt was free of her head, he tossed it aside and caressed her nakedness with his eyes before he touched her. Then he captured her breasts and fondled them.

Tess enjoyed the sensations for a moment before she reached for the elastic waist of his briefs and took them down, freeing him of the garment's restriction. His hands tightened on her breasts as she took liberties that were still familiar.

The contact was warm and pulsing, awakening an insistent need in Tess for a more intimate connection.

''Could we get into bed now, Peter, please—''

''Anything you say. I'm all yours, baby.''

His husky lover's words had a sweet ring of familiarity, bringing back the days of their wild, young lovemaking. Tess spoke in the same vein, telling him what she wanted and how much she desired it, for him to be on top and inside her.

Getting into his bed and lying on her back, she had no sense of impropriety. Her self-consciousness was titillating, not embarrassing, as he leaned over her, giving her an intimate inspection. His dark eyes were full of possessiveness.

He lowered his head to lick one erect nipple with his tongue. Tess arched her back at the rough, warm contact. He moved over the other breast, tasted it and then kissed a path down her body. Tess's legs opened gradually in a reflex response.

He kissed her tender inner thighs and then sent rockets of ecstatic sensation through her as he found her sensitive nub with his mouth. Tess gasped his name helplessly and opened wider, lifting her hips. He penetrated her molten wetness with his tongue, setting off quivers of deeper need.

"Now, Peter, please," Tess begged him.

"Now, sweet thing," he agreed, raising up and positioning himself for the entry that she demanded. He wanted it as much as she did. Tess could feel the tremor in his body as she embraced his shoulders. She could read the intensity of his need in his eyes as he looked down into hers.

The union of their bodies was deep and total, bringing them right to the brink of ecstasy. "God, Tess," he said. "I was afraid of this. It's almost too much for me."

"For me, too." Tess hugged him, understanding that he wasn't just talking about the sexual pleasure that threatened his control. He was having difficulty, just as she was, coming to grips with his emotion at the moment of joining his body to hers and possessing her once again. The sense of oneness and completion was overwhelming.

"I still feel like you're mine, Tess."

His confession was tender and yet sober as he shared with her the state of mind that defied his own comprehension and wasn't of his choosing. He would have gotten over her long ago, if only he could have figured out how.

"I know. Make love to me, Peter."

He took them both to the peak of pleasure with deep, hard strokes that exploded the core of sensation inside Tess that she had been storing up all those years apart from him.

She cried out for release. When it came, devastating body and mind, she blurted out her own joyous bewilderment that he was the one man who could satisfy her perfectly.

As soon as the words were out, Tess wished that she could take them back, but it was too late. She hadn't meant to raise the subject of other lovers and spoil their satisfaction in each other with jealous speculations. That was exactly what she'd done, though.

Still inside her, Peter braced himself on his elbows, gazing down at her and looking as though she had just admitted being unfaithful to him. "I can't stand the thought of you with another man, Tess." His voice held an accusing note.

"I feel the same way about you and other women," she replied, adding reproachfully, "In ten years, there had to be quite a few." His guilty expression was her answer and caused a stab of pain.

"Not so many, and it was never the same with anyone else."

"If there weren't a lot of different women, you must have had long affairs." A possibility somehow even more unacceptable than short flings.

"Several that lasted quite a while. I tried to fall in love again."

"So did I. I've only been to bed with men that I was seriously involved with. I didn't sleep around, Peter, and there was never any comparison to sex with you."

"I guess that should please my male ego, but it doesn't." He sighed and leaned down to kiss her on the mouth, withdrawing. Tess got up to go to the bathroom and closed the bedroom door on her way back to bed. Peter turned off the lamp, and they lay close, holding each other in the darkness, drawn together by regrets and sadness.

"You were a virgin," he recalled, resuming the conversation.

"But not really what you would call innocent," Tess reminded him. "I had gone steady in high school."

"The fact that you weren't entirely innocent only made that first time more meaningful for me. I was the guy you gave yourself to."

"It didn't seem wrong with you." Nor did tonight seem wrong, even though they weren't married and weren't committed to each other. "I didn't intend to get us into all this discussion," she lamented sorrowfully. "I spoke without thinking earlier."

"Don't feel bad. It was inevitable anyway." He kissed the top of her head, consoling her.

Tess sighed her agreement. The word *inevitable* seemed to apply to their whole relationship. "If I had given in and gone out to Denver with you, Peter, it wouldn't have worked out. I'd have worried myself sick about Daddy, felt guilty and taken everything out on you."

"Nor would it have been a viable solution for me to turn down the Denver job and work in New Orleans so that you could be close to your father. I resented him too much at that point to get along with him. The situation would have been impossible. You'd have been caught right in the middle." And would have had to choose between him and her father. "It would have been an even harder adjustment, losing you after I'd sacrificed my career." Which was what he would have been faced with.

His quiet, resigned analysis hurt Tess more than a bitter tirade would have. She wished with all her heart that she could honestly tell him that he was wrong, that she wouldn't have broken off with him and stuck by her father. But she couldn't.

"If our marriage was going to go on the rocks anyway, it was probably best that we split up and went our separate ways," she summed up sadly.

He didn't answer, but stroked her hair and then caressed her back and hips and buttocks, awakening her body as his own came to life. They made love again, taking longer this time to reach the same high peak of passion. Tess cried out at the moment of release, as she had done before, her voice blending with Peter's.

Afterward, he cradled her in his arms and told her good-night in a tender voice. Tess replied in the same tone. It was achingly, sweetly reminiscent of long ago nights with him, except for the missing words, *I love you.*

Tess wanted to say them, but she held them back, for the same reason, she knew, that Peter was holding them back, too. Loving each other hadn't kept the two of them together ten years ago, and it wouldn't be enough now to reconcile them. There was too much hurt and disappointment standing in the way of a fresh start.

## Chapter Eight

Tess roused the next morning and gave the most fleeting consideration to easing out of bed, getting dressed and leaving. Then she rejected the idea, reasoning groggily that she would wake Peter in the process. They lay on their sides, spoon fashion, with Tess facing out, her body curled into his and Peter's arm over her.

With a deep sigh of utter contentment, Tess snuggled even closer and went back to sleep. Some time later she partially awakened herself with a sound of protest and her own reflex movement as she turned over toward Peter. The weight of his arm had lifted, and he was inching free of her.

"I'll be back, baby," he promised tenderly, hugging her. "I'm just going to put on some coffee."

"What time is it?" Tess inquired drowsily, her voice muffled against his chest.

"Nine o'clock." He sounded complacent and relaxed.

"That late? I have to get up," she mumbled, not stirring.

"Do you have anything pressing to do today?"

"Nothing pressing."

"Then what's the rush? Stay right where you are and catch a few more winks, sleepyhead." He dropped a kiss on the top of her head and promised in the same indulgent tone, "I'll bring you a cup of coffee when it's made. Later on I'll even serve you breakfast in bed."

"That's hard to turn down," Tess said, lying on her back and opening her eyes when he released her and climbed out, standing for a moment and stretching. His dark, fine hair was rumpled, and he had a shadowy growth of beard, she noted, before she took in the rest of his lean, naked form appreciatively. Her drowsiness was fast vanishing.

"You sure you don't want me to help?" she asked as he left the room.

"Not with the coffee," he answered lazily over his shoulder. "But I was thinking that I'd come right back while it was brewing and take a quick shower. You could wash my back for me."

Flushed with warm anticipation, Tess got up and went into the adjoining bathroom. She was standing in front of the vanity mirror, brushing her hair with his hairbrush, when he returned.

"I didn't think about buying a shower cap, and you may not want to get your hair wet." He came up behind her and put down a handful of her hairpins that she'd left in the other bathroom.

"It takes forever to dry," Tess replied, meeting his eyes in the mirror.

His gaze lowered to her bare breasts as he observed, his voice softening, "I think you put those couple of extra pounds in my favorite places. Back here—" he caressed her buttocks with his palms and then brought his hands around

to cup her breasts "—and up front, here. Your waist is a
tiny as ever, and your stomach is flat."

"I'm sucking it in," Tess admitted. She was also swelling
her breasts to their utmost fullness for him.

"You feel like satin around your nipples."

They both watched him trace the dark brown circles of
her aureoles with his fingertips. Her nipples came more
prominently out of hiding and ached with the need to be
touched. Tess leaned against him as he pinched them,
awakening sharp little spasms of weak pleasure. She could
feel his arousal pressing against her.

"You have such a luscious, sexy figure for being small-
boned and slim," he went on, recapturing a rounded breast
in each hand and squeezing.

"Flattery like that will get you a back wash every time,"
Tess told him.

His smile was unabashedly male and suggestive as he met
her gaze in the mirror. "I'm hoping to get more than my
back washed, sugar. How about turning on the shower
while I get rid of these rough whiskers?"

"First, I want to pin up my hair."

Tess took her time, standing next to him in front of the
mirror and watching him lather his face with shaving cream
and then start to shave. She felt utterly seductive. He was
looking at her more than at his own reflection.

"Have a heart, baby, and get done with that," he pleaded
when he nicked himself with the razor. "I can't pay attention to what I'm doing with you standing there with your
arms raised in that centerfold pose."

"I was having my own problems concentrating," Tess
retorted with a bold glance in the mirror. He was fully
aroused.

She stuck in the last couple of pins and went over to the
large tiled shower, turned on the spray, adjusted it and then

got in and slid the glass door shut. The warm water felt wonderful on her tingling body. She tilted her head back and let the water run down the front of her.

"Did you cut yourself again?" she inquired sympathetically when Peter cursed.

"You must want me to bleed to death," he accused.

"Sorry," Tess said, not pretending not to understand. He found her stance provocative, as she had intended him to. She turned around, tilting her head forward and letting the water run down her back. "Is this any better?"

"Not much, but I'm almost finished carving myself up."

When Peter slid the shower door open and stepped in with her, Tess was genuinely distressed when she saw the several little cuts, crusted with blood, on his face. "Do they hurt?" he asked, caressing his face with tender concern.

"They burn a little." He reached for the bar of soap and handed it to her. "Some warm lather will take care of it."

Tess looked up at him uncertainly as she wet the soap and lathered her hands. He stood there, patiently waiting.

He grinned when Tess raised a soapy hand hesitantly to his cheek, and he caught it. "Oh, you thought I meant I wanted you to wash my face."

"I knew you were putting me on." Tess tried to keep from smiling back at him sheepishly and couldn't. In retaliation she soaped his chest and shoulders and arms thoroughly.

Finally he grabbed her hand and guided it, cajoling, "Come on, baby."

Tess ended his punishment with pleasure. She gave him the bar of soap to hold for her while she attended to every inch of him. He groaned at the slick, warm contact that was having its own arousing effect on her body. Her nipples were tight little knots of sensation, and the hub of her femininity ached with the emptiness that he could fill.

"I think I'm clean enough, baby. Thank you." The pained note in Peter's voice was a warning that Tess understood and heeded. Anticipation rose up in her as he lathered his hands. "Now that I don't have a razor next to my face, how about giving me one of those sexy poses while I wash you?" he requested.

Protesting that she felt self-conscious, Tess raised her arms and clasped the back of her head. In actuality, it was incredibly erotic, lifting her breasts and thrusting them out for him. When he massaged them with his long-fingered soapy hands, she sighed with the pleasurable sensations and tipped her head back, too.

His warm, slick touch was heavenly. She murmured encouragement as he worked downward, washing her waist and hips and stomach. "That feels wonderful...."

"Is that good enough?" he asked when he'd made her so weak with his ministrations that she clutched his shoulders

"I'm ready to rinse off," she told him, putting her arms up around his neck.

"And get out and dry off?" he queried softly.

"We haven't done our backs yet."

He smiled. "No, that's right, we haven't."

They took turns standing under the warm spray, helping each other rinse off and heightening the stimulation. Then they made love there in the shower, implementing techniques that they had used successfully in years past to compensate for the dissimilarity in height.

"Are you sure I'm not too heavy?" Tess asked the same question she'd asked when she was nineteen.

Peter gave the same answer, lifting her, "No, baby." And then, "Oh, Tess..." as he coupled their bodies.

Later, when they had showered again and were towelling each other off, he brought up the subject of birth control for the first time.

"It's a little late for me to be asking, but is there any worry?"

"No," Tess replied. "Otherwise I wouldn't have let anything happen."

He was silent a moment, and she could tell that he hadn't finished with the subject. "You're on the pill?"

"Yes. It's practically foolproof," she assured him.

"You told me you weren't sleeping with Buford." If that was true, why was she taking precautionary measures?

"I haven't, up to now, but in the event that I did, I wanted to be safe. I'm a little past the age for slipping up and getting myself pregnant. You and I were lucky," she reminded. Several times they had taken chances and gotten away with it.

Peter shrugged. "Maybe we were and maybe we weren't. Turn around, and I'll get your back."

Tess met his sober gaze questioningly before she obeyed slowly. The light, playful mood had dissipated. "What does that mean?"

"If we had had a child to consider, divorcing wouldn't have been such a simple matter. Didn't the same thought ever occur to you?"

"Yes," she admitted. "But the fact that it did is just further evidence that I was much too immature to be a mother. A child isn't a bargaining chip and an excuse for maintaining communication."

Peter draped the towel around her shoulders. "No, you're right, but I can't tell you how much I regretted not getting you pregnant." Tess turned to face him. He went on gravely. "I reasoned that being a father and the head of our own little family would have given me extra clout. Later on, I looked back and realized how immature and selfish my thinking was, but I was still sorry, for different reasons."

"You were?" Tess's question stuck in her throat.

"Yes. Even after I was certain that you would have re-married and had children with another man, I wished that we had had a little girl or a little boy as a by-product of our relationship. It just seemed too bad that what we had together came to nothing."

"But a lot of memories." So many of them painful, making the rest sad. "I'd better get dressed and go home now."

"No, don't go. Stay and have breakfast with me."

"But it's hopeless, Peter."

"Please don't run off, baby." He wrapped his towel around his neck and bent over to kiss her gently on the mouth. "The coffee maker has had more than enough time to do its job. Doesn't a cup of coffee sound good?"

Tess accompanied him into his bedroom, full of uncertainty. She knew that she shouldn't go along with another truce just to be with him. She should be strong and force him to admit that things couldn't work out between them now, either. Wandering over to the bed, a queen-size, she began making it up just for something to do. The pillows were bunched close together with side-by-side indentations, she noted.

"Don't bother with that." Peter had taken a clean pair of briefs from a bureau drawer and was putting them on.

"I don't mind."

"No, leave it."

"Okay. I'll just go and put on my clothes then." It was silly of her to feel rejected, but she did. He hadn't meant to drive the point home that she wasn't his wife anymore and had no domestic responsibilities, but was there strictly as his invited guest.

When she had gotten dressed and joined him in the kitchen, he insisted that she sit down in the breakfast bay drink the coffee that he served her and enjoy the view. His condo overlooked one of the large marinas at West End and, beyond it, the lake. Tess glanced at the vista and commented appreciatively, but she was far more interested in watching him as he got breakfast ingredients out of the refrigerator.

Dressed in jeans and a T-shirt, with his hair wet and combed slick, he looked clean and masculine. "Do you do your own laundry?" she asked. The jeans were pressed.

"No, I drop it off at a cleaner's and pick it up when it's done," he replied absently, getting a bowl down from a cabinet.

"You have maid service, I suppose."

"Once a week." He cracked eggs into the bowl. "I'm cooking scrambled eggs, if that's okay."

"Fine. Are you sure I can't help? I feel so useless, just sitting here."

He looked over with a teasing smile. "It's going to be edible. I promise."

"I'm not worried. You look as though you know what you're doing." Who had taught him culinary skills anyway?

"Think of all those times I sat and let you wait on me," he reminded. "I didn't lift a finger to help you in the apartment, and then I had the nerve to be critical."

"I wasn't the world's best cook or housekeeper."

"We were both full-time students. I was too much of a male chauvinist at the time to realize how unfair it was to expect you to take on the duties of a housewife."

"But you had a job besides, and you studied and made good grades. Plus, you took care of any mechanical problems with the cars, even the one my father gave us. I didn't have any complaints about you, along any of these lines," Tess said a little shortly.

She wasn't pleased with the whole discussion and changed the subject before she could ask him where he had acquired his liberated ideas about the roles of men and women. The answer was all too obvious, and she really didn't want to hear it: he had gotten them from feminist types that he had been involved with.

In addition to scrambled eggs, he cooked bacon and made toast. When Tess suggested that she could at least set the table, he consented. It touched her how pleased he seemed when she complimented his breakfast and ate every morsel on her plate. After the meal, he permitted her to help him clean up and then proposed that they take a walk. She agreed, stipulating that afterward she would drive on across the lake.

Peter didn't argue, but warned, only half jokingly, "Then it'll be a long walk."

Outside, the day was as sunshiny and delightful as the previous one had been. Pretending that she was struck by a novel impulse, Tess suggested that they might stroll through the marinas and look at boats. Peter applauded the idea just as facetiously and went along with it.

Tess noticed that he was stopping to look at smaller boats than the ones that he had expressed interest in on Saturday. She questioned him about whether he'd changed his mind about the size of boat he wanted. He admitted that he had.

"I've decided against investing a large amount of money in a sailboat," he added without explaining his reason.

Tess could supply it for herself. In a year or two when he was transferred and wanted to sell the boat, he might have difficulty finding a buyer if the state economy hadn't improved by then.

"How many slips do you have altogether in your marina?" he asked, changing the subject.

She answered, telling him the number of open slips and covered slips that made up the total.

"You get more rent for the covered slips, I presume?"

"Yes." When he seemed interested in knowing how much, she told him.

"What about the fuel-dock business? I know it varies seasonally, but what kind of income do you earn from it, say on an annual basis?"

He quizzed her thoroughly about her financial affairs, and Tess indulged his curiosity, trying to hide her disappointment when it became apparent that he wasn't going to bring up her refusal to rent him a slip.

Next he wanted to know what steps she had taken toward getting property appraisals on her house and the marina and whether she had spoken with any banks yet about obtaining a loan. Tess admitted that she had done nothing, but was relying on Will.

Peter frowned his disapproval.

"Will is a lot more qualified to handle matters like this than I am," she said defensively. "Besides being a lawyer, he has connections in real estate and banking. Last, but not least, he's a man."

"It's all of those things put together that bother me," Peter said grimly.

"I can understand that you might have taken an instant dislike to him, but it isn't fair to question the integrity of someone you don't even know," Tess pointed out.

Peter looked unrepentant. "Buford wants you, Tess. He'll use whatever tactics are necessary. I sized him up in about ten seconds."

"Well, I happen to have known him for fifteen years," she retorted indignantly. "Forgive me if I go on my own judgment. His opinion of you isn't all that high, either, you'll be interested to know."

From the set of his jaw, Tess knew that he was keeping back a sarcastic reply. "Just answer me this. Has Buford tried to bribe you into marrying him since all this came up? Has he made any offers of a personal loan with strings attached?" He read Tess's face and nodded, looking disgusted. "That's about what I thought. Has it occurred to you at all, Tess, that this bind that you find yourself in is made to order for him to put pressure on you?"

"What are you implying, Peter? That Will engineered this whole thing for his own purposes? That it's all a hoax?" she scoffed, and then eyed him incredulously when he didn't make a denial. "You're not seriously thinking that my half brother is a fake and that Will is in cahoots with him? Will isn't a crook!" she protested indignantly. "Give me some credit for being a judge of character!"

"I'm not implying anything, just considering all the possibilities," he said, unperturbed. "It concerns me that you're putting so much trust in Buford. Has he presented you with any proof that your half brother is who he says he is?"

"No, but I didn't ask for any. Will spent a whole week in north Louisiana investigating. Your suspicions of him are ridiculous, Peter!"

"Another thing. By your own admission, he has opposed your getting in contact with your half brother."

"Will liked my father and admired him!" Unlike Peter himself. "He's afraid, just as I am, that if news of my half brother gets out, people will draw their own wrong conclusions. I've explained all that to you, and I refuse to discuss this any more!"

Deep down Tess was disappointed that Peter's efforts to discredit Will were so reasoned and unemotional and that they were directed toward undermining Will as a legal and financial adviser, not as a potential husband. There was a hint of frustration in his manner, though, and a strained note in his voice as he requested that she at least give some thought to his reservations about her trusting attitude toward Will.

"It's just not wise to be personally involved with your business attorney. I can empathize with his conflict of interests," he added, squeezing her hand.

That was the closest he came to suggesting that Will was a rival. And he didn't ask Tess whether she was any closer to a decision about marrying Will now, after spending the night with Peter and making love with him. If he had questioned her, she would have told him that she was going to turn Will down.

"One other matter that I would like to suggest to you," Peter said. "Don't you think that it would be a good idea to go ahead and get an estimate on upgrading the marina and try to borrow enough money to cover that, too, while you're at it?"

Tess agreed dully that it was a good suggestion and that she would follow through on it herself and not ask Will to handle it.

"I would be more than happy to come over and talk to a contractor with you," Peter offered, but he didn't press her when she declined, telling him that it wasn't necessary.

He did extend the walk, overruling her every time she asked if they shouldn't be heading back. He bought her lunch at one of the popular West End restaurants that all featured fresh seafood. They dawdled over the meal and took a roundabout route of his choosing back to his condo, where he invited her to stay and postpone going home until later, even the next day.

Tess was terribly tempted and could have been swayed, if he'd insisted. Instead he just looked disappointed when she said that she had things to do at home and accompanied her down to her car. She got her keys out of her purse and let him unlock her door. He gave her a goodbye hug and kiss and helped her behind the wheel.

It was all so affectionate, but casual rather than emotion-charged, as it should have been. Tess was expecting some significant exchange that would allow them to broach the future, but Peter was acting as though she came and went as a regular welcome visitor.

"Drive carefully," he said, and bent to kiss her again on the lips, lingeringly. "I'm planning to be over on the North Shore Saturday. I'd like to see you. Will you be at the marina?"

"More than likely, I will."

"Then could I come by? Between now and then I'll do some research on computers for you and bring the information." On their walk, he had followed up on her mention the night before of getting a computer for the marina and was strongly in favor of the idea. "If you're free, we could have dinner together over there. I've been hearing about what great restaurants you have. Afterwards, maybe we could find a place with some good dance music."

"And what about when we leave that place, Peter? What then?" Tess asked, a ragged edge of desperation in her voice because she wanted to make the date with him so badly. "I thought we agreed last night that having an affair wouldn't be good for either one of us."

"After we leave the place, I'll take you home and drive back here by myself."

"Peter, you and I can't just 'go out' together!" she protested.

"We can't just not see each other, either," he said simply. "You don't have to decide about Saturday night right this minute. We'll just leave it open. Goodbye for now, and take care."

For a second she thought that he was going to lean in and kiss her again, but he checked himself and closed her car door. Tess started up the engine and backed out. Her foot didn't seem to want to press the accelerator. The last time driving had been such an act of will was the day she'd moved out of their Lafayette apartment and come home permanently to Maryville.

Glancing back at him before she pulled out onto the street, she wondered if he weren't remembering the same day. He was standing and watching her drive off, his expression somber. Whatever he was thinking—and his thoughts obviously centered on her—it didn't make him happy or optimistic.

Yet Tess was never more certain of anything than what his answer would be if she went back and asked him if he was sorry that he had asked her to come over yesterday to spend Mardi Gras Day with him. Despite the strained moments and the painful revelations, despite the absence of any hopeful outcome, he wouldn't have missed their time together.

And neither would she have missed it.

On Saturday she would see him again. By then, she hoped to have gained some positive momentum. Tess was about to take charge of her life. On the ride across the Causeway, she made a mental list. The number-one priority was getting things straight between herself and Will. She had to have an honest talk with him and turn down his marriage proposal. As much as she hated disappointing him, it was a relief not to have that decision hanging over her head anymore. Tess would also give him the opportunity to rid himself of her as a client, but she didn't expect him to agree.

While she didn't take any of Peter's suspicions seriously, she did intend to be more businesslike and inquiring about her own financial affairs, rather than rely totally on Will's judgment. It wasn't fair to him, she would explain, to take advantage of friendship and put the burden of decision on his shoulders. Later, if there were any complaints, she would have to take responsibility.

Next in importance, after clarifying matters with Will, was contacting her half brother. If Tess wasn't able to obtain his number from Information, she would have to call or write his lawyer. She wasn't going to be deterred.

Then, getting to less stressful duties, she needed to line up a building contractor to oversee the needed repairs in the marina. Peter was right. They couldn't be put off much longer. It would make her feel good to have the marina in tip-top condition.

By the time she arrived in Maryville, Tess was almost cheerful. Driving past her house, she went to the marina office and looked up an invoice from eight years ago, when her father had hired a Baton Rouge contractor to rebuild the fuel dock. David Johnson remembered the job he had done for her father and was agreeable to giving her an estimate, warning her, though, that he was currently backed up with work.

"It may be a couple of weeks before I can even get over there—unless you'd want to set up an appointment for this Saturday," he suggested. "I'm going to a friend's fishing camp over in Slidell and will be driving through on Interstate 12. I could stop by and take a look at what you need done."

"What time on Saturday?" Tess asked, hoping that he was passing through early in the morning, before Peter had arrived. She would just as soon meet with the contractor by herself, with no help or interference.

"Oh, say, about eleven or twelve. I'm afraid I can't be exact."

Tess consented to the appointment rather than wait two weeks. It was only after she broke the connection that she happened to think that Will could very well be present in the marina on Saturday, too, if the nice weather held up.

Her next call was just as successful. The long-distance Information gave her the number listed in the Shreveport area for Jake Davenport. Tess wrote it down and then sat there, staring at it and working up her courage before she punched out the digits, hoping that no one would answer on this first attempt or that she would get an answering machine and could just leave a message.

On the second ring, a child answered. Before Tess could get out more than a hello, she found herself engaged in friendly conversation.

"My name's Becky, and I'm almost four years old. What's your name?"

"My name's Tess."

For a moment, that was all Becky wanted to know about her caller. "I have three brothers," she confided. "Hank and Ted are big boys, and they're nice to me, but Brad is mean. He teases me and makes me cry. My daddy's going to have to spank him. Do you have any brothers?"

That was a very difficult question coming from a little girl who might be Tess's niece. "I just have one brother, Becky. Could I talk to your mommy or daddy?"

"My daddy's not home. He's at work. And my mommy is in the bathroom. I like to watch *Sesame Street* on TV and cartoons. My mommy watches *As the World Turns* every day, and my daddy likes Westerns." Becky paused in the interest of conversational give and take.

"I liked watching cartoons when I was your age, too." And even after she was older.

"You sound like a grown-up lady. Mommy says it's not polite to ask grown-up people how old they are."

"I'm thirty years old," Tess divulged with a smile in her voice.

"Here comes my mommy out of the bathroom." Becky was obviously reluctant at the prospect of turning over the telephone. Tess could hear the exchange between her and her mother, Tess's sister-in-law.

"Who is it, sweetie?"

"It's a nice lady. She just has one brother, and she used to like watching cartoons, too. I didn't ask her how old she was, Mommy, but she told me. Except that I don't remember."

"Hello, this is Betty Davenport speaking." There was amusement and apology mixed in with the inquiring note.

"Betty, I'm Tess Davenport, your husband's half sister." Tess paused for some reaction, immediately finding the going awkward.

"Would you hold on a moment, please?" Betty requested in a formal tone and then spoke firmly to her daughter, "Becky, go to your room and play with your toys while Mommy is on the phone."

She didn't want her conversation with Tess to be overheard by the little girl.

"Where are you calling from?" she inquired, on the line again.

"From south Louisiana near New Orleans, where I live. It's come as quite a shock to me to learn that I have a half brother living in Shreveport. Until recently, when your attorney contacted mine, I wasn't aware that my father had a son from an early marriage," Tess explained. "As far as I knew, I was an only child."

"J.D. didn't know about you, either," Betty replied, on her guard and prepared to deal with any unpleasantness. "Until a couple of months ago, he didn't have the vaguest idea where his father had gone or whether he was still alive."

Nor did her husband have the vaguest interest in knowing, Tess's sister-in-law implied with her tone. "It was me who insisted on getting a lawyer after we got that phone call. I talked J.D. into swallowing his pride for his kids' sake. Whatever inheritance he gets will go toward their education."

"Someone notified you of my father's death?"

Betty hesitated as though looking for some trap in Tess's puzzled query. "Some man who wouldn't identify himself except to say that he was a friend of your father's and wanted to right a wrong, on your father's behalf. He said your father felt guilty about J.D. on his deathbed."

"And this was about two months ago?" Peter had moved to New Orleans a little over two months ago, but that was just odd coincidence.

After another suspicious silence, Betty reluctantly named the exact date and the hour of the telephone call.

"My father had been dead ten months by then," Tess reflected. Why had her father's so-called "friend" waited that long?

"According to our lawyer, J.D.'s claim is still valid," Betty informed her in the formal tone.

"According to my lawyer, it is, too," Tess said quietly. "I didn't call to question your husband's legal rights, Betty." Somehow Tess felt shy about using her half brother's name. "Or to try to talk him out of claiming his share of my father's estate. I just wondered if he might not want to speak to me in person, too."

"You can leave your telephone number, and I'll tell him that you called."

Tess gave her both numbers, the one for the marina and Tess's home phone. Then neither of them said anything during an uncertain silence.

Betty broke it. "I didn't mean to come across as so unfriendly. If I know J.D., he'll return your call. He puts so much store by family, and you two are brother and sister."

"Does he have any other half brothers or half sisters?"

Now there was no hesitation in answering. "No. His mother was killed in an automobile accident the year after she had moved to Texas with him, when he was just a baby, to live with her sister. His aunt and her husband raised him as one of their kids, so he did grow up as close to his cousins as if they had been his brothers and sisters."

"Was my father informed of her death?" Tess asked, against her will. She didn't want to hear any of the details, but couldn't help herself from inquiring.

"J.D.'s aunt made an effort to contact him, but he had left north Louisiana in the meanwhile, and she didn't pursue it. She figured that he had gone back to New Orleans, where he was from originally, but knew that he was in no position to take on the job of raising J.D., even if he'd been willing. He was barely a grown man. He and J.D.'s mother had had to get married because she was pregnant. She only stayed with him until J.D. was born and then divorced him and went off to Texas without telling him where she was going."

"So he didn't know where she and J.D. were?"

"That's a question only your father could answer. It wouldn't have been that hard for him to track her down, but apparently he didn't. J.D. moved back here to Shreveport with his aunt and uncle when he was in high school and has lived here ever since. He has no memory of his father at all, of course."

"He was never interested in looking him up?"

"No." Betty hesitated. "Are you sure you want to hear this?"

Tess swallowed and forced out the words, "Yes, please."

"J.D. isn't bitter. He considers himself fortunate for having had a good upbringing in a loving family. In his opinion, his father just wasn't anyone he could have respected, since he shirked his responsibility to his wife and son. Things tend to be black-and-white with J.D. when it comes to family," Betty added almost gently. "He feels very strongly about being a father himself."

Her half brother sounded like the kind of man that her father could have been proud to have as a son. "I'm so sorry that J.D. never got to know my father," Tess said regretfully. "I'd like to make excuses. He was such a wonderful father to me, a good husband to my mother and a highly respected man in the community."

"It sounds as though he started off with a clean slate and did everything right the second time around," Betty suggested kindly. "Do you have children, Tess?"

"No, I was married and divorced when I was very young and never remarried. Your little girl mentioned that she has three brothers."

"Yes, Hank, our oldest, is sixteen. Ted is thirteen, and Brad, seven. I'm sure Becky told you that she's 'almost four.'"

"As a matter of fact, she did. She sounds adorable and very bright."

"Well, I'm prejudiced, but she's both. If you're ever in Shreveport, you'd be welcome to visit," Betty invited hesitantly but sincerely.

"Thank you. That's very nice, and I may take you up on it," Tess replied. She bit into her lower lip, regretting that she couldn't extend the same open invitation.

Hanging up the phone after her parting words with Betty, Tess thought about how much fun it could be entertaining her nephews and little niece. The boys especially would more than likely find the marina fascinating. She could arrange a boat ride for them and a fishing trip. In warm weather, she could see that they had a chance to water ski.

*I get a kick out of being an uncle,* Peter had said. On top of everything else, Tess resented that she was going to be denied the opportunity to find out if she wouldn't enjoy being an aunt. Oh, she could sneak up to Shreveport periodically without telling anyone where she was going or make up a phony excuse for the trip, but the furtiveness would spoil everything.

And it would be risky, in the long run. At some point in the future, if she got to know her nephews and niece, they might take it upon themselves to come down to Maryville and look her up.

The only way that Tess could visit her brother and his family and become acquainted was if she decided to acknowledge him and divulge the personal history that her father had kept secret. One part of Tess hoped that J.D. wouldn't call, so that she wouldn't have still another difficult decision to face.

But he did call her several hours later, after she'd gone home. Tess almost broke down when she first heard his voice because he sounded so much like her father. It was awkward and strange, conversing the first time with a thirty-nine-year-old brother, asking him questions like, what did he do for a living?

He was earnest and quiet-spoken and careful of her feelings. Tess was touched by the way he steered clear of any critical remarks about her father, *his* father, too. His favorite topic obviously was his children. He was very proud of all four of them.

Tess found herself reassuring him that he was entitled to his inheritance when he brought the subject up, admitting his own strong reservations. It was incredible to her, even as she spoke, that she had come to that state of mind. Paying him his share was still going to be a financial hardship, but she felt much better now about the whole thing.

He seconded Betty's invitation at the end of the call, wording it differently, "If you could come up and visit us, we'd sure like that."

Tess answered with tears in her throat, "I'd love to, J.D. I want to meet you and Betty and the kids."

"Just let us know when. And, Tess, I'm all in favor of sitting down and settling this inheritance business between us and then telling our lawyers what we've worked out."

Tess managed to keep from crying until she had hung up, and then she let the tears flow, crying because of all the years that she hadn't had him for a brother. Because of what all three of them had missed out on, J.D. and herself and her father.

## Chapter Nine

"Les, could I have a minute?"

Les Morgan looked up from scrawling his signature and smiled a welcome at Peter. "Sure, Peter, come on in and close the door." Les sprawled in his chair, tossing the pen down. "Have a seat. I wanted to talk to you anyway. I'm thinking about sailing over to Biloxi Saturday and wondered if you'd be interested in joining an all-male crew. No? Other plans, huh?" He read Peter's expression, looking shrewdly unsurprised.

"I appreciate the invitation, Les, but I have to pass it up." Peter dropped into a chair. "I was wondering if you could recommend a good broker who deals in commercial property on the North Shore. Someone who's really up on the current market and knows what's available in commercial loans."

Les's eyebrows lifted. "You're thinking about buying commercial property on the North Shore?"

"No, I'm doing some legwork for Tess. She's going to need to use her marina as collateral to borrow money to meet a sizable financial obligation and also to do some necessary renovation."

Les shook his head doubtfully. "From what I hear, commercial money is really tight. The banks and thrifts are running scared, with all the bad loans they've had to foreclose on in the oil-patch states the last few years. She might run into problems getting a mortgage of any size."

"That's what I'm afraid of."

Les frowned at Peter's grave tone. "She isn't in danger of losing the marina?"

"Not if I can help it," Peter said soberly. "Before I'd let that happen, I'll sink every penny I have and pull out my retirement."

"You'd have to quit the company to do that, Peter."

"I know. I'm hoping like hell that I don't have to, but I will, if necessary."

Les gave a resigned sigh. "I could read the handwriting on the wall Mardi Gras Day when I saw you two together. You're going to marry her again, aren't you?"

"I still love her, Les."

"Then marry her, but for God's sakes don't go in for any false heroics like sacrificing your career to save her marina. If she loves you, she won't let you throw away your future. Hell, man, think about how sorry you're going to be if your marriage goes on the skids again."

"That's just a chance I'm going to have to take. Look, Les, I've thought this all though, and I'm not overjoyed with any of my alternatives, but my number-one priority is having a life with Tess. I'm not going to lose her again."

"So when's the wedding?"

Peter's smile was rueful. "There's no date set, since Tess doesn't know about it yet. I have to eliminate my competition and convince her. Heard of a lawyer named Buford over your side of the lake?''

"I've encountered Buford a time or two. He's a member of the boat-owners' group that sponsors the boat parades at Mardi Gras and Christmas. Stocky fellow, a good bit older than Tess. Has a big power boat. Isn't he on the board of a bank?''

Peter nodded grimly.

"From a monetary standpoint, at least, I would think that you have some pretty stiff competition in Buford," Les reflected.

"Tell me something I don't know."

"Tess didn't strike me as a materialistic type of woman."

"She isn't, or Buford would already have a big diamond ring on her finger." Peter didn't try to hide how repugnant that thought was to him. "He's a flashy bastard. Drives a white Cadillac. You've seen his boat. Damned thing hardly fits in the slip."

"He keeps it in Tess's marina, I take it." Les waited for Peter's abrupt nod of confirmation before remarking with sympathetic irony, "How convenient for him. So he definitely has the edge on you with proximity and easy opportunity, too."

"That's not all. He got along with Tess's dad and was his attorney. Buford was there for her when the old man died. His wife had passed away recently enough that they had grief in common. Tess gets along with Buford's two sons. She's known Buford half her life. He's accepted in her circle of friends. He's Catholic." Peter ticked off each item on a finger.

"There's the age difference," Les put in helpfully, but then added candidly, "Buford's a vigorous man, though."

"Yes, he must be frustrated as hell, going out with Tess a whole year," Peter commented with a kind of savage satisfaction.

"You don't mean..." Les didn't have to spell out his question, any more than Peter had to answer it explicitly. The two men exchanged a glance that imparted the information that Buford hadn't been able to get Tess into bed with him. "That evens things out a bit," the older man said shrewdly. "A blind man could feel the sparks between you and Tess."

"She's really something, Les. But it's more than just sexual attraction with us. I've never had as much fun with anyone else. Never felt the same closeness to any other human being, not my parents or my brothers or my best friends. That's why it tore my guts out when she left me."

"And why you're going to give her another shot at leaving you in the same condition."

"I never completely recovered, and I don't think she did, either. That's the reason that she hasn't married Buford or anybody else before now."

Les sighed again, giving up. "I've been there, Peter, and I don't believe in romantic fairy tales, but I hope I'm being too pessimistic, for your sake. You asked about a broker over on the North Shore. Philip Giraux is your man, and he happens to be a neighbor of mine. Feel free to mention my name and say that I sent you to him."

"Thanks, Les. I will. I found a sailboat," Peter announced, grinning as the other man's face lighted up at once. "It's right there in the marina by my condo building. The owner lives just five minutes away. When I called him yesterday afternoon to make inquiries, he offered to come over and take me out sailing. It handles like a dream and is in real nice condition. He's moving up to a bigger boat and is eager to sell. I closed a deal with him at a very reasonable price, contingent on a survey that'll be done on Friday.''

Les whistled. ''You aren't wasting any time. That's great news. I just assumed, from what you were telling me just now, that you'd changed your mind about buying a boat.''

''I probably would hold off, to keep from spending the money, but being a boat owner is as much a necessity as a luxury right now.''

''You plan to keep the boat in Tess's marina and have your own excuse for being there, with sleeping accommodations if you want to stay overnight.''

Peter grinned an admission. ''That's my strategy. I'd be lying, of course, if I didn't admit that I was glad for an excuse to go ahead and buy a boat. I'm really looking forward to taking Tess out sailing, for one thing. Maybe Sunday, if all goes according to plan.''

''You have in mind taking the boat over on Saturday?''

''In the afternoon, providing everything is okay with the survey, and I expect it to be. While the boat is up on the ways, I thought I might as well have the bottom painted. She'll be back in the water by noon Saturday.''

''You don't let any grass grow under your feet,'' Les remarked.

''There's a lot of time to make up for,'' Peter replied, rising to leave and return to his own office.

After a call to Philip Giraux, which Peter scrupulously charged to his own home number, his weekend schedule was even more jam-packed. Giraux suggested a Saturday-morning meeting, and Peter agreed to come over at nine.

It was a strong temptation at odd minutes during the day, and especially that night after he got home, to pick up the phone and call Tess, but he resisted the impulse. He might find himself weakening and telling her about the boat. That would naturally lead to the question of where he planned to keep it. No, the surprise element was all in his favor. It was better not to give her any more than a few hours' notice that he needed a place to tie up the boat temporarily. Peter was planning to use the foot-in-the-door tactic.

When the phone rang about nine-thirty, he was looking through a stack of information on computer software that he'd picked up during his lunch hour and after work. He picked up the receiver, expecting the caller to be some stranger selling something. The surprise of hearing Tess's voice made his heart leap with gladness, but her troubled note immediately set off an alarm.

"Hello, Peter. This is Tess."

As if she had to identify herself with more than the hello. "Hi, baby, what's up?" he inquired lightly, preparing himself for discouragement. She'd had time to think over seeing him on Saturday and decided against it.

"Last night I tried to call you."

The faint reproach in her tone that he had been out somewhere eased Peter's tension slightly. "I'm sorry I wasn't in. I went out for a bite to eat with a fellow I met who lives here at West End." Accurate, but sketchy. He and the sailboat owner had come to terms over beer and poboys at a local restaurant after they'd come in from sailing.

"Yesterday afternoon after I got back here, I telephoned my brother's house in Shreveport. He wasn't home, but I spoke to his wife. Later on, he returned my call."

Peter breathed in a sigh of relief without losing any of his concern. Her call had nothing to do with their relationship. "You sound upset. Was your half brother unpleasant to you?"

"Not at all. He's a very nice person. So is his wife. They have four children, three boys and a little girl."

"Did you get the story on his background?" Peter asked, trying to draw out of her what was the matter. His guess was that she had learned something damning about her father.

"I learned the bare facts," she admitted reluctantly. "His mother was pregnant with J.D.—that's the name he goes by—when she married Daddy. They were even younger than you and I were. She was eighteen, and he was nineteen. He'd gone up to Shreveport to work. After J.D. was born, his mother left Daddy and took J.D. to Texas, without telling Daddy where she was going. She died in a car accident when J.D. was a year old. Daddy had left Shreveport in the meantime. He must have come back down here. J.D.'s aunt and uncle didn't try to locate him. They raised J.D. themselves and apparently did a very good job."

"So he never knew your father at all?"

"No."

Peter could hear sadness in her voice, but, surprisingly, very little defensiveness. He did his best to sound objective, speaking aloud his thoughts, "This sheds some light on your father's attitude toward our marriage. I wonder if he just didn't look upon it from the first as the same kind of mistake he had made in his youth."

"I thought about the same thing. He begged me to wait until I was older, as you know, and then he gave in, as he always did, when I used every means to get my own way. When we separated and I came back home to live, he just accepted our breakup. The same with the divorce. He never suggested it, but he never tried to talk me out of it, either."

Peter didn't trust himself to say anything further on the subject. Insight was one thing. Forgiveness was quite another.

"When there was no word from you, he had nothing critical to say about you," Tess went on. "I guess he might have seen a parallel."

She meant no offense, but it was more than Peter could stomach. "I didn't go off and leave you with a baby to raise, Tess," he objected harshly. "There's no way in hell that I could have done what your father did."

"I knew that you'd be glad to hear all about his failings—if you didn't already know, that is," she added.

"Of course, I didn't know. How could I?" Peter was puzzled as well as exasperated and annoyed with himself.

The brief silence was suspenseful.

"You haven't asked how J.D. learned about my father's death," Tess said.

"Well, how did he?"

"An anonymous telephone call from a man. Two months ago."

Her tone was uncertain, inquiring. Stunned comprehension hit Peter, leaving him at an utter loss for several seconds. "For chrissake, Tess, you don't think that I—" He broke off, cursing in a kind of outraged astonishment. "I can't believe that you'd actually consider me capable of doing something that sneaky and underhanded. *Why* would I?" The insult was vying with his incredulity.

"Whoever did call him did the right thing," Tess evaded. "I'm glad, after all is said and done, that I know about my half brother. I don't resent having him come in for an inheritance now that I've talked to him and found out the circumstances."

She was encouraging him to make a clean breast of it and confess! Peter had to overcome another bout of speechlessness. "Just out of curiosity, how do you suppose this anonymous do-gooder of yours stumbled on your father's secret, Tess?" he asked her grimly.

Her hesitation had nothing to do with thinking up a reply. She'd been mulling over the same question. "A private detective or perhaps by tapping into some kind of computer data base. I got J.D.'s telephone number through directory assistance. It would have been no problem to trace him down."

"My first knowledge of your half brother came from you, but I refuse to discuss this any further on the telephone. I'm coming over tomorrow night."

"I have a date tomorrow night with Will."

"Break it."

"No, I don't want to do that."

Peter cursed under his breath, gripping the receiver hard while he struggled to control his jealousy and frustration. "Between now and tomorrow night, when you see Buford, give this some thought, Tess. Who was more likely to be in your father's confidence than his lawyer, who made out his last will and testament?"

"I've already given it some thought," she admitted, sighing. "The timing was what threw me, the fact that you moved back to Louisiana approximately two months ago. And you have a lot of resentment toward my father. But I believe you if you say that you didn't make that call. You've never lied to me. It may always be a mystery."

"Not to me. Buford made that call. He was running out of patience and needed a way to put pressure on you to marry him." It was crystal clear to Peter. How could she not see how the pieces all fit, too?

"I just find it so difficult to accept that he could betray my father's trust and cause me all the worry I've been going through."

"But you don't find it difficult to believe that I could do you harm. I guess I know where I stand in your opinion now, in relation to Buford, Tess. Remind me not to put you down as a character witness," Peter said heavily, too wounded to muster sarcasm. He told her good-night and hung up the phone.

Cursing violently, he hurled the stack of software brochures with all his strength, sending them flying all over his living room. Then he went around and gathered them all up again and reorganized them in the order in which he would present them to Tess for her consideration.

If Peter had only slammed down the phone, half deafening her the way the younger Peter would have done, Tess might have not felt quite so bad. The quiet way he broke the connection sent a wave of depression through her.

He had changed, matured, become more rational. She couldn't deal with him intuitively now, reading him and touching the spring releases of his emotions. Her old confidence was lacking. Once she would have blurted out what was more a doubt than a suspicion, instead of being so roundabout and giving him a chance to volunteer that he had made the anonymous call to J.D.

It was because he had changed that she'd even entertained the possibility. The younger, impetuous Peter whom she had married would have confronted her with the damaging information that he had uncovered. He would have been righteous and open about any vindictive motives.

This more self-contained Peter hadn't approved when he'd learned of her intention to maintain secrecy about her father's past, but he hadn't argued with her. He hadn't agreed with her when she declared having no intention of contacting her half brother, but, once again, he hadn't stated unequivocally that she was wrong.

Instead he had questioned calmly whether she had a clear perspective and was doing the right thing. He had planted seeds of doubts, knowing that they would take root, because he knew her. He knew that she had a conscience, that she was inherently truthful and fair-minded.

He also knew that she was stubborn and prone to making emotional stands. Was Peter dealing with her differently, taking past experience as a lesson?

Or was he just more detached now?

Tess might have called him right back if she hadn't guessed that the latter explanation was the true one. She felt on tenuous ground, in spite of Mardi Gras Day and spending the night with him. He hadn't spoken one word to raise her hopes about a future together.

Because he didn't see them as having a future together, any more than she did.

Tonight when she'd told him about her date with Will the next evening, he hadn't insisted that she break it to see him instead. Even though he was jealous of Will, not once had Peter said in so many words, "You can't marry Buford." He hadn't even pressed her on whether making love with him didn't have some influence on arriving at an answer on Will's proposal of marriage.

That answer was still an apologetic no that Tess would deliver tomorrow night. Her low state of morale following the telephone conversation with Peter didn't change her decision. She couldn't marry Will.

Tess didn't know if she would ever remarry, but at least now she had come to terms with the reason that she hadn't so far: in her heart of hearts, she had never divorced herself from Peter. That had been his problem, too. The tragedy of it was that their emotional ties were only going to cause them more heartache.

Will arrived promptly at seven to pick her up. Tess had initiated the date herself. Wanting to be able to talk to him in privacy, she had called him and invited him to come over to her house for supper. But he had overruled that suggestion, saying that he had made dinner reservations at one of the better restaurants and was about to call her himself.

Tess was nervous. She dreaded the whole business of telling him her decision and wished that she could get it over with at once. Will gave her a keen glance or two, but he didn't ask her if anything was wrong. His own mood was jovial, and he didn't give her any opening, requiring very little of her in the way of conversation.

At the restaurant, he acted as though it were a special occasion, ordering champagne.

"Are we celebrating something?" Tess asked in a wan voice.

"You might call it an advance celebration," Will declared, toasting her. "Here's to the future and putting a happy smile back on that pretty face of yours. I talked to Joey Dumas, and he's promised to get those appraisals on the marina and your house over to me by the end of next week. That's pushing him, but he owes me some favors. Then I'll be ready to play hardball with a certain Shreveport attorney. We'll close the books on the last month and get on with life."

Tess sipped her champagne and put down her glass, smothering a sigh. "I don't know what I would have done if I hadn't had you to turn to during the last month, Will. You've been a good friend. It won't be necessary to play hardball with my brother's attorney, though."

"Careful of what you say, hon," Will cautioned, glancing around to remind her of diners at nearby tables who might overhear. He frowned when Tess didn't show instant alarm.

"I've decided to tell my friends, Will. This isn't something that I can keep locked up inside me, even if I didn't want to get to know my brother and his family. And I do. I've talked to him on the telephone," she explained quickly before Will could break in with the strong protest written on his face.

"Now why did you go and do that?" he demanded, and answered his own dismayed question, shaking his head. "You're not thinking straight, hon. You've been under an awful strain and are in no condition to make decisions that you're going to be sorry about later."

Tess covered his big hand with hers. "I have been under a strain, but I am thinking straight finally, about a lot of things," she said gently.

"This isn't you talking, Tess. I can't stand by and let you shame your daddy's memory. Neither you nor I—nor anybody else—has the right to sit in judgment on him."

"I don't mean to be sitting in judgment, Will, but I can't be ruled in my actions by what my father did. My main regret is that I grew up without knowing my brother. Now I have the chance." Tess removed her hand, signaling the end of that aspect of the subject. "I discovered the reason that he didn't try to claim his inheritance earlier. He had no knowledge of his father's whereabouts or whether he was dead or alive until a couple months ago."

Will nodded as though the information came as no surprise. His expression was cynical. "And how did he find out? I'll be interested to learn if my own personal theory is correct."

Tess had been watching him closely for some telltale sign of guilt. Now she regarded him with surprise. "What is your theory? You haven't mentioned it to me."

He shrugged. "I had no proof. The pieces of the puzzle all fell into place when Roussell showed up in New Orleans. I figure he found out somehow and tipped off your half brother out of spite."

"But it wasn't Peter. I asked him, and he denied it."

Will frowned. "Didn't your half brother say who contacted him?"

"He doesn't know. He got a telephone call from a man who wouldn't identify himself."

"It was Roussell, then. That sneaky bastard. I'd like to get my hands on him." Will shook his head disgustedly. "Here comes our waitress with our salads. Let's change the subject, before I get a bad case of indigestion."

But Tess couldn't leave the matter there. After they'd been served, she picked up her fork and held it, contemplating the plate in front of her with no appetite. It might have held plain lettuce instead of the delicious Caesar salad that the restaurant was noted for.

"Peter was always honest, Will. He wouldn't lie to me."

"Have it your way, hon," he soothed. "I can understand that you don't want to believe the worst of the guy. After all, you were married to him. Come on, eat your dinner."

She managed to get down a bite. "He's just as certain that you're the one who made the call. I defended you to him, too."

Will put down his fork and took a sip of water. "Well, it's only natural that he'd try to point the finger at someone else, and I'm the obvious target. Roussell's probably kicked himself a hundred times. Something tells me he might not have realized how much money was involved. My guess is that he sees his mean trick now as a classic case of cutting off a nose to spite a face."

"What do you mean?"

"Come on, Tess. Roussell shows up after ten years and starts to hang around after it dawns on him that his ex-wife has come into a nice little inheritance."

"Peter's not interested in my inheritance!" Tess protested, remembering all the questions that Peter had asked her about her finances and about the value of her house and the marina.

"I trust your judgment on a lot of things, hon, but not where he's concerned."

Will changed the subject, and Tess didn't try to bring it up again. Between thinking about the disturbing conversation that they'd already had and the one she would introduce later, she was able to get down very little of her food. He urged her to have her favorite dessert on the menu, cheesecake with a topping made of fresh strawberries. When she refused, he ordered it with two forks. Tess ate a few bites to please him.

In the car she debated about whether to go ahead and tell him what she had to say or wait until they arrived at her house. Deciding on the latter, she was prepared to decline a suggestion that they go somewhere and dance, as they frequently did after eating out on a Friday or Saturday night. He didn't mention the idea, but he wasn't driving directly to her house, Tess realized, and she spoke up quickly to raise an objection.

"I'd rather not go anywhere else tonight. We need to talk, Will."

He glanced over with a smile. "We can talk at my house after I give you the present I have for you."

"What kind of present?" Tess asked, dismayed. She hoped that he hadn't bought her some expensive piece of jewelry that he would only have to return.

"No hints. You'll just have to be patient."

His house was a large two-story colonial in one of the country-club subdivisions. He parked his car in the circular drive and took her through the front entrance that had ornate bevelled glass doors. A crystal chandelier shed soft light in the spacious foyer, and Tess had glimpses of the formal living room and dining room on the way back to a more cozy family room.

"I just rattle around in this big house by myself," he remarked, and excused himself after leading her over to a sofa and seating her. Tess's heart sank when he came back minutes later with an open bottle of champagne on a silver tray with two fragile long-stemmed tulip glasses. He certainly wasn't making this easy for her. She accepted the glass of champagne that he gave her as he sat down next to her, holding his own glass.

"Will, before you give me your present—"

He leaned over and cut her off with a kiss. "I can't wait another moment, hon. It's been burning a hole in my pocket all night. Here. Let's see how it fits." He put his glass down and produced a jeweler's box from a breast pocket of his suit jacket. From the box, he took out a ring, a huge diamond solitaire, and slid it on the third finger of Tess's left hand.

Tess stared down at it, appalled. "This is an engagement ring. I wish you hadn't . . ."

"Don't tell me you don't like it." He feigned disappointment.

"It's beautiful, but I can't keep it." Tess tried to take the ring off, but he stopped her.

"Come on, hon, wear it. I bought it for you. It'll be worth every penny I paid for it if you'll just give me a smile and a sweet little peck on the lips."

Tess sighed, lowering her eyes to his big hand grasping hers. "I feel so awful about this. Will, I've decided not to marry you. You'll have to take the ring back."

He took her champagne glass from her and put it on the coffee table by his, then slid closer to her, putting an arm around her and tilting up her chin with his free hand. "Tess, you can't make me believe that you don't care about me."

He held her face when she tried to turn aside and avoid his kiss. "Come on, hon, loosen up," he urged softly against her mouth. "Kiss me like a woman kisses her man." He pressed his lips hard against hers, moving his head.

Tess pushed against his chest, but he only exerted more strength and held her closer, trapping her hands. She tried to cry out, and he immediately deepened the kiss with a little guttural sound of pleasure, misreading her whole intention as she opened her mouth. Tess struggled harder, beginning to panic. He was powerful, and she could feel his chest rising and falling with his breathing as he became excited.

"Go ahead, turn into a hellcat, hon," he encouraged, pushing her back on the sofa. "It's what you really want, deep down." She grabbed his hand and tried to pull it free as he captured one of her breasts and squeezed it, but he was much too strong for her. Lowering himself on top of her to kiss her again, he chided her when she jerked aside her head, "Don't be like that." Kissing her neck, he murmured, "You're such a sexy little thing. Don't you know you can drive a man crazy?"

His low gravelly voice was full of male frustration. Tess felt a little pang of fear. She hadn't meant to string Will along and keep alive his hopes, only to disappoint him. Going limp, she stopped all resistance.

"Please, Will, let me up. You're not the kind of man to force yourself on a woman."

His hand relaxed on her breast, and he rose up enough to look at her. Tess met his gaze, apologizing mutely for her role in causing his behavior. With a deep breath, he levered himself up and sat on the edge of the sofa, slumped forward with his elbows on his knees, holding his head in both hands. His whole posture spoke shame and discouragement.

Tess wanted to touch him and console him somehow, but didn't dare. "Will, I'm truly sorry. I do feel affection for you, but it's not enough. You need more from a woman. I'll understand if you'd rather not continue being my attorney."

He shook his head. "No, hon, I'm a bigger man than that. I still want to look out for your interests. I promised your daddy I would."

"I'm glad," Tess told him. "Is there a chance that we can still be friends?"

He pushed his hands on his knees and straightened the bulk of his upper body as though it were an effort, sat back and gave her a strained smile of reassurance. "Sure thing, hon. I'd still like to take you out. What happened here tonight won't happen again. I can promise you that."

"I'm not afraid in the least, and I'd like to go out with you occasionally, too, as long as you date other women. My answer tonight is definite, Will," Tess said gently, taking off the ring and returning it to the little velvet box. "You need to look for someone else."

On the drive to her house, Tess searched for some topic of conversation and came up with her appointment with David Johnson, the Baton Rouge contractor, the next day.

"I was planning on coming to the marina in the morning anyway," Will said. "Let me talk to him for you."

Tess thanked him for the offer and refused tactfully, adding, "I'll discuss his estimate with you before I make any decision on hiring him."

"At least introduce me and let me be there while you're talking to him," Will suggested. "It won't hurt anything, hon, for a man, especially your lawyer, to be present."

Tess knew that he was right. Not wanting to hurt his feelings any more than she already had, she agreed, reflecting to herself that after her telephone call to Peter last night, he might not even be coming over tomorrow.

As much as Tess didn't look forward to handling a situation where Will and Peter were both in the marina when Johnson arrived, she would prefer the awkwardness to Peter's not showing up at all.

## Chapter Ten

Dave Johnson was a man in his fifties with thinning, straw-colored hair and a tanned, seamed countenance. Of average height, he obviously once had had a ruggedly powerful build that was now going to fat. Tess heard him drive up to the marina office, and she went out to see him as he stepped down from a new pickup truck, wearing jeans, a Western shirt and cowboy boots. He transferred his clipboard to his left hand to shake hands with her cordially, but he wasn't there on a social call.

"Let's take a walk around and see what you have here that needs doing," he said after they'd exchanged greetings.

Will was already on his way over from his boat. When Tess introduced the two men, Johnson's manner didn't change in the least. He was as friendly and businesslike as he had been with her and showed no sign that it mattered to him, one way or the other, if Will tagged along.

Tess liked the way Johnson directed his comments and questions to her as the three of them began their tour of the marina. It came as no surprise to her, though, that Will found it impossible to stand back and listen. He put in a question or two and a remark here and there at first, and then gradually asserted himself, until Johnson was dividing his attention between Will and Tess.

Tess could sense that Johnson was asking himself, Exactly who was in charge here? If he took this job, who would he be answering to?

She tried not to let the situation bother her, since she wasn't going to point-blank tell Will that he was overstepping his bounds and make him lose face in front of the other man. Somehow she would manage a private word with Johnson before he left and assure him that he would be submitting the estimate to her. She was the owner and no one else.

There was no sign of Peter so far. Tess thought about him and breathed in a despondent little sigh as they came to the entrance of the marina and started back toward the office. She would rather have been on pins and needles over the possibility that he could show up at any minute. Instead she had the heavy intuition that he wouldn't be coming at all.

At the sound of a car engine, she glanced over her shoulder with little hope of seeing his car. Her heart leaped as she recognized the BMW. She waved to him as he passed. For a second she thought that he might stop, but he speeded up and drove on toward the office, much to her relief. Tess had a glimpse of his face, and he looked grimly inquiring.

Johnson's pickup truck would provide an explanation for him of who Johnson was. Lettered on the doors was David Johnson, Marine Construction. Tess knew that it was probably too much to hope for that Peter would wait for her inside the office building, but she was more relieved and glad that he was here than worried about a hostile scene between him and Will in front of Johnson. The contractor would be in a hurry to leave, and she would get rid of Will.

A minute or so later the sight of Peter coming back on foot told Tess that she had been overly optimistic. He walked with a long, brisk stride, and his bearing, like his determined expression, said clearly that he intended to be included in the conference that had started without him. Tess's heart sank at the prospect of unpleasantness, but she responded to his tall, lean build and his clean-cut masculinity with a little surge of welcome. He wasn't wearing jeans, she noted, but tailored slacks and a long-sleeved shirt, opened at the throat.

"Look who's coming to butt in," Will said to Tess. He spoke low for her ears alone, but the contractor obviously overheard and glanced to see who was approaching.

Tess was appalled at the loathing in Will's tone and saw the same emotion on his face as she tried to make eye contact with him and request silently that he please be civil, for her sake. But, his big hands clenched into fists, Will was watching Peter. Just for a moment, Tess relived struggling helplessly against Will's brutish strength and felt her old fear for Peter, when violence threatened.

"Hi." She greeted Peter and took several steps to meet him when he had come within eight or ten yards of them. "Did you have to go into your office and work this morning?" She grasped his arm as he came to a stop, meeting her gaze unsmilingly. Tess held her nervous smile in place, making the same plea she'd failed to communicate to Will, *Please behave civilly.*

"No, I had a business appointment over here on the North Shore. It looks like you're in the middle of one yourself." He sounded accusing and offended as well as angry.

"A business appointment?"

"I'll tell you about it later." He glanced pointedly at David Johnson, who was waiting impatiently, while Will looked on with a glowering expression.

Tess held on to Peter's arm as she led him over to introduce him, but then she had to let go when he shook hands with the contractor, ignoring Will.

"I've been making some inquiries on Tess's behalf, and you have a good reputation," Peter told Johnson. "On the basis of what you've seen, what kind of ballpark figure are we talking about to get the marina back in shape? I realize, of course, that you'll have to do a lot of computations to come up with something firm."

Johnson looked at Tess questioningly, as though seeking her go-ahead to answer. Just who the hell was Peter to be asking? he was obviously wondering. Tess was still caught up in surprise over Peter's opener, which had brought a muffled growl from Will and a disgusted, knowing headshake.

"It's none of your goddamned concern, Roussell," Will spoke up to inform Peter.

Tess grabbed Peter's arm again as he balled both of his hands into fists. "I was wondering the same thing myself, Dave," she said quickly. "If you can just give me a rough idea of what to expect, I could get started on the financial end of things."

Johnson stuck his pencil behind his ear, tucked his clipboard under his arm and started them walking at a fast clip toward the office, talking as he went. Peter was the only one who had no problems keeping up.

"I'd rather not just pull a number out of the air, Tess. For one thing, I'm real backed up with work, like I told you on the phone. If you're in any hurry, I probably shouldn't even put in a bid."

Tess knew that it wasn't the time element that was causing him to have serious second thoughts about giving her a bid. "I'm not in a big hurry, Dave," she replied with as much dignity as possible.

Johnson agreed without any enthusiasm to prepare an estimate and promised to get back with her as soon as he'd worked it up. He didn't waste a second making his departure, getting into his truck and driving away, leaving Tess standing there with Will on one side and Peter on the other.

"I hope you're both happy!" she said, mustering more indignation than she actually felt in the effort to shame them and defuse the tension. "He's probably going to hike up his price just so I can't afford him."

"I don't think he's the type to do that," Peter disagreed. "He seems like a real straight shooter. I'll call him next week and talk to him."

"You'll do no such thing, Roussell," Will objected threateningly. "I'll call Johnson. When I do, I intend to give him my personal assurance that you won't be coming around and sticking your nose into Tess's business again."

"Neither one of you is going to call Dave Johnson!" Tess declared. "I'm going to call him myself and try to undo the damage, if it isn't too late to convince him that I'm the owner of this marina."

Neither man paid her much attention. They were eyeing each other with open hostility.

"You have a hell of a nerve, you know that?" Will demanded of Peter with a contemptuous sneer. "Don't you realize how obvious you are, man? If you think for one moment that I'm going to let you get your greedy hands on Tess's inheritance, you're dead wrong."

"Will, please, go back to your boat, and, Peter, you go inside." Tess gave each one of them a little push, but they didn't budge.

"If you think for one moment that I'm going to let you bulldoze Tess into marrying you, Buford, *you* are dead wrong," Peter replied through clenched teeth. "Your underhanded scheme for getting her into your clutches isn't going to work."

"Both of you, please, there are other people in the marina!" Tess reminded desperately. "Don't embarrass me by getting into a brawl right here!"

"It wouldn't be much a brawl, hon," Will jeered, directing his words to her, but keeping his eyes on Peter. "Just one or two punches ought to do it. Then maybe this bastard will get the message that he can't throw you away and then take up with you again when your daddy's died and left you well fixed."

"I didn't throw Tess away, you lying sonofabitch—"

Tess launched herself at Peter, hugging him around the waist and pushing with all her strength to stop his forward motion.

"*Please*, Peter, don't fight with Will. For *my* sake," she begged.

"Let him go, Tess. Don't protect him," Will taunted. "Don't you think your ex-husband can take care of himself?"

"You shut up, Will, and quit acting like some high-school bully!" Tess's voice blazed hotly over her shoulder. She clung tighter as Peter tried to remove her arms from around himself without exerting force and hurting her. "If you don't go back to your boat now, you can just find yourself a slip in some other marina!"

"Tess, you don't mean that!" Will protested in a hurt voice. "After fifteen years? Your daddy would turn over in his grave if he saw you and heard you right now."

The tension hadn't dissipated, but suddenly the threat of violence was gone. Tess released Peter and took a step away from him, but she'd clearly chosen sides. "Daddy would never think you were capable of behaving this way," she pointed out to Will defensively. "He'd be very disappointed. You know what his attitude was about settling differences with fistfighting in his marina."

"It was strictly against his rules," Will agreed in the same injured tone. "But you and I both know, Tess, that in this situation, he'd be calling the police to come and toss Roussell out on his ear, not be threatening me."

"I only said that to bring you to your senses, Will. I know from experience that there's no getting through to Peter with words once he's lost his temper." Tess tried to explain away any suggestion of partiality in her method of intervention. "Aside from the embarrassment, do you two know how bad I would feel, watching you hurt each other?" she demanded of both of them. Neither looked repentant or appreciative of her concern.

"Why don't we all three go inside your office." Peter surprised her with the terse suggestion. It would have been more in character for him to invite Will to go elsewhere, off the premises, where they could take up their quarrel. "I have some things to say to Buford in front of you, including an answer to his snide accusation that I'm after your inheritance."

"I can't wait to hear it," Will said with heavy sarcasm. "How about you, Tess?"

Tess met Peter's dark, penetrating gaze with a telltale uncertainty. She was interested in the explanation behind his unexpected interest in her financial affairs. He turned, his expression grim, and led the way inside.

Billy was out on the fuel dock handling a transaction with a customer. Tess was relieved that he hadn't been in the store to overhear the altercation outside. Inside her office, she started to go behind the desk to sit down and then hesitated.

"It's okay," Peter said, reading her mind. "Buford and I aren't going to start taking swings at each other. Right, Buford?"

Will sullenly acquiesced, and Tess sat down in her chair. The two men both remained standing, even though there were a couple of other chairs. Peter took charge.

"This morning I had an appointment with Philip Giraux, in Mandeville. I assume you know him?" He addressed Will, who had stiffened with surprise.

"Sure. I know Giraux. What did you talk to him about?"

Tess was mentally seconding the question. She didn't know Philip Giraux personally, but recognized his name. He was a well-known real-estate broker.

"As you're undoubtedly aware, Giraux specializes in commercial property on the North Shore. He's put together a number of big deals with developers. I wanted to pick his brain about what Tess's marina is worth." Peter was still addressing Will, who shot Tess a knowing glance.

"Why should you want to find that out?" he drawled.

"Because I ascertained from talking to her that she was relying entirely on you for advice and information, and I don't trust you," Peter replied bluntly. "Talking to Giraux, I was able to confirm what I had already suspected. In the present economic climate, Tess isn't going to find it easy to borrow the amount of money she'll need, using the marina as collateral, with her cash-flow situation. Commercial money is very scarce."

Will crossed his arms across his chest and looked bored. "There's always money to be had, if you have the right connections." Which Roussell, of course, didn't, he implied with his smug tone.

"The problem with 'right connections' is what kind of strings are attached," Peter said grimly. "Tess isn't going to be put in the position of either marrying you or losing her marina, Buford. I'm going to see to that, even if it means drawing out my retirement in addition to investing every penny that I have accumulated in savings."

"Peter!" Tess blurted out his name in amazed disbelief. Both men glanced at her and then resumed their tense discussion.

"That's real big of you, Roussell, but what kind of strings are you attaching?" Will inquired cynically. "Don't tell me you're not going to want some paper on your investment. Like a marriage certificate, for example?"

"If and when Tess and I get married again, it will be for the same reason that we got married the first time, not because I had to resort to bribery," Peter replied scornfully. "I expect to have to cosign the mortgage note, but the marina will still belong to Tess."

"If there's any signature besides hers on the note, it won't be yours. And Tess won't need a penny of your money. This is all a lot of hot air to impress you, hon," Will confided to Tess in a disgusted voice. "When it comes right down to it, I'm the one who's going to see to it that you hold on to what your daddy left you."

Tess stood up to assert herself. "No, you aren't. And neither is Peter. It might disappoint you both to know that I'm not in any danger of losing the marina." She looked from one to the other, annoyance growing at the patience and male indulgence in their faces. "My brother and his wife aren't the money-hungry kind. They would never force me to sell if I can't borrow enough to pay him in full for his share."

"Did he say as much when you talked to him on the phone?" Peter asked, skeptical, but hopeful, too.

"Not in so many words, but I could tell the type of person he is. He's all in favor of the two of us getting together and working something out, without lawyers."

Will spoke up at once, questioning the wisdom of that idea, but Tess hardly heard. Her attention was all on Peter's reaction. He wanted very badly to believe that her estimation of her brother's character was on the mark.

"I wish you'd mentioned that when you called Thursday night," he said with mild exasperation.

"I didn't dream what you had in mind, or I would have," Tess replied. "It would have come as a relief to you, I'm sure, to know that you didn't have to go to such lengths to save me from Will. This marina is without a doubt the last investment that you'd choose to sink your money into."

He couldn't deny it, not even with Will standing by and observing and listening. "To pull out my retirement, I'd have to terminate my employment and take whatever job I could get with another company," he explained.

That was the major sacrifice for him, to give up his future with the company that had hired him out of college. The future that he'd chosen over staying married to her. Tess's answer was full of bitter pride.

"I appreciate the fact that you'd be willing to do that, but I wouldn't let you. I'd sell the marina first."

"You'd never have to do that, hon," Will put in.

Peter glanced over at him with frowning impatience, obviously hampered by his presence, then glanced at his watch. "How late are you going to be here at the marina?" he asked Tess.

"Billy has to leave at three o'clock. I'll probably stay until dark," she answered, surprised by his quick change of subject. "It's been busy on the river today, and I can't afford to close up and lose business."

"I have to go back to New Orleans now, but I'll be crossing the lake again. I should make it here before dark, unless I run into unforeseen problems. We can finish this conversation then—hopefully in private," he added with pointed irony.

"He needs some time to make up more lies, hon, and try to pull the wool over your eyes," Will drawled, standing aside so that Peter could leave the office without getting any confirmation from Tess that she would be there when he returned.

Tess sat down, filled with a sense of anticlimax and dissatisfaction. What kind of pressing commitment did Peter have on a Saturday afternoon that took precedence over the discussion that they had been having?

"Please, Will, I'd like to be alone," she told the man who remained. He was closing the door behind Peter.

"Tess, you don't believe all that bull that Roussell is trying to lay on you, do you?" Will inquired, eyeing her worriedly.

"Yes, I do believe him," Tess replied without my hesitation. "Peter isn't devious, Will. He doesn't have any profit motive. The last thing that he would ever want is to own any interest in this marina. It has only unpleasant associations for him because my father built it." She sighed, not trying to hide how unhappy her own explanation made her. "That was the reason that Peter took back his slip-rent money. He couldn't stand the thought of keeping a boat here."

"If that's the case, then why get messed up with him? How are you ever going to be happy with a man who has hard feelings against your father? Answer me that. If you marry him, Tess, you might as well resign yourself to pulling up roots and selling this marina that Jake put his heart and soul into."

"It's not even that simple," Tess replied dully. "Peter doesn't have in mind marrying me, or he would have said so today, in front of you."

"You misjudged him once before, Tess," Will reminded.

Tess wanted to reply that she only wished that she were wrong in her insight now. Instead she smiled wanly. "Neither one of you puts any stock in my ability to judge character where the other one is concerned. You're both good men, Will, you and Peter. I want you to know that he hasn't changed my good opinion of you, either, with all his jealous suspicions."

"Thank you, Tess," he said gruffly, obviously touched. "I wouldn't do anything to harm you, for the world. And I'm not going anywhere at the whim of some big oil company. I'll still be around when Roussell's gone, to pick up the pieces." He came over, gave her a gentle pat on the cheek and left, closing the door behind him.

Tess blinked at hot tears of emotion, chief among them regret that he was still fostering hopes that were futile. Hearing young voices and laughter in the adjoining room, she got up and went out to wait on a party of teenagers who'd pulled up to the fuel dock in a high-powered ski boat. They wore T-shirts over wet bathing suits and were so carefree and full of high spirits that Tess envied them and felt sorry for herself, stuck there all afternoon.

Time didn't hang heavy on her hands, luckily. Between customers at the fuel dock and visits from boat owners in the marina, who dropped in at the office building for a purpose or just to chat, Tess didn't have much opportunity to watch the clock and mope. Things quieted to a lull in the late afternoon, though. When six o'clock came and Peter still hadn't driven up, she began to get restless and impatient, watching the open door.

From the direction of the lake she heard the quiet *putt-putt* of an engine grow louder as a boat came in from the lake. Then, also from the river, came a man's voice hailing her. "Tess!" He sounded remarkably like Peter. Tess listened and heard him call her name again, "Tess!" That *had* to be Peter!

Mystified, Tess walked out on the fuel dock. Approaching was a sailboat—with Peter at the helm, grinning broadly and waving to her. His dark hair was windblown, and he looked exhilarated and thoroughly pleased with life.

"How do you like my new sailboat?" He turned the engine down to idle and headed toward the fuel dock.

"Did you sail all the way from New Orleans?" Tess called back, walking closer to the edge of the dock.

"I motored part of the way." He coasted up alongside. "But this southeast breeze we had today was made to order. I had a great sail. Can I tie up in one of your empty slips for the night?"

"Is someone driving over to get you?" Tess ignored his request for the moment. It apparently hadn't occurred to him that she might enjoy making the trip across the lake with him, instead of spending a boring afternoon.

"No, I plan to sleep aboard, unless you have some objection."

"There's no restriction against staying overnight in the marina," she assured him. "You can tie up in number 14."

"Thanks. Come over and have a beer with me," he urged. "I want you to see the inside of the boat."

"I'll walk over and give you a hand with the lines."

"Great." He flashed her a good-natured grin, his teeth even whiter against his sun-darkened skin. Like Tess, he tanned easily. This afternoon he would have taken off his shirt, and his whole upper torso would be brown and sleek.

The mental picture that accompanied the conjecture quickened Tess's pulse.

She locked up and hurried over to the slip that she'd assigned him, her bad mood fast dissipating. Apparently he planned to sail back the next day or, perhaps, take his boat to another marina, but he was here for the night, with no transportation.

Peter had the boat in the slip when she got there. Together they secured it, no instructions necessary. Tess fastened her end of each of the mooring lines to a piling, and then Peter tightened the line and cleated it off. He moved around on deck nimbly, she noted, and seemed thoroughly in his element.

He'd left the engine running. When all four lines were tied, he stepped down into the cockpit to kill it and then came back up on deck again, holding out his hand to Tess. She took it and came aboard.

"This is one of the boats we looked at on Wednesday, isn't it?" she asked, standing in the cockpit. With hindsight, she realized now why he had decided to buy a smaller, less expensive boat.

"It sure is," Peter confirmed cheerfully. "I called the owner right after you left, and he came over to show me the inside. We took it out for a trial sail."

"He lives at West End?"

"Five minutes away from the marina by my condo building. Go on down below and take a look."

The sailboat owner was the "fellow from West End" he had been out having a bite to eat with when Tess had tried to call him on Wednesday night. Why had he been so vague?

"When did you make up your mind to buy the boat?" she asked, preceding him down the companionway ladder.

"I made an offer, contingent on a survey, when Bob and I got back in from our sail." Peter followed her down. "It's compact, but comfortable, don't you think?'' He gestured proudly to indicate the boat interior.

"It's very nice," Tess complimented sincerely. "And roomier than I would have expected. You even have standing head room."

"There's no refrigeration, but I have a big ice box that holds a lot." Peter lifted the lid so that she could peer in and see plastic containers in addition to beer and soft drinks and a bottle of wine. "The sink has pressure water, which is convenient." He went on to point out the features of the galley. "A two-burner stove and an amazing amount of storage space." He slid open the doors of several cabinets, revealing grocery staples and neatly stacked plastic dishes.

"It's a regular little kitchen," Tess said. "It's cute."

"The cushions are in good condition, but they could be reupholstered." He walked into the cabin area, sat down on one of the two long settees running along either wall and patted the spot next to him for Tess to sit down, too. She obligingly did. "This bunk that we're sitting on pulls out into a double," Peter told her, as though it were relevant information she'd be interested in.

"It seems to be plenty long enough for you," she replied.

"The head is small, but it even has a shower." He got up and opened the door to a small compartment. Tess went over by him to look inside when he encouraged her with a smile to come and inspect it. She noted the shower head fitting that was designed to be detached from the wall and held in the hand.

"Taking a shower is strictly a one-person affair," Peter lamented cheerfully, reading her thoughts. He grinned down at her. "That's my one regret about this boat, but then there are other compensations, like anchoring in a private spot and swimming nude."

Tess wanted just to smile back at him and share his infectious pleasure in being a new boat owner. She resisted with an effort, pointing out, "You should have gone ahead and bought a larger boat, like those we looked at that first day."

"Don't you like her?" Peter looked genuinely crestfallen.

"I think this boat is really nice," Tess hastened to assure him. "She has all the appearance of having been extremely well cared for."

"Wait until you see how she sails." He closed the door to the head and ushered Tess toward the companionway. "Why don't we sit out in the cockpit? I'll fix you a rum and Coke. I have a bottle of good Barbados rum on board. We'll use our imaginations and pretend that we're down in the Caribbean islands."

Rather than tied up in her marina, the last place that he would have chosen voluntarily to dock his new sailboat. Tess didn't speak her thought aloud. She tried for a light touch as she stepped up the companionway ladder. "That may take quite a lot of imagination if the mosquitoes are out."

Peter was standing behind her, holding her lightly by her waist and lending unnecessary balance. He tightened his hold, stopping her ascent as he replied softly, "Then we'll just have to come inside."

Tess looked at him over her shoulder, her heart beating faster at his tone. His expression erased any doubt that she'd imagined the message in his voice. She let him turn her around carefully so that her feet didn't slip from the ladder tread.

"Not perfect, but not bad, either." He pulled her into a close embrace and hugged her tight against him. "The next step would be a little high, don't you think?"

Tess put her arms around his neck and smiled back at him, sweet joy and expectation swelling up inside her.

Nothing else mattered for the moment except being there with him. His kiss tasted of sunshine and open water and exultation. It also told her what he hadn't said with words: he wished that she had been with him today on his lake crossing.

## Chapter Eleven

I'd better make those drinks," Peter said in a husky, reluctant voice as he parted his lips from hers and drew back to look into her face, without loosening his tight embrace.

Using her fingers, Tess combed his fine, dark hair into a windblown semblance of his neatly trimmed style. Then she touched his lean cheekbones and cleanly chiselled nose.

"You have a suntan," she accused.

"Tomorrow you can get one. I'm going to take you out sailing with me." He kissed her on the lips as though settling the matter, gave her a hard hug and then released her, saying teasingly, "This time I won't watch you and maybe you can make it out into the cockpit. That back view is much too tempting in those jeans." He gave her a little slap on her bottom as she turned and climbed the ladder.

Outside the western sky was a vivid canvas of oranges and shades of fuchsia. "You have to see this sunset," she said, sticking her head into the hatch to tell him.

He was in the midst of pouring rum into two glasses and stopped to climb up a couple of steps and look out. He whistled softly. "Look at those colors! How could the Caribbean possibly top that?"

It was exactly what Tess was thinking. He finished making the drinks and brought them out. They watched the sunset fade, keeping their voices low in the hushed quiet that seemed to magnify sound. Occasionally there was the splash of a fish breaking the surface of the water. Several other boats had people aboard them, and there were outbursts of laughter now and then and snatches of conversation.

"God, this is peaceful isn't it?" Peter remarked with deep contentment, not really requiring an answer.

"With all the time that I've spent in this marina, I've really never appreciated this aspect of it."

Her comment pleased him. For the first time, Tess felt the awakening of hope. Even if it was impossible for them to start afresh, perhaps they could build something new and strong on top of all that had gone wrong in the past.

With darkness, an insect chorus piped up shrilly. Peter tossed his ice cubes into the water. "Hungry?" he asked.

"A little." Tess hated to leave the boat and go out among people. "We could pick up a couple of fried-chicken dinners and bring them back here."

Peter stood up and reached a hand to her. "I brought supper. It'll just take about thirty minutes to put it all together."

"We're going to cook? What fun!" Tess exclaimed, letting him pull her up.

"No, I'm going to cook. You'll just sit back and look pretty."

"But I want to help."

"The galley's a little small for two people."

"So I noticed."

He grinned and bent down to kiss her. Then he hugged her hard and held her. Tess could sense his amused delight turning to seriousness even before he spoke.

"I never stopped missing you, Tess. Even after enough time had passed that I didn't think about you often anymore, my life was flat somehow. Nothing had quite the meaning that it should have had."

"Like some key ingredient had been left out," she said, nodding her head so that her cheek rubbed against his chest. "It was like that with me, too."

"I still love you."

"I still love you, too."

He hugged her so tight for a moment that she couldn't breathe. Then he loosened his embrace and ran his hands possessively down her back and over her hips and buttocks. His voice was tender and happy as he suggested, "Let's go down below and see about making supper, shall we, baby?"

Tess preceded him down the companionway ladder, aglow with her own emotion that answered his. Getting their feelings for each other out in the open wasn't going to work magic. It wasn't going to sweep aside all the hurt and disappointment or erase the very real problems that they faced in making a commitment. But now wasn't the time for facing up to reality. It was the time for basking in the special thrill of loving and being loved in return.

Her old confidence was back. She took advantage of the liberty to touch him as he busied himself in the galley after he'd put a tape on to play for background music and opened out the drop-leaf table. They were having fettuccine Alfredo and a shrimp-and-crabmeat salad with remoulade dressing. He'd bought the salad at a West End restaurant with the dressing separate.

While he made the sauce for the fettuccine, using a packet of mix and a carton of half-and-half, Tess served the delectable-looking salad into bowls, feeding Peter a whole pink shrimp with her fingers when she stole one for herself.

She finished her tasks before he did and watched him, getting so near that he barely had room to work. Even after seeing him in his condo kitchen, she was intrigued at the sight of him doing what he'd considered woman's work when he was younger. She couldn't resist teasing him.

"You look good with a wooden spoon in your hand," she commented. "Much sexier than any chef I've seen on a TV cooking show."

"Yeah?" He feigned an interested, vain expression. "I turn you on stirring a pot?"

Tess caressed his back, enjoying the supple tautness. "You turn me on, whatever you're doing." For her candor, she was rewarded with a kiss. "I don't want to make you bigheaded, but you've gotten even better-looking, and I didn't think there was any room for improvement before."

"I didn't think it was possible for you to get any prettier or sexier than I remembered you, but the grown-up Tess knocked me off my feet," Peter confided.

"I did?"

He smiled at her delighted tone that encouraged him to elaborate.

"You've changed very little in your outward appearance. The measurements of your figure are almost the same. You still have the same dark brown eyes that can flirt one second and commit murder the next, the same pretty face that tells whether you're on top of the world or down in the dumps, the same long, wavy hair that you wear in the same hairstyle. But now you're a woman, not a girl." A transition he found very exciting, he told her with his voice and eyes.

"You're so much surer of yourself. And you've learned self-control, but there's still that reckless, devil-may-care streak in you that always made you so much fun."

"You're more poised, but every bit as outgoing. Not nearly as big a flirt as you used to be, but seductive as hell."

"I wasn't a big flirt!" Tess protested. "And I don't come on to men."

"It's probably just innate, not conscious."

"You always had a jealous imagination," she scoffed. "After I met you, I never had eyes for any other guy. When I'm with you now, I don't even notice another man."

"I just wish I could put blinders on the rest of the male population," Peter admitted. "I'm still jealous, baby. That's one respect in which I definitely haven't changed."

The fettuccine was ready to be drained. They both transferred their attention to last-minute steps of getting their meal on the table. Peter opened the bottle of white wine that Tess had glimpsed in the ice box, and they sat down to eat, the disrupted conversation forgotten.

The boat cabin was cozy and intimate, the food and wine delicious, their pleasure in each other too complete to allow for discussion of weighty topics.

After they'd finished, they were in no hurry to clean up the galley, lounging back and sipping their wine to the accompaniment of music. When they did stir themselves, Peter insisted that he would wash the few dishes and the two pots that he'd used. Tess dried. It took them a mere ten minutes.

Peter held out his wet hands for her to dry them with her dish towel after he'd let the water out of the sink and given it a quick rinsing.

"If you're not careful, you'll end up with dishpan hands," she warned lightly to cover up her little stab of emotion at the sight of his ringless left hand. By now she should be used to it, but she wasn't. So far she had managed not to ask him what he had done with his gold wedding band. "There." She smiled up at him.

His dark eyes were questioning. "What's wrong?"

"Nothing."

"Yes, there is." He took the dish towel from her and spread it on the counter. Then he took both her hands in his. "Come on. Tell me."

Tess sighed. "It's something that I've been wondering about that I don't really want to know. And if I bring it up, it will spoil the wonderful time that we're having."

"Does it have anything to do with my hands?" he probed quietly.

"Yes."

He brought her left hand up between them, turned it over, knuckles up, and rubbed her bare third finger with his thumb. "Your hand looks so naked every time I see it."

"So does yours. I still have my wedding rings." She answered the question that he hadn't asked her before now because he dreaded knowing, too.

"I've never gotten rid of mine, either."

"You haven't? I thought surely that you would have by now."

"I couldn't bring myself to." He hesitated.

What he was thinking would cause her pain. "Go ahead," Tess forced herself to say.

"Without going into details, I wouldn't have stayed single if I could have managed to dispose of it." He squeezed her hands apologetically as she bit her bottom lip hard.

"You were on the verge of marrying someone, and she found the ring and refused to let you keep it?"

"I hadn't hidden it. It was with my cuff links and other jewelry."

Tess had to deal with the unbearable thought of some other woman having the freedom of his bedroom. "You gave her an engagement ring and made wedding plans and everything?"

He nodded and looked down at her hand. "The kind of ring I had wished I could give you. I thought of that when I bought it." He drew in a breath and caressed her ring finger again. Tess could read the question in his mind and knew that her answer was going to cause him the same pain and rejection that she was feeling.

"I was engaged very briefly about a year after we were divorced. And then about five years later to someone else. Now you see why I said a minute ago that nothing was bothering me," she said unhappily. "I knew that I was going to get us into another one of these horrible question-and-answer sessions."

"We've been apart ten years, Tess. I know it's rough on both of us, but we have to work through all this." He drew her into his arms and held her against him. "I love you."

"I love you, Peter."

They hugged each other tightly for a long moment, seeking solace and taking comfort.

"Before we have dessert, I need to try out that shower," Peter said. He loosened his embrace to caress her back and shoulders.

"You brought dessert?" It was his lack of privacy that piqued Tess's interest, not the prospect of dessert. He would have to undress in the cabin. "What are we having?" she pulled back from him enough to look up and inquire.

He smiled down at her. "I'll give you a hint. It's the kind that's good any time of day or night. The problem is that it can leave you hungry for more."

"Is it fattening?" Tess had a good idea by now of what kind of after-dinner treat he had in mind.

"No, in fact you can lose weight, especially if you over-indulge in it."

"Then I'll probably just gorge myself. You are sure that it's something I like."

"You've always seemed to enjoy it. In fact, some times you've been a little greedy."

They smiled at each other.

"I'll just help you get undressed and hurry things along." Tess unbuttoned his shirt. "After you take your shower, I think I'll hop in and take one, too." She tugged his shirt free of his jeans and took it off. "Look at how brown you are!" While she was stroking his chest and shoulders, Peter un-snapped his jeans and slid the zipper down.

Tess took over, tugging his jeans down over his lean hips and helping him step out of them. Next she took off his briefs. "You'd better be careful and not run into any-thing," she cautioned with a suggestive glance, stroking a finger along the jutting length of him.

"Tell me that when I get out of the shower, you little tease," he came back threateningly.

"I'll just undress myself or else we might start fooling around," Tess said, grasping the ribbed waist of her knit top and pulling it over her head. Peter took both of her hands in his and stopped her before she could undo the front clo-sure of her bra. He didn't unclip it, either, but caressed the bared tops of her breasts curving out of the lace-and-satin cups.

"That's a sexy bra," he told her, pushing his forefinger down into the narrow valley of her cleavage. Tess sucked in her breath, making it even narrower, when he leaned down and trailed his tongue along the cleft.

To her utter disappointment, he straightened up to un-fasten her bra and take it off. When her breasts were fully exposed to him and aching to be touched and kissed, he circled the dark peaks lightly with his thumb and dropped his hands to unsnap her jeans.

"Now who's being a tease," Tess complained, throwing back her shoulders.

"I'm afraid I won't be able to take just a taste and wait, baby," Peter told her softly, but he bent down and suckled each breast while he was slowly unzipping her jeans. Tess moaned with the exquisite sensations.

She put her arms around his neck and kept him eye level with her as he started to straighten again.

She drew his head to hers to kiss him with moist parted lips. He made a passionate sound in his throat as she found his tongue with hers.

"We could have a sample of dessert before we take our showers if you don't think that we'd be spoiling our appetite," she murmured against his mouth.

"I don't think there's any danger of even taking the edge off mine," he replied. "I have this terrific hunger."

He finished undressing her, and they made urgent love, right there in the galley, passion bringing out the resourcefulness of their youthful days in adapting to any location.

Afterward Tess reminded him teasingly that he had remarked earlier during supper preparations about the counter level in the galley being lower than the standard kitchen height.

"Were you thinking ahead?" she asked him.

"Baby, with you I have to be ready to improvise in the heat of the moment," he came back.

"Are you complaining?"

"Never."

They took turns in the tiny bathroom. Even though the door had to be closed, since the compartment itself formed the shower stall, they talked and laughed, sharing the novelty, enjoying the intimacy.

Peter pulled out the bunk that made into a double bed. Putting on the bedding together was a joking, lighthearted affair, and, with both of them naked, more than a little stimulating. They made love again, at more length, kissing and fondling and taking pleasure in arousing each other to a state of urgent need again. Then they satisfied each other in a more conventional position than before, reaching the same high peak of sensory devastation.

"Thank you." Tess hugged the lax body slumped on top of her. Her lips twitched into a smile that she kept out of her voice. "That was very nice."

She could feel his initial surprise at her words turning into a lazy comprehension. He rose up and scowled down at her. "Nice? Can't you come up with something a little more complimentary than that?"

"I just hate to use up all my superlatives, since the dessert course is definitely your specialty," she explained.

"If that's a hint for more, I'm afraid you're going to have to wait until morning." He dropped a kiss on the tip of her nose. "The chef has had a long day. A good day." He got up to turn off the lights in the cabin.

"I should get dressed and go to my house." Tess's voice expressed her reluctance. "The word will spread all over the marina tomorrow that I've spent the night with you on your sailboat."

Peter came back and got into the bunk with her. He pulled the sheet up over them and drew Tess close to him. "This is my first night aboard my own sailboat. I want you to sleep with me and be here in the morning."

Tess badly wanted the same thing. "It's not just the thought of people talking about me. I hate causing Will embarrassment," she confessed, knowing that her pangs of conscience weren't likely to meet with sympathy. "It's going to be a real slap in the face for him that I've dated him a whole year and never spent the night aboard his boat.''

"He might as well go ahead and deal with the sting," Peter replied in a hard voice. "Buford will have to get used to the idea that we're sleeping together because I plan to be over here every weekend and probably some evenings, too."

"What do you mean, 'here'?" Tess asked hesitantly.

"Here in this slip, unless you throw me out."

She was silent a moment, her gladness at war with caution. "Is this a spur-of-the-moment decision?" One made in the aftermath of lovemaking?

"No. I bought this boat with the intention of keeping it here in your marina," he admitted. "The reason I didn't tell you was that I didn't want to give you a chance to refuse renting me a slip again. Once I was here, I hoped you wouldn't evict me. Can we give it a shot, on a trial basis?"

"On a trial basis," she agreed. No amount of clear-headed judgment could win over the allure of having him keep his boat right there in her marina, making it so convenient to see him. "And on one condition."

"What is it?"

"It has to do with taking guests out sailing."

He rubbed his cheek against her head. "The only guest I'm going to be taking out is the bossy little marina owner who runs the show around here."

She snuggled closer. "I don't anticipate any problem, then."

"Good night, baby. I love you."

Tess told him good-night and spoke her own words of love. He fell asleep almost immediately.

Tess was getting dressed while Peter made coffee, whistling a cheerful tune.

"You went out like a light last night," she remarked.

"I hope I didn't snore."

"No, you didn't."

"Sailing gives you a good kind of physical exhaustion. Tonight you'll see what I mean."

His tone was complacent, and he resumed his whistling as he measured coffee grounds. Did he envision them being tired together that evening or separately? Tess wanted to know.

"Are you planning to go back to New Orleans tonight?" she asked him.

He glanced over at her, his expression quizzical. "That's what I had in mind. I have to be at work fairly early in the morning."

"You're counting on having me drive you?"

"Is there a reason that you can't?"

"No, but there easily could be," she pointed out. "When were you going to bring it up?"

He glanced at his watch as though to assure himself that the hour was as early as he'd thought it was. "After I'd had a cup of coffee?" he suggested mildly.

Tess didn't answer. She turned her back to him as she pulled her blouse over her head and then went into the head to use the woman's hairbrush that he had brought aboard, along with other feminine toilet articles. His forethought rankled more than pleased her in her present mood. He certainly seemed to be taking a lot for granted where she was concerned.

The door to the small compartment was open. Peter had hooked it securely to the bulkhead after their showers the previous evening so that the dampness could dry, and neither of them had closed it for privacy that morning. Tess considered shutting it, but didn't because of the limited space. Bumping her elbow into the wall as she began to brush her hair, she muttered an unladylike oath.

"Here. Let me do that." Peter had come up behind her and put his hand over hers on the hairbrush. Tess held on to it for several seconds, meeting his gaze rebelliously in the mirror. He smiled at her coaxingly, refusing to engage in a battle of wills. She surrendered the brush to him and stood, straight-shouldered.

He set to work, being gentle but thorough. Tess tried to resist the physical enjoyment, tried not to relax, tried not to watch his reflection. He looked so thoroughly engrossed. When he started talking, she lost the battle on all three fronts.

"I knew that I might find myself stranded," he confided. "Just like I knew I might have to tie up at the town dock tonight. Might have to spend a whole evening alone here on my boat. I prepared myself, as best as I could, for having my whole plan for this weekend miscarry. Then I hoped for the best. Am I being too rough?" he inquired.

"No, it feels wonderful," Tess admitted.

"I'm just taking one step at a time, Tess. It isn't easy to go slow, but there's too much at stake not to be patient." He met her eyes in the mirror. "Trust isn't something that can happen overnight."

Especially not between them, when they'd let each other down so badly once before.

"I hope you don't plan to keep me in suspense from one hour to the next, though," Tess said. "As much I like surprises and doing things on impulse, I can't sit around and twiddle my thumbs on the chance that you'll show up. I need some advance notice."

"Okay," he agreed. "I'll start giving you a complete itinerary. Today, for example, I thought we'd go out sailing for three or four hours. You probably won't want to leave your high-school boy to handle the fuel dock and the store by himself on a nice Sunday afternoon when things could get pretty busy." He paused to look inquiringly at her.

"No, I really shouldn't, as much as I hate to cut your sail short. I suppose you could go out again by yourself."

He shook his head. "No, I'll enjoy puttering around here on the boat and doing little odds and ends. Plus I can come over and visit you. If you aren't too busy, we can go over some computer information that I've gotten together for you. After you close up the office, we'll either have dinner out over here or on the New Orleans side of the lake, whichever you prefer. Afterward, we'll go to my condo, watch a little TV, and you'll spend the night with me. Is that good enough?" He held the brush poised over her head.

"Yes, thank you." Tess took the brush from him. "My hair hasn't had that good a brushing in ages."

"I'll see that it does. Often."

Leaving her to pin up her hair, he went to pour them each a cup of coffee. Tess hummed along with the tune he was whistling. To sound that happy, he must be at least cautiously optimistic about them.

The whistling stopped, though, as he slid the hatch open. Coming out into the cabin, she saw that he had climbed partway up the companionway ladder and was looking out at the marina.

Was the sight repugnant to him? she wondered. Was he thinking to himself how much he'd like to take back his statement of his intention to keep his boat there?

Noticing his wallet lying on the floor, where it had evidently fallen out of his jeans pocket, Tess bent and picked it up.

"You dropped your wallet," she told him.

"Just put it in the cabinet with the tapes, will you?" he replied. "It's not a good idea for me to carry it when I'm out sailing."

Her heart sank at his quiet, reflective tone. "Aren't you worried that I'll look inside it and find pictures of all your old girlfriends?" she asked.

He didn't say anything for a moment. "I hadn't thought of that." He stepped back down into the cabin.

Tess eyed him uncertainly. She had been expecting a teasing comeback. Did he have some pictures in his wallet of women he'd dated?

Peter gestured, giving her permission to go ahead and look, if she wanted to. "I don't carry but just a few pictures. They add too much bulk."

"Maybe I shouldn't be so nosy," she suggested.

"You won't find any old girlfriends," he assured her. "Other than yourself."

Tess stared at him in surprise and then opened the wallet under his gaze. There was a studio photograph of his mother and father, looking older than her memory of them.

"When was this taken of your parents?" she asked him.

"On their thirty-fifth anniversary last year."

The only other pictures were a school photo of a nephew, who was also his godchild, he explained, and the snapshot of Tess that he had carried in his wallet when they were married.

"Did you just run across this recently and stick it in your wallet?"

"No."

"You don't mean . . ." Surely he hadn't been transferring it to each new wallet all these years.

He nodded and then went on to answer her unspoken question, why? "The first time I changed wallets after we were separated, I hadn't given up on being reconciled with you. The other times, I bargained with my pride in various ways to keep from discarding your picture."

"Like putting another picture on top of it?" she guessed, and winced when he made a self-derogatory face, giving her her answer. The other picture, of course, had been of another woman.

"That and by playing the cynic. I told myself that keeping your picture was a healthy sign of indifference, but I knew, deep down, that I was lying to myself in the teeth. Actually it was just the opposite." He picked up her cup of coffee and held it out toward her. "Your coffee's getting cold. Would you like to sit outside in the cockpit? The sun's coming out."

Tess accepted the cup and took a hasty sip as she handed him his wallet. "No, I'd better run. I want to go home and change clothes and get a few things for our sailing trip, then get back in time to open up for Billy."

He didn't argue with her. Tess was all too sure as she left him to make breakfast for himself that he was glad for some time alone.

The discovery that he'd been carrying her picture through the years that they'd been separated and divorced might have been a thrill, if only doing so had brought him any joy, which obviously it hadn't. She'd wanted to ask him if he'd ever looked at it and smiled and felt glad that he'd known her, but she hadn't dared, knowing that he would answer honestly and the answer would hurt.

The reason he was there, tied up in her marina, was his inability to toss the old picture of her in a wastebasket. The question was whether he was going to be able to replace it with a more recent one that would be a tangible reminder of the missed years.

## Chapter Twelve

Peter flipped open his wallet after Tess had gone and gazed down at the snapshot of her. So many wasted years, he reflected with sharp regret, mentally comparing the young Tess in the picture to the grown woman. There was no getting those years back, and yet they kept intruding upon the present.

It was going to take time. Eventually he and Tess would be able to put the past behind them. Peter clung to that belief during low points, like the previous evening, hearing that two other men had put their engagement rings on her finger. He felt the same sick jealousy and sense of betrayal now, remembering, the same apology and guilt he'd felt at causing her pain with his own confession that he'd put a ring on another woman's hand.

With time would come all the necessary adjustments. Peter had to believe in that, too. He wasn't going to lie to himself. He wished with all his heart that he and Tess could work out things between them somewhere else, make a life for themselves in a location other than this one.

But that wasn't going to happen. Peter was resigned to living permanently in close proximity to Maryville, to working permanently in New Orleans, to sharing all the headaches her father had dumped upon her shoulders and helping her operate her marina.

There couldn't be any halfhearted commitment or any spirit of martyrdom. He did draw the line at living in her parents' house, right next door to the marina, though. They could at least have their own place, preferably not in Maryville, and furnish it from scratch.

And Buford had to go.

Those were Peter's only two conditions, and he thought they were reasonable enough.

"I wish we didn't have to go back in," Tess said wistfully. "It's such a beautiful day, and that was so much fun. But I hate to leave Billy in the lurch."

They'd had a wonderful sail out on the lake and were heading back to the marina. Peter was being such a good sport about cutting his sail short on her account that she felt twice as bad.

"Is there anybody else you could get to help him out on weekends?" he asked. "I'll pay the extra wages."

"I couldn't let you do that," she protested.

"It would be worth it, to free up your time," he replied. "If you can, line up someone for next weekend. We could sail over to Bayou Liberty, anchor out and spend the night, and come back on Sunday."

"That sounds like fun," Tess said. "I'll see about hiring some help for Billy."

"We can do some weekend cruising over on the Gulf Coast, too," Peter went on. "Les Morgan takes his boat over to Biloxi for the summer and sails out of there."

Tess greeted that suggestion with enthusiasm, too, but she could hear her own hollow note. After one weekend, he was thinking of ways to escape her marina and spend as little time there as possible.

In the channel they met a number of boats heading out. Up ahead, anchored at the spit of land in the mouth of the river called the Point, Tess could see a whole cluster of powerboats that she recognized. They were all from her marina, and Will's powerboat was among them.

"I think I'd like something cold to drink. What about you?" she asked Peter, getting up.

"I'll split a beer with you," he offered, reaching out his hand for hers and squeezing it. He was having to concentrate on steering and apparently hadn't spotted Will's boat or he would have objected, she knew, to her getting out of sight to spare Will the humiliation of watching her come in from sailing with Peter, with Will's boat-owner neighbors from the marina looking on.

Tess dawdled down below, paying a visit to the head. A glance through a port on her way back to the galley showed that they had motored past the Point. She got an ice-cold beer out of the icebox, opened it and handed it out to Peter.

"You can come out now," he told her shortly, and then glanced back, his lips tightening. "Or maybe you'd better put on a life jacket. Buford has pulled up anchor. I wouldn't put it past the bastard to try to sink me."

"Will's a member of the power squadron," Tess protested mildly. "He wouldn't disobey any rules of water safety."

"Oh, yeah," Peter said grimly. "Seriously, Tess, hang on down here. He's kicking up a hell of a wake."

Tess could hear the powerful engines and the churn of water, but she still couldn't believe that Will would operate his boat recklessly. "I'm sure he'll slow down," she said, coming out into the cockpit. "See. He's eased back on the throttle."

"The sonofabitch didn't know you were aboard." Peter's voice was hard with both contempt and satisfaction. "Otherwise, he'd have tried to wash me up on the bank."

She sighed, knowing that it would only make things worse to come to Will's defense. If she dropped down onto the seat opposite Peter instead of sitting next to him again, that was going to offend him, too, so she remained standing and waved as the big powerboat gave them a wide berth, kicking up practically no wake. When it was past, it speeded up with a powerful forward surge and quickly left them behind.

"You can sit down now," Peter told her.

Tess did sit down, on the opposite seat. "I can understand Will having a grudge against you, but not vice versa," she said, exasperated. "You're the one I spent the night with last night, the one I was out with on his boat today. Don't you realize how much Will would like to change places with you?"

"I realize that all too well," Peter replied, completely unmoved. "Buford would go to any lengths to get you, including committing a serious breach of legal ethics."

"You have no proof that he's done anything unethical, Peter. That's just your suspicion. He's equally certain that you tipped off my brother out of spite and that you have ulterior motives for coming back into my life."

"He's a liar. He knows damned well I didn't make that call."

"I can't take any more scenes like the one yesterday morning," Tess warned, giving up on reasoning with him. "The two of you are going to have to behave when you run into each other."

"If it comes to blows between Buford and me again, we'll take our quarrel somewhere else," he promised her.

"I want you to give me your word that you won't fight him at all," Tess insisted. She moved over to sit next to him. "I happen to like your face just the way it is."

"Is Buford an ex-boxer?" he asked, not really mollified. "You gave me the impression yesterday that you were protecting me from him."

"He's a very strong man. You can see that by the way he's built," she added quickly when Peter looked at her sharply.

"He's never tried to manhandle you, has he?" His voice was dangerously toneless.

"No, of course not!" Tess lied.

Peter didn't press her for the truth, but his white-knuckled grip on the tiller didn't relax. He stared fixedly upriver, his whole body taut. In her role of peacemaker, she had inadvertently just made things worse.

"I enjoyed our sail so much," she told him miserably, her tone completing the rest of the thought. She was sorry that it had had to end this way, with tension between them.

He put his arm around her. "You don't know how much I've looked forward to having my own boat and taking you out sailing with me."

"Next weekend I'll plan to take off all day Saturday and Sunday."

He hugged her. "God, that'll be great, two whole days together out on the water."

In the marina Tess helped him tie up the boat and then went immediately over to the office building. Will's boat was back in its slip, too, but he hadn't left. With a little sigh, she noted the white Cadillac and walked over to give Will the same warning that she'd given Peter. She wasn't tolerating any more violent outbursts of temper.

Will wasn't out on deck. She tapped on the varnished cap rail. He came out immediately, looking injured and inquiring, but his low rumbling voice was warm with welcome as he greeted her.

"Hi, hon. Come on aboard."

"I don't have time to visit," Tess explained as she stepped aboard after a moment's hesitation. It would be more private inside his boat, and there wasn't any reason she should feel inhibited. "I just wanted a quick word with you."

"Sit down," he urged her. "What can I get you to drink?"

"Nothing, thank you." She perched on the edge of a settee. "I have to get over and give Billy a hand. That's why Peter and I came in."

His face hardened with contempt at the mention of Peter's name. "That guy's got some nerve. Shoots a big line about all the money he can come up with and then buys a raggedy-ass little sailboat like that. I'd be surprised if he could scrape up five or ten grand."

Tess sighed. "Will, Peter is going to keep his boat here. I'll understand if the situation is too awkward for you."

"Is that a nice way of asking me to take my boat somewhere else, Tess? Are you kicking me out, after fifteen years?"

"No, I wouldn't think of doing that," she denied sincerely. "But I won't put up with any fighting, Will."

"You're afraid I'll beat the pulp out of him, aren't you?" His speculation held a kind of grim satisfaction as well as reproach for her partiality.

"Promise me, Will."

He shrugged. "Don't worry, hon. I won't cause any trouble here in your marina. If he loses his cool, though, don't blame me."

"The same rule applies to Peter. If he can't behave himself, he'll have to rent a slip somewhere else."

"Fair enough."

Tess left Will's boat, feeling once again as though she'd tried to defuse a bomb and failed. Just the thought of Will and Peter confronting each other filled her with dread.

Billy was glad to see her. Business had picked up in spurts after lunchtime. When several boats pulled up to the fuel dock at once, it was impossible for one person to pump fuel and handle the cash register inside, too. A responsible youth, Billy didn't like leaving it unattended.

During lulls, they chatted. Billy had asked her about sailing, and she was giving him an enthusiastic accounting when Peter walked in, carrying a manila folder. Tess smiled her welcome, noting that after being out in the sun today, he had tanned even a deeper brown.

He came behind the counter, where she sat on a high stool, gave her a casual hug and kiss and joined in the conversation. She appreciated the way he was able to strike up a rapport with Billy immediately. It came as no surprise when he took the boy's hint and offered to take him out sailing soon, much to Billy's delight.

Peter had always been generous and quick to empathize. That was part of the reason for his popularity, along with his gregarious, outgoing nature. He liked people, as did Tess herself. When they were dating, they'd spent time alone with each other, but also enjoyed going to parties and socializing with friends. Even during those couple of months of married bliss before her mother became ill, they hadn't closeted themselves totally.

Tess didn't doubt that he'd be accepted quickly by her circle of friends, and she was confident that she could win even Les Morgan over. She and Peter were so compatible in their personalities when nothing was wrong between them, she reflected, enjoying the sound of his voice and his laughter.

Two boats pulled up at the fuel dock, and he went outside to give Billy a hand. Tess got up and went to stand in the door, when two young women in their early twenties aboard one of the boats engaged Peter in conversation. He glanced back at her and smiled, telling her with his dark eyes that she had no cause for jealousy.

She was jealous, and possessive. He was tall and lean and virile in faded jeans and a T-shirt.

"I never noticed that your eyes had a green tint," he said in a low, teasing voice, for her ears alone, as he handed her the money he'd accepted in payment and accompanied her back inside, his arm loosely around her shoulders.

"It's not good for business to carry the friendly routine too far," she informed him tartly. "I thought for a moment those two women were going to pull you on board bodily."

"Not a chance." He hugged her shoulders. "Why don't we go into your office and take a look at that computer information I've compiled for you?"

Tess didn't need any urging. Leaving Billy with instructions to give her a yell if he got swamped, she led Peter to the small adjacent room that had been her father's office and now was hers. She turned around and waited for him to close the door. Then she took the folder from him, tossed it onto the desk and went eagerly into his arms.

He held her against him in the way she adored. Tess wrapped her arms around his neck, her face on a level with his.

"You know that no other woman in the whole world holds a candle to you in my eyes," he told her in a tender, indulgent tone.

"Don't tell me you didn't notice the size of the chest on that blonde."

"She was way out of proportion. I happen to like small voluptuous brunettes, one in particular." He bumped his nose against hers. "Now, could I have a kiss?"

"With a line like that, how can I refuse?"

Kissing him was such sheer pleasure. Tess loved the pressure of her lips against his, the warm, moist, intimate mating of their tongues, playful at first and then more and more hungry and ardent.

"That's enough, baby," he murmured. "I'm getting all turned on."

"Me, too," she murmured back. They pulled back a few scant inches, looked at each other, smiled and kissed again, lingeringly. Then Peter put her down, setting her carefully on her feet, not sliding her down his body.

"It's going to be really crowded in here with a computer table," he commented.

"There isn't a whole lot of space," Tess agreed. The office didn't extend the full depth of the building. An inside wall partitioned it from a storage shed, accessible from the fuel dock.

"You could get by with a smaller desk, couldn't you?"

"Yes, I suppose," Tess replied, reacting negatively to the idea of replacing the huge old desk that had been her father's. She hated to speak her feelings honestly, though, and disrupt the harmony. "Couldn't a computer just go on top of the desk?"

"It wouldn't be an efficient arrangement at all. The keyboard wouldn't be the right height."

"Well, getting a computer is only in the thinking stages now."

He looked at her questioningly.

"That old desk is like a fixture."

"Why didn't you just say that?"

"Because I knew you wouldn't be in sympathy. If I turn it around and push it against the wall, then there might be room for a computer table, don't you agree?"

His jaw tightened. "There might be."

Tess walked around behind the desk, reached for the folder and opened it. "Do you want to bring a chair around and explain all this to me?" she asked, sitting down.

"That all depends on whether you're really open to converting to a computer," he said. "It would mean giving up your father's old-fashioned way of keeping books."

"If a computer will cut short my time spent in this office doing bookkeeping, I'm all for it," Tess declared. "I'm just intimidated at the idea of learning to use one."

"It's not that difficult." He picked up a chair and brought it around behind the desk. Tess scooted her chair over. She smiled up at him inquiringly when he didn't sit down immediately. Her smile faded in instant comprehension, and she sighed, following his gaze. She was so used to the framed enlargement of a candid snapshot of her father and her together that she hadn't given it any thought.

"That was taken about three years ago," she volunteered. "I wanted to remember him when he was still in good health. He got so frail."

Peter sat down and reached over to pick up the photograph. He studied it briefly and put it back in precisely the same place.

"What was wrong with him?"

"His heart."

"It must have been rough on you."

"Yes, it was." Tess was warned by the compassion in his expression and in his voice, even if it was entirely for her, not her father, his enemy. Then before her eyes, his face hardened as they both listened to a conversation in the outer room.

"How are things going, Billy. Is Tess in her office?"

"Yeah, Mr. Buford, she and Peter are both in there. They're going over some stuff on computers."

"Tess needs a computer like she needs a hole in the head," Will scoffed. "Somebody must have been selling her a bill of goods."

Billy made a noncommittal reply.

Tess held her breath, hoping Will would leave. Her heart sank at the sharp rap of knuckles on the office door. Peter made a move as though he were going to get up.

"Please," she implored, grasping his forearm. It was rock hard, and his whole body was tense. "Come in," she called out.

Will came in and closed the door behind him. He ignored Peter altogether, addressing Tess. "Hate to interrupt, but it slipped my mind when you came by the boat earlier. I should have those appraisals Wednesday. Either you can come by the office or I'll bring them over, and we can go over them together."

"I'll come by your office," Tess said. "What time?"

"Come around noon. We'll go out and have some lunch. Also, I wanted to remind you that the Lions Club benefit shindig is Friday night. I'll pick you up—"

"Tess isn't going anywhere with you on Friday night, Buford," Peter interrupted, coming up out of his chair like a shot. Tess stood up with him, still clinging to his arm.

"That's for Tess to decide, not you, Roussell," Will informed him. "She and I made this date before you ever showed up on the scene. I paid a hundred bucks apiece for the tickets, but that's no big thing.''

"I'll reimburse you for her ticket," Peter said tersely, reaching to his hip pocket and then dropping his hand. "I left my wallet aboard my boat. I'll send you a check."

"I won't hold my breath."

"Will, I'm sorry, but I would like to cancel," Tess spoke up apologetically. Aside from not wanting to trigger Peter's temper, she preferred to spend Friday night with him.

"We'll just leave it open, Tess. I understand that you don't want to set Roussell off and cause a big ruckus."

"Tess doesn't have to worry about 'setting me off,' Buford." Peter's voice dripped contempt. "She knows that I won't cause a 'ruckus,' because I've given her that assurance. And you can leave your Friday nights open until hell freezes over, but she won't be going out with you."

"Peter, that kind of talk isn't necessary. Will, I'll see you on Wednesday. We'll have lunch."

"I don't pay him any attention, hon," Will told her. "Talk is cheap."

"If you'd like to go somewhere and carry on a different kind of dialog, Buford, I'm ready when you are."

"You don't know how tempting the thought is, but I promised Tess I wouldn't hurt you."

"Will, I didn't ask you not to hurt Peter!" Tess protested indignantly.

"Not in so many words," he admitted.

She met Peter's dark gaze, full of outraged masculine pride. "I went by Will's boat on my way here and told him exactly what I had told you," she explained. "That I wouldn't stand for any fighting."

"And the offender would find himself without a slip in your marina," Will reminded her. "That puts me between the devil and the deep blue sea, Roussell. If I could just figure out some way to make you blow your cool and get off scot-free myself, I'd sure do it."

But Peter wasn't paying Will any attention. He was searching Tess's face. "You said that?" he asked her. "You told Buford that you would put me out of your marina?"

"Don't cry, Roussell. So long, Tess. See you for lunch on Wednesday." Will spoke his parting words in a satisfied tone.

"Get the hell out of here, you bastard," Peter told him wearily. "You've accomplished what you came to do." He waited until Will had closed the door behind him and then looked back at Tess, still waiting for her to answer him.

"You had given me your word, Peter. I knew that I wouldn't ever have to put you out."

"I'll be over on my boat," he said, and walked out.

His long stride didn't falter when Tess followed him from behind the desk, imploring, "Peter, please come back...."

By the time she reached the office door, he was making his exit from the building. She would have had to run to catch up with him, and then she doubted that he would slow his pace. He was too hurt and angry. Even if she ran along beside him, he wouldn't listen to her until he had calmed down. Even then, she doubted that she could undo the damage.

"Damn, damn, *damn*," Tess murmured, overwhelmed by frustration and discouragement. She closed the door and leaned against it. Why had Will had to barge in, particularly at that moment? For the first time, Peter had opened up the subject of her father's illness and death, giving Tess a chance to share that difficult period with him.

When Tess saw Will on Wednesday, she was going to give him a revised ultimatum. She wasn't going to tolerate his needling Peter, the way he had done today, whenever the two men encountered each other.

The problem was only a temporary one. The antagonism would die down, even if it never disappeared altogether. Will would become involved with someone else and not resent Peter so much. Tess would hire someone to help Billy and arrange to take off the next few weekends, even though she had qualms about not keeping an eye on things herself and couldn't really justify paying a second employee.

It would be worth the uneasiness and the extra expense to be with Peter in surroundings that were free of tension. She would try to convince him to keep his boat somewhere else on the North Shore, where they could still go sailing and spend time together. He would agree, she was all too certain.

Tess straightened away from the door with a little sigh of effort and went around behind the desk again, skirting its bulk with heavy steps. Edging in between the two chairs, where she and Peter had sat side by side, she started to close the folder of computer information he had compiled, but then noticed a handwritten notation on the top page.

On impulse she looked through the thick stack of brochures and found more comments and questions in his familiar scrawl. He'd also underlined and blocked off sections of printed text. He hadn't just given the manufacturers' explanations of their products a cursory reading, but gone to some trouble.

A picture rose in Tess's mind of Peter sitting with a textbook and reading an assignment, having no difficulty concentrating even though she had the TV or the stereo playing. She could see herself, making a bid for his attention every now and then, sitting down next to him on the sofa or passing by the kitchen table and stopping to kiss him on the cheek or ruffle his hair.

He'd never complained or seemed to mind her interruptions. He would stop and watch a segment of a TV program with her, talk to her a few minutes, pull her down on his lap and give her a hug and go back to his studying.

The memory made love well up inside her, but it was accompanied by regret so sharp and painful that Tess clutched the edge of the old desk that she'd protested replacing because of sentimental attachment. Tears blurred her vision, and she blinked hard to focus on her father's kindly face smiling at her from the framed photograph.

"It was wrong for me to leave him, Daddy," she whispered. "I wish you hadn't let me. I forgive you, but I'm not going to lose him again over this marina."

She put away the folder in a drawer, shoved her chair into place and dragged the other one back around the desk. Then she went out into the store, feeling as though an enormous weight had been lifted from her shoulders.

"Let's pack it up early, Billy," she told the high-school youth, who looked at her a little uncertainly.

"Sounds good to me," he said.

Tess emptied the cash register and made out a deposit slip while he took care of his closing-up chores. They finished about the same time. She locked up, got into her car and drove over to Peter's slip, noticing that Will had departed in the meantime.

Peter wasn't out on deck or in the cockpit. The hatch was open, though, she saw with relief, as the possibility struck her that he might have gotten a ride with someone and gone.

"Ahoy," she called out as she stepped aboard. "It's me."

"I'm down below."

"I'll come down," she invited herself, although she could sense from his voice that he hadn't stirred.

"I went ahead and closed up," she explained, climbing down the companionway ladder. "When I didn't see any sign of you just now, I panicked, thinking that you might have decided to hitchhike instead of waiting on me."

"The thought occurred to me."

He was lounging on the bunk opposite the one that made into a double. A boating magazine was open on his lap, and he had a beer at hand. His impassive air and calm, sober expression gave Tess a sinking feeling in the pit of her stomach.

"You don't seem upset the way I expected," she ventured, glancing at the magazine. "Before, you would never have been able to settle down and read this soon after you'd gotten really mad at me."

"I wasn't reading. I was thumbing through and looking at the pictures," he corrected her.

"Probably wishing that you'd bought the kind of boat you really wanted and were sitting aboard it, tied up in any other marina in the world except this one."

"I don't regret buying this boat. It's my choice to keep it here in your marina, but that's going to depend on you. You're going to have to decide between renting to me and renting to Buford." He issued the ultimatum quietly and tonelessly and waited for her reply, showing no emotion.

Tess walked over to him. When he didn't make room for her to sit on the bunk, she remained standing.

"Are you saying that if I don't ask Will to take his boat somewhere else that you and I are through?"

He didn't have to think over his answer, but delivering it didn't come easy to him. "No. Just that I'll move my boat over to Mandeville, and your marina will be off-limits to me."

"Peter, aren't you just using Will as an excuse?" Tess asked gently. "You can't possibly consider him a threat. I've never been to bed with him. I don't love him. I've turned down his marriage proposal and given him no hope that I would ever change my mind. That's the reason he's acting the way he is toward you. His pride is hurt, and he's very disappointed."

Peter slowly pushed himself up to a straighter sitting position, still resting his back against the bulkhead behind him and extending his long legs on the bunk cushion. "You didn't tell me that you'd turned Buford down."

There was room at the foot of the bunk for her to sit, but she didn't. "Friday night. That's why I didn't want to break the date with him when you asked me to. My whole purpose in seeing him was to give him my answer. I wanted to get it over." She sighed, remembering. "He didn't make it easy for me. He had bought me an engagement ring and tried to give it to me. I felt terrible and still do, because I let him keep his hopes alive so long."

Peter tossed his magazine on the table. It landed with a little *splat*. "The bastard read the handwriting on the wall and made a last-ditch effort. I'll bet the ring he bought you had a whopping big diamond that would knock your eyes out."

"It was a beautiful ring, but I didn't have any desire to wear it."

"Buford hasn't given up, Tess. He's just biding his time, hoping that I'll strike out with you again. He'll be hanging around you, trying to undermine our relationship every chance he gets."

"Not for long. He needs female companionship. Now that I won't be dating him, he'll start going out with other women and find someone else."

"So the bottom line is that he stays and I go," Peter said flatly.

"No, that isn't the bottom line, but there's more involved than you've considered. If I put Will out for no justifiable reason, it could well lead to a mass evacuation by the long-time renters among the powerboat owners. He's well liked by all of them, and they might follow him and leave me with even more empty slips than I have now. But I'll risk the repercussions and live with my own conscience if you can honestly say that you wouldn't be happier in another marina. Could I sit by you?'' she requested before he could speak.

He swung his legs down to the floor and then swivelled sideways so that she still wouldn't be able to sit close to him.

''What I really had in mind was sitting on your lap,'' she confided ruefully.

''Is this where you soften me up and get back in my good graces?'' he asked, but he put both feet on the floor, one hand on either side of him. He didn't reach for Tess or touch her after she had settled herself on his thighs and put her arms around his neck.

''Do you remember how I used to bug you when you were trying to study?'' she asked him.

''There isn't much that I don't remember.''

''I looked through that folder after you left and saw the notes that you'd written. It brought back memories of what a good student you were, without ever being a grind. Did you realize how proud I was of your being so smart? I bragged about you to anyone who'd listen. And to anyone who wouldn't,'' she added, smiling.

He didn't smile back, and hers faded.

She sighed. ''You're not helping much, and I could really use some encouragement. What I'm leading up to isn't at all easy to say. I was wrong for asking you not to take the best job you were offered, Peter. You had worked hard and earned the opportunity to have a bright future.''

He stared at her, as though not believing that he'd heard her right. ''I wanted that future for both of us, not just me.''

''I know you did.''

He went on, as though she hadn't agreed with him. "It was important to me to be able to buy us a nice house, to earn a good income so that we could have a few luxuries and raise our kids without scrimping, the way my folks had to do. It wasn't just for my self-esteem that I wanted a good job. I tried to explain all that to you, Tess, but you wouldn't listen. You were only concerned about what was best for your father."

Tess nodded sadly. "I should have put you first, Peter, but I didn't. I wish I had, but there's no going back and changing that now."

He shook his head with a kind of despairing concurrence. His arms came around Tess, and he held her tightly against him. "Somehow I thought that hearing you say all this would help, but it doesn't bring back one wasted moment."

"No, nothing can."

"I blame myself, too, Tess. If only I hadn't been so goddamned proud. I should have called you or written and told you how much I missed you and wanted you there with me. I should have taken the next plane here after I got those divorce papers, asked you face-to-face if you really wanted to go through with it."

"I'd have said no." Tess pulled back and framed his face with loving hands. He looked into her eyes, letting her see his self-recrimination and naked regret. "All we can do is try to take advantage of now, Peter. We have to put our mistakes behind us and not waste any more precious time." She kissed him on the forehead. "I have a proposition to make you. Would you like to hear it?"

## Chapter Thirteen

A proposition?" he repeated.

"Yes, *proposition*, not *proposal*," she reassured him. "I agree with what you said this morning. It's going to take time for us to work things out and learn to trust each other. But do we have to live apart? I could move in with you and drive back and forth across the Causeway. It would give us a chance to find out if we're compatible as grown-ups, and we could take it from there." She paused hopefully, not sure of exactly what his response was going to be. She'd taken him by surprise, and he didn't seem opposed to the idea, but he didn't show any eagerness, either.

"I could get a place over here and do the commuting myself," he suggested. "If we lived in Mandeville, I'd be right there near the Causeway."

"No, you enjoy living at West End, and it would be a nice change for me. There would be so much more to do for entertainment over on that side of the lake."

"We can try it and see how it works out."

Tess could have done with a little more enthusiasm. "If you find that you want a night to yourself every so often, you can just tell me. I'll still have my house over here."

Peter's kiss was an answer in itself, but he followed it up with words anyway. "Baby, I'm not going to want any nights to myself. You can rest assured of that. Don't you know how much I'm going to look forward to coming home and spending my evenings with you?"

Appeased, Tess gave him a kiss and rubbed her nose against his. "I'll be a lot more considerate now that I've grown up than I was when we were married. When you're reading, I won't bother you. If you're tired and not in a talkative mood, I'll just leave you alone. I'll be much neater and more organized."

"Doesn't sound like very much fun living with such a reformed version of your old self," he remarked. "I could have gone to the library if I hadn't wanted you to interrupt me when I was studying."

"Except you know that I would just have tagged along with you, giving you my solemn word that I was going to do an assignment, too."

They smiled at each other, sharing sweet reminiscence that for once held no sting of bitterness.

"I was so head over heels in love with you, Tess. And I still am." He kissed her again, tenderly but with depth. "Let's go pack up your clothes. I want to take you home with me."

"Are you sure? You didn't exactly act bowled over."

"I was, though. The idea of going to bed with you every night and waking up with you every morning is going to take some getting used to. It's almost too good to be true."

"I know what you mean. I feel the same way."

Tess loaded a cooler with perishables from the boat's ice-box while he gathered up the few items that he wanted to take with him. It was all so companionable, but not casual. They were making a new beginning. Every time they met each other's eyes and smiled, they shared the thrill but also the tentativeness. The harmony seemed fragile as well as precious.

As they left the boat and got into her car to leave, Tess was hypersensitive to every inflection of his voice and every flicker of expression on his face, trying to read his thoughts.

"What year model is this car?" he asked.

She couldn't detect any note of disdain. After she told him, she added the obvious. "It's five years old." When he just nodded, she went on, "It's in good running condition. The gas mileage isn't the greatest, but the car is paid for. That's its strong point." Her father had always paid cash for his cars, but she didn't pass on that information. "Compared to your car, it's like driving a tank, but it gets me from here to there," she finished up philosophically.

"If money was no object, would you want a new car?"

Tess's look told him that that was a silly question. "Why, yes, especially now that I'll be crossing the Causeway twice a day. I'd get something more fun to drive, with some get-up-and-go."

"We'll go shopping for a car for you, then. If you pick out something that I like, I'll trade off with you and let you drive my car every other week." He smiled at her. "That should give you some idea of how high you rate."

"I hope that offer stands when I can afford a new car. I really can't right now."

"Luckily I can, since I economized on a boat."

"That's sweet of you, but I can't let you buy me a car. I wasn't trying to make you feel sorry for me. Honest." She patted him on the thigh.

"Why do you think I brought up the subject?"

He wanted to buy her a car that she would enjoy driving, one that suited his taste in automobiles, too, but he hadn't felt as though he could come right out and tell her. Instead he'd fished around to find out if she was sentimentally attached to this car, like she was to the old desk in the office, because it had been her father's.

If Tess had answered differently, she would never have known what he had in mind. The realization disturbed her, but she didn't confide her concern about communicating in such a roundabout fashion. They would get over this sense of walking on eggshells, she told herself, pulling into the driveway of her house.

"Can you believe that it was just a week ago, Saturday, that you showed up here on my porch?" she demanded as she unlocked the front door. "You were wearing gloves and a parka. Now look at the weather. The temperature was up to eighty degrees today. Aren't you coming in with me?" she asked in surprise when he hung back instead of following her inside.

"I'll just wait out here and not get in your way," he said. "When you're packed, I'll carry your suitcases out to the car."

He didn't want to spend any more time in her house than absolutely necessary. Like the marina, it had unpleasant associations, reminding him of the years she'd spent living with her father instead of with him.

"I can't think of anyone I'd rather have get in my way," she told him brightly, trying to act as though her insight didn't bother her. "But if you're not going to keep me company, I'll just pack what I'll need for tonight and be right out. It probably makes more sense for me to transport my clothes gradually, anyway. That way I can cull out what I don't wear."

He shrugged and stepped over the threshold. "There's lots of closet space in my condo. We might as well take what will fit into your car. Tomorrow after work I can drive over and we can load up both cars."

"There's probably not much point in my taking all my winter clothes," Tess reflected, leading him through the house to her bedroom. "We may have a cool spell or two, but our cold weather is over."

He didn't answer, but his silence wasn't acquiescence.

In her bedroom he glanced without curiosity, his dark eyes taking in the furnishings and decorations of the room where she'd slept the ten years that they'd been separated. "This is your same room," he commented.

"The same bedroom set," she replied cheerfully. "Do you want to help?" She pulled out a dresser drawer that contained lingerie and dangled a pair of lacy red bikini panties, bargaining with him, "I'll let you pack my underthings."

He came over, took the panties from her and held them up to examine them with male interest. "I like these. You'll have to model them for me. Do you have a bra that matches?"

"Bras are in this drawer." Tess lifted the hinged brass pull on another drawer and let it drop. "You can find out for yourself while you're putting the stuff in all these drawers into a suitcase for me."

"Where are the suitcases?"

They both set to work, filling her set of matched luggage and several other old suitcases with the contents of her dresser and chest of drawers and the shelves of her closet. Tess teased him about taking so long and examining individual articles of her clothing.

"It would go a lot faster if you didn't unfold things and then fold them up again," she pointed out as he shook out a nightgown.

"I can see we're going to have to go shopping and get you some sexy nightgowns," he observed. "These are entirely too modest."

"They're the kind you wear for sleeping in, not for taking off."

"Exactly."

While he started loading the car, Tess packed personal toilet articles and her makeup from both her bedroom and the old-fashioned bathroom that had been all hers for a year now.

She was struck for the first time by the permanence of her move. If her hopes proved true and living with Peter led to their remarrying, she would never return to this house except as a caretaker or a visitor. It would no longer be her home. As excited as she was, she was also sad. As much as she wished that she could share her emotion with Peter, she didn't dare, not wanting to spoil the camaraderie. Her best bet for not giving herself away was to hurry things up and leave.

"There's still plenty of room," he announced, returning from his last trip. "Do you have some cardboard boxes?"

"That's enough for today," Tess said. "Let's just each grab some hanging clothes and call it quits."

He gave her a close look and then glanced at her dresser, chest of drawers and bedside table, all bearing knickknacks and feminine clutter. "Don't you at least want to take your jewelry box?" he asked.

"Oh, yes, of course, I forgot about it."

What she'd wanted to prevent had happened anyway. He apparently sensed something was wrong, but didn't ask her what it was. Probably he'd guessed and didn't want to discuss it. Tess was back to wondering what he was thinking as she led the way out, her jewelry box under one arm and the other draped with hanging clothes.

He arranged those he carried, then hers, closed the trunk and reached into his pocket for her keys. Tess took them and went back to lock the front door while he got into the car.

"Do you want me to come over tomorrow afternoon and help you get the rest of your things or not?" he asked when she slid behind the wheel.

"It isn't really necessary. There's no big hurry." She couldn't tell whether he wanted a yes or a no. "I'll just invade your space a little bit at a time," she added with an attempt at lightness.

He didn't answer, and she thought the subject was dropped. On the way to the Causeway, she made several efforts at impersonal conversation and got minimal response.

"You aren't already having second thoughts, are you?" she inquired when they were on the southbound bridge.

"I had reservations when you suggested moving in with me," Peter replied. "It isn't going to work, Tess, unless you think of my condo as our place, not mine. There's a big difference between us living together and you visiting me."

Now Tess knew the answer he'd wanted back at her house. "In that case, why don't you plan to come over tomorrow afternoon. I'll see about getting some boxes."

Some to use to transfer her personal belongings that she would move, including treasured memorabilia and picture albums. Others to pack up cherished possessions that she would put in storage—her mother's best dishes, her father's collection of carved wooden ducks, odd and ends of bric-a-brac and keepsake items that she couldn't bear to part with, even if the time never came when she could have them in her and Peter's home.

She would also store a few pieces of furniture that she loved, the cherry-wood corner cabinet in the dining room, a small gateleg table that had belonged to her Grandmother Ames and a wicker chest. The rest of the furnishings and contents of the house she would sell or give away. Once the house was cleared out, she could rent it.

Tess didn't speak any of these thoughts aloud to Peter. There was too much emotion involved that he couldn't empathize with. She was also a little hurt that he hadn't perceived any of her sense of finality about moving out of her house that had made her sad. Otherwise he would have known that she didn't have in mind visiting him.

She might have been a houseguest arriving from out of town for a long stay, though, from the way he talked, growing more relaxed and lighthearted as they left the North Shore behind them. He mentioned restaurants he wanted them to try, outings they could take together and events that were coming up, like the Jazz and Heritage festivals. His whole focus was on how much fun they were going to have in their leisure time. Tess almost got the impression that he was trying to cheer her up and sell her on her decision to move over to the New Orleans side of the lake.

"You really seem to like living in New Orleans," she observed.

"I like living in a large city," he replied. "Or at least on the outskirts of one within easy driving distance of downtown. I do like New Orleans," he added. "It has its share of problems, like most major cities, but it also has a lot of character and historical interest. The food is great, and the people really know how to enjoy life. Any excuse for a party." He reached over to squeeze her hand on the wheel. "Now I think I'm going to be very happy in New Orleans."

"It sounds as though you would have a hard time adjusting to living in New Iberia again."

"I definitely would," he said. "I've changed too much in my attitudes to ever want to go back and live in my hometown. I thoroughly enjoy visiting my folks on holidays, getting together with my brothers and their families and looking up a few old buddies, but I don't have a lot of common interests now with my brothers or my old friends. Their idea of a great weekend is to get away from their wives and go off to a camp with a bunch of other men, play cards and hunt or fish. They can't understand why I don't get a thrill anymore out of shooting an alligator or gigging a frog. Now, instead of going shrimping or crabbing, I'd rather go sailing. Instead of spending my vacation deer hunting, I'd rather go skiing."

"You probably don't relate to their views on a lot of things now," Tess speculated. Like he wouldn't relate to the views of some of the husbands of her friends.

"I don't," Peter admitted. "I don't share some of the same prejudices and bigotry. One of the pluses of my job has been coming in contact with people from every part of the country."

"It shows that you're not a small-town boy anymore." He'd broadened his horizons and ventured out into a bigger world, while she hadn't. Could she keep up with him? Some of Tess's wistfulness and uncertainty crept into her voice.

"There's a lot to be said for living in a small town. It's nice to know your neighbors and not have to be so security conscious. When there's a large city in close proximity, it's like having the best of two worlds. That's why the North Shore has built up the way it has."

She hadn't been living in the backwoods, he seemed to be reassuring her. Liberalizing influences had come to her.

"A large majority of the married guys in our New Orleans office live over on the North Shore and commute," he went on to comment. "There's a lot of carpooling."

"I'll be headed in the opposite direction of most of the Causeway traffic, both coming and going," Tess observed. "I can just settle back and listen to the radio."

She smiled over at him. He met her glance, looking a little put out, as though she'd changed the subject abruptly on him. Had he been leading up to something? Another offer for him to do the commuting?

"Your new car will have cruise control and a good stereo," he promised her. "The only thing that worries me is weather conditions. But then you're your own boss. You don't have to punch a time clock, do you?"

Tess assured him that she could go over late and return early, when necessary. That apparently eased his qualms. She didn't volunteer that she really didn't have enough work to keep her busy at the marina, all day, every day during the week. Weekends and holidays were when she needed to be on hand to mind the store and the fuel dock. He, on the other hand, would have regular office hours from Monday through Friday, would cope with the pressures of his job and be free and ready to relax on weekends.

Their schedules were exactly opposite.

At his condo building, it took a couple of trips to unload the car. In the process, they encountered several residents that Peter knew, and he introduced her as Tess Davenport and mentioned matter-of-factly that she would be living there with him. There was no reason that he should have identified her as his ex-wife, but Tess was conscious that he hadn't. Some intuition told her that he was conscious, too, of not disclosing their past relationship.

"That is how you wanted me to introduce you?" he asked her out of the blue when they had finished moving her things and had sat down in the living room to take a breather.

"It's my name, and I don't guess the fact that we're divorced adds any element of respectability."

"Is the situation awkward for you?"

"No," Tess replied. "I guess it's because I was married to you, but it isn't awkward at all. I feel like I have every right to be sleeping with you."

"I feel like you do, too."

"Did I seem embarrassed?" Tess asked, wondering what was behind the whole conversation.

"No, not really."

"Do you have a problem with introducing me as your ex-wife, or do you just think that it's nobody's business?" she probed. "I noticed at Mardi Gras that you didn't mention to any of your co-workers that we were formerly married, but I didn't think anything about it."

"I have a problem introducing you as my former wife, Tess Davenport," he said bluntly. "Hasn't it occurred to you that I would?"

It hadn't occurred to Tess. "I never really stopped to consider that you would feel awkward, having people wonder whether I took back my maiden name or else married someone else in the meanwhile. I never had the chance to really get used to being Tess Roussell," she confessed. "One reason I figured I might as well change my name legally back to Davenport was that everybody called me Tess Davenport anyway."

"I can imagine that it does take a while to adjust to having a different last name," he reflected. "Some women now don't take their husband's name when they marry. I guess it is a sexist tradition."

Had the woman he had come close to marrying been a feminist? Tess wondered jealously. "Well, personally I like it," she said. Wanting to end the subject before it went any further, she scooted over closer to him on the sofa, put her arms around his neck and kissed him. "If we end up getting married again, I'll want to take your name." End of subject, she added with her tone.

"You will?"

He looked and sounded so pleased that it dawned on her that he might have been feeling her out on her opinion indirectly. She thought for a second that he was going to say something else, but then he kissed her instead. Tess felt a moment's disappointment that he hadn't spoken, but it faded and turned into pleasure as she kissed him back.

"Do you want to unpack before we go out and get something to eat?" Peter murmured against her lips, tugging her blouse free of her jeans.

"No," Tess murmured back, tugging up his T-shirt. "I'll unpack tomorrow."

He slipped both hands up under her blouse, undid the front closure of her bra and captured her breasts. "You want to change clothes and go somewhere fancy?"

"No, let's just go somewhere casual." She unsnapped his jeans and unzipped them enough to reach her hand down inside.

"Have I ever mentioned that your breasts are perfect?" he asked.

"Maybe, but I've forgotten," she encouraged.

"Well, they are. Help me take your blouse off. Don't you think we should celebrate the occasion and dress up?"

He was back to the discussion of plans while he pulled her blouse over her head. Tess let him lay her back on the sofa. She made room for him to stretch out beside her and guided his head, bringing his mouth to first one aching breast and then the other.

"Whatever you want to do," she gasped, arching her back. "I'd agree to almost anything when you're doing that."

"'Almost anything,'" he repeated, rising up to take off her jeans and bring her bikini panties off with them. "Is there anything that I can do to remove every last shred of resistance?"

His intimate inspection sent a rush of weak pleasure through her and awakened anticipation. "You know there is," she told him.

"Tell me when you reach that point." He opened her thighs wider and leaned down to arouse sensations so exquisite that Tess writhed her hips without modesty, moaned and gasped out her helpless pleasure. "Now?" he paused to ask.

"Don't stop," she begged and demanded.

"Then tell me yes to whatever I'm thinking."

"Yes!"

Unhurriedly, he brought her to a state of mindless selfish need, on to a solitary release that shattered her to bits and left her quivering with the aftermath. Then delicious languor stole through her body, melting her into the sofa.

"That was wonderful," she murmured, stretching and watching him as he stood up and stripped off his clothes.

"Aren't you worried about being under my power now? You promised to do whatever I had in mind at the time."

She smiled at him, lazily seductive, then dropped her gaze to his aroused body. "No, because getting a promise like that works two ways. I know how to cancel mine out."

Later when they were showering, she quizzed him about what demand she had saved herself from, and he wouldn't tell her, denying all her teasingly absurd guesses.

"Did you really think of something?" she asked when they were drying off, expecting him to admit that he hadn't.

"Yes," he answered.

"What?"

But he refused to satisfy her curiosity.

"Maybe it's something I'd want to do anyway," she suggested.

"I'm in trouble if you don't," he said, then kissed her and patted her on the bottom. "But I'd rather not go into it now."

His serious note made her want to pursue the matter even more, but also discouraged her. It was obviously something that would give rise to heavy discussion. The fact that he had any doubt at all about her reaction gave her clues.

He hadn't been buying a yes to a marriage proposal. There could hardly be any question of her willingness. Her guess was that if he were granted the one request in the world he would most like to ask of her, it would be for her to sell her marina and house, liquidate her ties of loyalty and responsibility to her father.

Tess inevitably was going to have to face up to that decision, but she needed some time. It was like a bridge that she had to cross over into the future, and when she did cross it, she needed Peter to be holding her hand and bolstering her courage. She needed to know that she had his trust, and she needed to be able to trust him.

Because there would be no safety net. Nothing to go back to.

They decided to dress comfortably and walk to one of the nearby seafood restaurants to have dinner. Neither of them was really in the mood for dressing up and dining elegantly, and they didn't have reservations anyway. Tess mentioned on the way that she'd had a hunger for boiled crawfish lately and elicited an immediate enthusiastic response from Peter.

"Boiled crabs sound good, too," he said, and she agreed.

They ended up ordering both along with a pitcher of beer. When the waitress brought a large metal tray heaped with crustaceans still in their shells, Tess and Peter both dug in. In a matter of minutes, their hands were sticky and the debris had begun to pile up. Eating boiled seafood was anything but a dignified affair.

"Never eat boiled seafood with a Cajun and expect to get your share," Tess complained happily, noting Peter's deftness as he decapitated a crimson-shelled crawfish and freed the tail of its hard protective armor all in one movement of his long, supple fingers.

"Is that ever a hint," he returned, and fed the tail to her.

She ate it greedily, and they smiled at each other. The tablecloth was plastic and the napkins were paper, but they wouldn't have traded a candlelight dinner for being there together, feasting in gory fashion, south-Louisiana style.

Strolling back to the condo, they walked with their arms around each other. "Do you know the last time I felt this happy?" Tess asked him.

"Probably the last time I felt this happy, too," he replied.

"Those first few months after we were married?"

"Yes. We didn't have a honeymoon," he added, but there was not the slightest trace of regret, only reminiscence.

"Sure we did," she contradicted him. "We didn't go on a trip, but we had a honeymoon, just like tonight we had a celebration."

It had been a long, eventful day. Within thirty minutes of their arrival back at the condo, Tess was yawning and her eyelids were drooping.

"I don't think I'm going to have any trouble with insomnia tonight," she told Peter.

"Let's go to bed, baby," he said. "I'm beat, too."

He didn't sound sleepy, and when Tess came out of the bathroom to climb in bed with him, he put down a magazine that had been lying on his bedside table. Evidently he'd been reading while he waited for her.

"The light won't bother me," she assured him, but he turned out the lamp anyway and held her close in the darkness. Tess hated to go to sleep on him instantly, but she could feel herself drifting off. She talked to stave off the drowsiness. "This bed is so comfortable. I like a firm mattress. Mine is too soft, and I was going to have to get a new one. Now I won't have to. Funny how things can happen so suddenly. When I got up this morning, I didn't dream that I might never be sleeping in my old bedroom again...."

He didn't answer. Tess had a moment's awareness that he was silent, and then she was sound asleep.

The next morning she opened her eyes to find him standing at the side of the bed, looking clean-cut and handsome, dressed in tailored slacks, long-sleeved shirt and tie. He smiled at her and bent down to kiss her on the lips, saying, "Good morning, sleepyhead." He kissed her again on her nose and straightened, leaving Tess with a lungful of his clean, masculine scent. "Do you want me to bring you a cup of coffee before I leave, or would you rather just catch a few more winks?"

"You're leaving? I was going to get up with you and cook you breakfast," she protested, rising up on her elbows. The sheet fell back to her waist, leaving her breasts partially hidden by her long hair. They tingled under his dark gaze.

"I had some cereal. That'll hold me fine." He reached down, picked up the edge of the sheet and pulled it up over her chest before he kissed her again. "Now I'd better get out of here or I'll be late for work. Go back to sleep."

"No. I'm going to get up. I'll have everything packed up in boxes this afternoon. What time do you think you'll be over?"

"You were right. There's really no great rush to move everything at once."

Tess was disconcerted by the turnabout. What had happened to change his mind? "So you're not coming over?"

"No, if it's okay with you, I won't. I'll just see you back here about five-thirty? If you'd like to wait until then, I'll help you unpack and put away your clothes. If not, go ahead on your own and rearrange my things anyway you want to free up storage for yourself."

"What about dinner?" Tess asked. "Do you want me to pick up some food to cook?"

"No, don't worry about it." He stroked her cheek in a farewell gesture. "Bye. Drive carefully, baby. I love you."

"I love you."

Tess smiled at him and blew him a kiss when he stopped at the door to look back at her. She listened for the sound of the door closing and got up, puzzled and disturbed.

Was the thought of meeting her at her house so repugnant that he just preferred to avoid the unpleasantness? Had last night been reassurance enough that she didn't intend to be a temporary guest?

Or was there some other reason he was no longer in favor of her moving all of her things to his condo?

He hadn't appeared to be upset. Tess took some reassurance in playing back the past few minutes and went out to the kitchen to pour herself a cup of coffee. She brought it back to the bedroom and stopped to take a sip at intervals while she checked out the contents of Peter's bureau, chest of drawers and closet.

It was more than just a practical investigation to determine how much free space was available. She was exploiting her freedom to look at his clothes and shoes and accessories, to pick up a pair of his briefs and fold them, to pull out a hanger and examine a jacket and imagine him wearing it. Satisfying her curiosity gave her pleasure, but also made her wistful and sad that she had had no wife's role in his accumulating his wardrobe. A pair of white tennis shorts came as a surprise and served as a reminder that she'd missed sharing a whole segment of his life. He hadn't played tennis before.

He had good taste and had obviously done his share of shopping in better men's stores, but there was a noticeable absence of trendy designer labels. She knew at a glance that he hadn't bought the plush velour Christian Dior robe. It had been a gift and probably not from his mother. Tess put it all the way at the end of the closet and jammed several garments against it.

She finished out her inventory by opening up a plain walnut-and-leather box on his bureau. Inside were cuff links and tie pins and several rings, including his high-school graduation ring, a signet ring...and his gold wedding band. Tess picked it up and caressed it, then slid it on her finger, remembering their wedding day.

She visualized his left hand now with the bare ring finger and ached with the wish to see the ring back on it, proclaiming to the world that he was hers, symbolizing his love and fidelity and commitment.

Tess returned the ring to the box with the utmost gentleness and reluctantly closed the lid. It was only then that she noticed.

Her jewelry box was open.

At some time since she'd placed it there on the bureau yesterday afternoon, Peter had looked inside and seen her wedding rings in their own little compartment. Had he picked up the narrow circle of gold and relived their wedding day, when he'd placed it on her finger?

She knew in her heart that he had.

Her certainty comforted her and yet wasn't a source of confidence because she didn't know whether he could ever recover completely from her having taken the ring off and broken the promises she'd made to him before God that day.

It wasn't a matter of whether he wanted to forgive her and believe that she wouldn't break them again, given the chance to prove herself.

Could he?

Tess postponed unpacking and got dressed to go to the marina. Before she left the condo, she made up the bed and briefly tidied up. Using the key that Peter had given her, she locked the door behind her, took the elevator down, got into her car and headed for the Causeway.

The whole routine was strange and unfamiliar. Without the insecurity, she could have enjoyed the novelty, but she had keys to two places of residence now, and neither of them was home. Her personal belongings were divided between Peter's condo and her house.

And he saw no hurry for her to finish moving in with him.

## Chapter Fourteen

Hi, Tess. What a nice surprise. Come in," Evelyn Laird invited warmly. "I'll put on a pot of coffee. This must be mental telepathy." She went over to the coffee maker while Tess made herself at home, sitting down at the kitchen table. "I tried to call you last night to see if you wanted to have lunch and go shopping this afternoon, but you weren't home. What's new?"

"Maybe you'd better sit down before I answer that," Tess suggested.

Evelyn glanced around curiously and then gave Tess a closer look. "Don't tell me. Let me guess. There's going to be a wedding."

Tess made a little face. "I hope that there will be one eventually."

Her friend raised her eyebrows in puzzled surprise. "What's the holdup? Don't tell me that Will's gotten cold feet now that you've finally made up your mind to marry him?''

"But I haven't. Just the opposite. I'm not going to marry Will. I've gotten back together with Peter. I'm staying with him. I warned you that you should sit down," Tess said ruefully as Evelyn's mouth dropped open.

"You've gotten back together with Peter. You're *staying* with him," Evelyn repeated incredulously. "When did this happen? That was just a week ago Saturday that you were with Will at Sherrie and Wayne's house. Wait." She held up her hand. "I think you were right. I'd better sit down to hear all this."

Tess waited until the other woman had dropped down into a chair opposite her, then she told her story.

"You two didn't fool around, did you?" Evelyn marveled, shaking her head and subjecting Tess to a searching scrutiny. "Why didn't he move in with you? Are you hoping to keep it a secret that you're living with him until you see how things work out?"

"No, the news is bound to get around, no matter what. I don't plan to make a public announcement, but I really don't care about gossip. It's my life. I moved in with him at my suggestion. Peter would have a problem living in the house where I had lived while we were apart. He has hard feelings against my father," Tess confessed. "I wanted to give us the best chance possible to make a go of things."

Evelyn got coffee cups down from a cabinet. "How's it going so far?" she asked, filling the cups and bringing them to the table. "You don't seem to be bubbling over."

"I'm up one minute and down the next," Tess admitted. "Oh, it's wonderful being with him, Evelyn. We have so much fun, but I feel like a pampered houseguest. Of course, it's only been two days." She sighed. "I want so badly to be his wife again, but he doesn't seem to want a wife. He won't let me cook, and he doesn't intend to let me do his laundry. He's contacted his cleaning service and is going to have them come in twice a week instead of once.''

"Sounds like a dream to me,'' Evelyn remarked, spooning sugar into her coffee.

"You know good and well that you wouldn't like it at all if Joe and the kids didn't depend on you,'' Tess scoffed. She took a sip of her coffee before continuing in a wistful voice. "Peter's so self-sufficient after being a bachelor for so long. Aside from my company, he doesn't need me. If he came home and found that I had moved my things out, he'd miss me, but he wouldn't be inconvenienced at all.''

"I take it he hasn't proposed a second time?''

"No. He doesn't want to rush into anything.''

"And you do?''

"There's so much time to make up for. And I want to put a ring on his finger,'' Tess confided, woman to woman. "He's gotten even better-looking, Evelyn. I have an attack of jealousy every morning when he goes off to work, looking like he could pose for a magazine ad of a successful young engineer. The world is full of women who would love to snap him up.''

"He's undoubtedly had his share of opportunities to marry one of them, and he hasn't. When we put you through the third degree that night at Sherrie's house, you told us that he'd stayed single. It sounds to me as though he's been carrying the torch for you all these years, Tess.''

"He has. I'm just going to have to be patient and give him time.''

"You've broken the bad news to Will that he's out of the picture, I assume.''

Tess nodded. "He doesn't know that I'm living with Peter yet. I have an appointment with him in an hour at his office, and I'll tell him. I don't want him to hear from someone else.''

Evelyn was thoughtful, her expression pensive. "I guess we won't be seeing much of you now that you'll be living over in New Orleans. And if you marry Peter, you'll be moving to some other part of the country in a year or two when he's transferred. Most of us, myself included, weren't that crazy about your marrying Will, but at least we wouldn't have lost you as a member of the crowd.'' She reached over and squeezed Tess's arm. "Don't mind me. I'm just being selfish and honest. I hope that things work out for you and Peter, Tess. You've been carrying the torch for him all these years, too, haven't you?''

"Yes." Tess's voice was husky with emotion. "And you're not losing me as a member of the crowd. I'll be driving over every day during the week. We women can get together for lunch and have our shopping sprees. Peter and I can come over for dinner or a party. You'll all like him.''

"Sure, we will," Evelyn soothed. "I can't wait to see the look on Sherrie's face. Have you talked to her lately?''

"I'll call her this afternoon.''

Evelyn poured them second cups of coffee, and they caught up on news, both making an effort to preserve the ordinariness of sitting together at Evelyn's kitchen table and visiting. Underneath, though, was the poignant awareness that occasions like this one were numbered if Tess married Peter.

She wouldn't be spending the rest of her life in Maryville, sharing the everyday problems, joys and tragedies of her good friends, like Evelyn. Already, with Tess having been reconciled with Peter just on a conditional basis, the status quo was gone.

When Tess announced that she really should be going to keep her appointment with Will, neither she nor Evelyn got up. They looked at each other, both fighting tears.

"This is so silly," Tess said. "It's not as though I would be moving away tomorrow, even if Peter asked me to marry him tonight."

"Maybe he won't be transferred for another five years. Or longer than that."

"And there's always the good chance that his company could send him back to their New Orleans office."

"If you held on to the marina and your house, you and Peter could come back to Maryville when he retires. By then surely he'd be over any grudge against your father."

"Holding on to the marina isn't very feasible, from a financial standpoint," Tess said sadly, getting up. "But that's a whole other story. I'll have to fill you in. How about lunch tomorrow?"

"Why don't I have you and Sherrie both over here?" Evelyn suggested. "I'll try out a recipe for chicken-curry salad that I clipped out of the Sunday paper."

Tess responded as enthusiastically as she normally would have. Evelyn walked with her to the kitchen door, as she always did. Their farewells were casual, and then they spoiled the whole effort to make Tess's exit painless when they embraced.

On the fifteen-minute drive to Covington to Will's law office, Tess conquered her emotion and braced herself for a different but equally difficult scene. It would have been a source of comfort and strength to her if she'd known that she could share all her thoughts and feelings about both Evelyn and Will with Peter that night, not just give a factual account of her day, as she'd done the two previous evenings.

Will's secretary sent Tess right in, saying that Will was expecting her. He opened the door almost immediately when Tess knocked, and he was warmly cordial.

"Let's get our business over with, and we'll go have some lunch," he said, leading her to a leather sofa. Then he got a legal-sized manila folder from his desk and came over to sit next to her. Balancing the folder on his knees, he took out a stapled sheaf of papers. "This is the appraisal on your house. As you can see—" He broke off to listen as his secretary's voice came over the intercom.

"Mr. Buford, I hate to interrupt, but Mr. Caulley is out here and says that it's urgent that he have a word with you."

"Excuse me, hon, I'll just be a minute. Why don't you be looking over this?" He gave her the appraisal and got up, putting the folder on the sofa before he went out.

Tess glanced at the first page, which had dimensions and factual information about her house and lot, and then flipped through until she found the market value the appraiser had come up with. It was about what she had expected.

What had the marina appraised for? That was the big question. Expecting the other appraisal to be in the folder, Tess opened it, but she didn't see a similar document on top of the stack of papers. Since the file obviously pertained to her legal affairs, she felt free to look through it. There was the letter from her brother's attorney, a copy of J.D.'s birth certificate and also one of the marriage license that proved J.D. was her father's legitimate heir.

Tess noted the name of J.D.'s mother, her father's first wife, Sue Ellen Trotter. When she visited her brother, she would ask to see a picture of the young woman who had been her mother's predecessor. Had her father confided in her mother that he had already been a husband and a father? she wondered, and sighed at the realization that she'd probably never know.

She looked through the rest of the file quickly, with little interest, until she came to a sheet of paper with nothing written on it but a telephone number and a date notation.

J.D's telephone number, which Will had claimed not to have. But that wasn't the damaging evidence. The date was mid-December, roughly two months ago.

Will had made the anonymous telephone call, just as Peter had accused him of doing.

"Sorry to be so long," Will apologized, coming back in. He took in her expression, glanced down at the open file and went gray. "You look disappointed. The price that Dumas came up with on your house was pretty good, I thought," he declared.

"How did you find out about J.D., Will?" Tess asked him.

His shoulders sagged. "Your daddy told me," he answered in a voice that matched his posture. He came over to drop down heavily into an armchair. "It weighed on his mind toward the end. Your mother had been against you ever knowing. Otherwise, he probably would have told you, Tess, before he passed on. I advised him against it, too, explaining to him that if you looked up your half brother, you could be letting yourself in for inheritance problems."

"Then you turned right around and brought all those problems on me yourself in the most underhanded way possible. I trusted you completely, Will. I considered you a very good friend." Tess didn't tone down her reproach or try to hide her disappointment in him.

"I wanted to be more than a friend, Tess. I wanted you to be my wife, and I was reaching the end of my rope, trying to make any headway with you. It didn't get me to first base with you that I'm worth several millions, but if I could come through for you and save you from losing your marina, I knew that would count for something."

"I defended you to Peter when he accused you of engineering the whole plot to put pressure on me. But he was right. He sized you up right away."

Will looked sick at the mention of Peter. "Tess, for God's sake, don't tell Roussell about this. Can't we just keep it between you and me? I'll move my boat and stay away from you. I'll get you the financing you need or make you a personal loan. Just don't give him the ammunition to smear my name and reputation, because I'll bring suit against him for slander, if he does."

"Will you bring suit against me, too, Will?" Tess asked. "Call me a liar in court?" She picked up the sheet of paper with the incriminating evidence and handed it to him. "Here. I don't need this. I have my brother's telephone number. But I'll take the rest of this file, since you won't be handling any legal work for me anymore." She closed up the folder, picked it up and stood. "Send me a bill for whatever I owe you. I'd like for you to have your boat moved by this weekend. Aside from Peter, I don't intend to tell anyone else about what was said here today, and he will keep my confidence. I can trust him to do that."

Tess walked out.

It was disillusioning to learn that Will had stooped to such shabby methods to get her in his debt. Her confidence in herself as a judge of people was deeply shaken. If Peter hadn't come along, Tess might very well have ended up marrying Will, with no inkling that he was capable of such dishonesty and trickery.

Adding to her depression was Will's revelation that her father in the last days of his life had been plagued with guilt, and she hadn't even known, hadn't shared his burden with him. At least Tess's mind had been put at ease on one point. Her father hadn't kept his past secret from her mother.

That was the only pinprick of light in a very gloomy day.

Tess drove back to the marina, with little more sense of purpose than killing hours before she returned to West End. She had nothing pressing to do in the store or the office. She could pick up boxes and pack up some of her possessions in the house, but there was no incentive. Tomorrow she would see about hiring another lawyer and check with the appraiser, Dumas, on when the marina appraisal would be finished. Today she just didn't have the heart to tackle anything.

The phone was ringing when she walked through the door. The caller was Dave Johnson, the contractor. He came to the point bluntly. He had decided against giving her a bid because he really wasn't interested in the job.

Tess thanked him for being honest with her and hung up. Now she had to get in touch with some other contractors. But she would leave that until tomorrow, too.

Moping around the marina wasn't going to boost her morale, though. Going to her house would only depress her more. She would drive back over to West End, Tess decided, go grocery shopping and get food for dinner, and then spend the afternoon being domestic, pretending she was Peter's wife.

Peter was later than he had been the last two afternoons. He hadn't called to say that he was delayed at work. Tess flipped off the TV after watching the thirty-minute local newscast, followed by the national news. She turned on the stereo and paced around the living room, listening for the sound of his key in the lock.

The sound of the doorbell made her jump. She went to see who was at the door, banishing a vision of a uniformed policeman with a grave face. Nothing had happened to Peter, she told herself.

But her sense of urgency kept her from taking the time to look through the peephole or putting on the chain and inquiring who was there. She unlocked the door and opened it to see Peter with a grocery bag in either arm.

"I went by the supermarket," he explained unnecessarily. "How does steak, baked potatoes and green salad sound for dinner? Baby, what's wrong?"

His concerned face wavered and blurred as Tess's eyes filled with tears that spilled over to make room for more. It was simply the last straw. She turned and headed blindly back to the living room.

"What's the matter, Tess?" Peter demanded in an alarmed voice, catching up with her. He'd evidently put his grocery bags down because he grasped her by the waist to stop her.

"*Everything*'s—the—matter—" Tess managed to get the words out between sobs. Peter turned her around and wrapped his arms around her, gathering her close.

"Don't cry, baby," he begged her. "Just tell me, whatever it is."

"You don't—want to—hear." Her words were muffled because her face was buried against his chest.

"Of course, I want to hear. Let's sit down over here on the sofa."

Tess let him lead her. He sat and pulled her down on his lap and cradled her as though she were a little girl. She poured everything out, her visit with Evelyn, her appointment with Will, the call from Dave Johnson, her afternoon of domesticity. She held nothing back, not one thought or emotion during the trying day, including her insecurities where he was concerned.

"Then you show up with food for dinner," she finished up tragically.

"I'm glad I did, since it caused you to open up like this," Peter said, giving her a hard hug and a tender kiss. He had listened without once interrupting. "Baby, the only reason I haven't asked you to marry me is that I thought you wanted time to be sure. There's nothing in the world I want more than to be your husband and to make you my wife. Will you marry me again, Tess?"

She sniffled. "Yes."

He kissed her lips and then each tear-stained cheek.

"Why did you change your mind about me moving all my things?" she asked.

"Because I didn't figure that our living over here would be permanent. I'd rather do the commuting myself, and it would be so much more convenient for you to live closer to the marina. You looked so sad Sunday when we got ready to leave. I know that house is home to you after living there practically your whole life."

Tess framed his face and kissed him. "I was sad, but I was excited, too. From now on, home is going to be wherever you and I live together. I'm planning to put the house up for rent, as soon as I get it emptied out. There are a few pieces of furniture and some other keepsake items that I want to keep, but other than that, I'll get rid of everything else."

"We could do some remodeling, get new appliances and turn it into a place that reflected both our personalities," Peter suggested.

"It's not worth it for the time that we'd be living there. In a year you might be transferred, and we would be moving," Tess pointed out.

"No, we won't. I've made up my mind to stay with the New Orleans office."

"If you think you're keeping me locked up in Maryville for the rest of my life, you have another thought coming," Tess told him, warmed to the core that he had every intention of sacrificing his career for her. "I want my chance to see how the outside world lives."

He searched her face. "You're just saying that. You know that you have deep roots, Tess. You'd miss all your good friends, like Evelyn. It would be a huge adjustment for you relocating to another geographical area."

"I'm sure it will be," she said. "The prospect is definitely scary, but it's exciting, too. I'm still a very outgoing person. You don't doubt that I'm capable of adapting and fitting in somewhere else, do you?" she asked earnestly.

"Of course not."

"It's settled, then. You're not turning down any promotions." She kissed him to settle the matter.

"We'll discuss it when the situation arises." His voice was resonant with his sincerity as he went on, "Whether we go or stay, Tess, I'm going to be happy with you. I love you so much that if I were offered the presidency of the company and it meant leaving you, I'd turn it down. And I mean that."

"I believe you. But I'm not just thinking of you. I'm thinking of *us*. Your future is *our* future. In about a year, I'm going to want to have a baby and get us started on that family of three or four kids." Her throat tightened at the emotion in his face.

"I'll settle for just a couple," he said, and kissed her tenderly.

"I guess we should put up those groceries you bought," Tess mused with a happy sigh.

"That's my last independent trip to the supermarket," Peter promised her. "From now on I'll only go with a list. I can't believe that I've been knocking myself out to be a model of a nonchauvinistic male, and I've only offended you."

Tess giggled. The earlier scene at the door was funny in retrospect. "Here you come home after working all day, with food to cook my dinner, and I burst into tears."

Peter chuckled. "I didn't know what the hell was going on. You took one look at me and teared up. I thought something tragic might have happened."

"We can have your steaks for dinner," she offered, managing to keep from smiling.

"No, indeed. We're having whatever you got for us to eat, even if it's hot dogs. What is our menu, just out of curiosity?"

Her smile broke out, giving her away. Peter joined in, speaking in unison with her, "Steak, baked potatoes and green salad."

Their laughter blended, too, in wonderful harmony. He dumped her off his lap onto the sofa and pushed her on her back to tickle her ribs. Tess grabbed his hands and wriggled and twisted her body, begging him to stop.

When he did stop, she didn't let his hands go, but settled them on her rib cage, just below her breasts. Peter took it from there.

*　*　*　*　*

## *Silhouette Intimate Moments*®

# It's time ... for Nora Roberts

There's no time like the present to have an experience that's out of this world. When Caleb Hornblower "drops in" on Liberty Stone there's nothing casual about the results!

This month, look for Silhouette Intimate Moments #313

# TIME WAS

And there's something in the future for you, too! Coming next month, Jacob Hornblower is determined to stop his brother from making the mistake of his life—but his timing's off, and he encounters Sunny Stone instead. Can this mismatched couple learn to share their tomorrows? You won't want to miss Silhouette Intimate Moments #317

# TIMES CHANGE

Hurry and get your copy ... while there's still time!